PRAISE FOR THE NOVELS OF ANGELA KNIGHT

Jane's Warlord

"What an awesome, scintillating, and sexy book! *Jane's Warlord* is intriguing, extremely sensuous, and just plain adventurous. A star is born." —*Romantic Times* (Top Pick)

"Chills, thrills, and a super hero and heroine will have readers racing through this sexy tale. Take note, time travel fans, the future belongs to Knight!" —Bestselling author Emma Holly

"[Angela Knight's] world is believable and her plotting fast-paced. Knight's fictional world seems to have a promising future." —*Booklist*

"Exhilarating . . . delightful . . . action-packed . . . [a] wonderful tale that showcases a new writing talent heading for the stars." —*Midwest Book Review*

"Solid writing . . . sexy love scenes, and likable characters. I look forward to [Knight's] next book." —*All About Romance*

continued . . .

Master of the Night

"Her novels are spicy, extremely sexy, and truly fabulous . . . complex and intriguing . . . loads of possibilities for future sensual adventures."
—*Romantic Times*

"A terrific paranormal romantic-suspense thriller that never slows down until the final confrontation between good and evil. The action-packed story line moves at a fast clip . . . Angela Knight is a rising star in the paranormal pantheon." —*Midwest Book Review*

MORE PRAISE FOR ANGELA KNIGHT

"Get ready for the adrenaline-rushing read of your life . . . the cream of the crop!" —*ParaNormal Romance Reviews*

"Will have readers . . . aroused." —*A Romance Review*

"Fresh . . . hot sex. You are sure to enjoy." —*The Best Reviews*

"Erotic . . . packed with violence [and] action . . . quite a story. The . . . love scenes are steamy and sensuous—some of the best I've read." —*SFRA Review*

"Ms. Knight has combined the erotic with the romantic and made a classic tale." —Susan Holly, *Just Erotic Romance Reviews* (Gold Star Rating)

"[A hero] to make any woman hot with desire." —*In the Library Reviews*

Mercenaries

Angela Knight

BERKLEY SENSATION, NEW YORK

THE BERKLEY PUBLISHING GROUP
Published by the Penguin Group
Penguin Group (USA) Inc.
375 Hudson Street, New York, New York 10014, USA
Penguin Group (Canada), 90 Eglinton Avenue East, Suite 700, Toronto, Ontario M4P 2Y3, Canada
(a division of Pearson Penguin Canada Inc.)
Penguin Books Ltd., 80 Strand, London WC2R 0RL, England
Penguin Group Ireland, 25 St. Stephen's Green, Dublin 2, Ireland (a division of Penguin Books Ltd.)
Penguin Group (Australia), 250 Camberwell Road, Camberwell, Victoria 3124, Australia
(a division of Pearson Australia Group Pty. Ltd.)
Penguin Books India Pvt. Ltd., 11 Community Centre, Panchsheel Park, New Delhi—110 017, India
Penguin Group (NZ), Cnr. Airborne and Rosedale Roads, Albany, Auckland 1310, New Zealand
(a division of Pearson New Zealand Ltd.)
Penguin Books (South Africa) (Pty.) Ltd., 24 Sturdee Avenue, Rosebank, Johannesburg 2196, South Africa

Penguin Books Ltd., Registered Offices: 80 Strand, London WC2R 0RL, England

This is a work of fiction. Names, characters, places, and incidents either are the product of the author's imagination or are used fictitiously, and any resemblance to actual persons, living or dead, business establishments, events, or locales is entirely coincidental. The publisher does not have any control over and does not assume any responsibility for author or third-party websites or their content.

First edition: September 2005

Library of Congress Cataloging-in-Publication Data

Knight, Angela.
    Mercenaries / Angela Knight.— 1st ed.
        p. cm.
    ISBN 0-425-20616-5
    1. Mercenary troops—Fiction. 2. Women soldiers—Fiction. I. Title.

PS3611.N557M47 2005
813'.6—dc22   2005050120

PRINTED IN THE UNITED STATES OF AMERICA

10 9 8 7 6 5 4 3 2 1

Contents

Dear Reader,

I grew up reading science fiction—wonderful stories of bold, adventurous men and women confronting strange new worlds, who learn something about themselves in the process. So naturally, I've always wanted to write those stories myself.

I got the chance a few years ago with the e-book versions of the first two stories in this collection. Because both novellas were in electronic format, I felt free to let my imagination run wild, pushing the envelope in every way that I could. As a result, fans of my Berkley novels will find "Trinity" and "The Thrall" a little more hard-edged and erotic than the rest of my work, and "Trinity" was also expanded from the original e-book. But though the heroes and heroines play with dominance and submission in the bedroom, you'll find they remain fiery equals everywhere else.

In the third story, created especially for this volume, I decided to write something a bit more in line with the rest of my Berkley work. I hope you find "Claiming Cassidy" just as deliciously hot and romantic.

Happy reading!
Angela Knight

Mercenaries

Trinity

Chapter One

SHE had to get off this planet.

Trinity Yeager watched grimly as Sheriff Makerson dragged the woman across the scaffold to the Sinner's Post. Beefy and broad, he towered over poor Mary Stevens, a delicately built woman whose long gray dress suggested something from another age.

Come to think of it, the entire situation seemed like something from another age.

With an ease that spoke of long practice, the sheriff lashed Mary's wrists to a ring driven into the seven-foot wooden stake. She watched him helplessly, eyes wide with a blend of shame and fear.

Trin winced in sympathy. She had an ugly suspicion it wouldn't be long before she ended up tied to that stake herself. Wouldn't be the first time. Anyway, far too many people thought she needed another lesson from the lash.

Most of whom wanted to marry her.

Elder Jones stepped closer to the post, one bony white hand clutching his copy of *The Teachings of the Prophet Orville,* pale eyes burning. Trin wasn't entirely sure whether the fire was born of righteous indignation or sick excitement. Probably both.

Mary's husband walked across the platform to join the trio, smirking at his wife. George Stevens was a plump man who ran one of the shops lining the square. Trinity had learned to count her change carefully whenever she bought anything from him.

The call had gone out that morning for the residents of Rectitude to gather in the town square for Mary's punishment. Trin had planned to harvest the kellum today, but she left the orchard when she'd heard the gathering bells. She'd rather be anywhere else, but she knew better than to court the sheriff's fury.

Now she stood on the edge of the crowd as far from the scaffold as she could get. Everybody in town was present—close to three thousand people, chatting and laughing as they waited for the entertainment to begin.

It was a pretty day for a beating. The sky was a lovely pink, and one of the three moons that orbited Orville's Paradise rode low over the horizon, rendered pale and ghostly by the afternoon sun.

Wooden shops in a cheerful rainbow of colors surrounded the city square. Gleaming picture windows displayed prim dresses, dry goods, and farming implements. Intricate gingerbread fretwork decorated the shops' front porches like swags of lace, giving the town the look of something from a pre-spaceflight trid.

But it was the Temple of Orville that dominated the square. Built of massive gray granite blocks, it seem to crouch, brooding. Twin white spirals thrust from its slate roof like horns, symbolizing the faith's foundations: piety and genetic superiority.

Something hummed past overhead, a flitter on its way to the shuttleport. Trin dared a quick upward glance at the gleaming wedge as it flashed across the cloudless sky. One of the mercenaries, she imagined, picking up supplies. Rectitude was one of the few towns on Orville's Paradise that allowed any contact with outsiders at all. Still, most chose to land at one of the larger settlements, so the town got very few visitors.

She'd rarely seen flying transports of any kind since she and her father had immigrated to Paradise ten years before. Orville taught that high technology corrupted the faithful with infidel values.

A movement drew Trin's attention: Elder Jones stepping to the edge of the wooden platform. The wind plucked at the black robes draping his narrow body, sending them fluttering like wings.

"Two hundred years ago the Prophet Orville led our ancestors to this world to live as the Maker intended." Though his face was pale and pinched, the elder's voice was beautiful, deep and mellow and hypnotic. Sometimes even Trin found herself falling under his spell. "Chief among the Prophet's teachings was that woman should submit to the dictates of her husband, for the Maker gave men superior judgment, just as he gave them superior strength." He paused to let the message sink in, scanning the crowd for any show of disbelief.

On cue the sheriff pulled the whip from his belt and shook it out, letting the long lash writhe on the scaffold floor. A faint smile of anticipation curved his mouth. Mary stared over her shoulder at him, her face ghastly white beneath the bruise that rode one cheekbone.

No doubt about it, Trin thought. *I definitely need to get off this planet.*

"But Mary Stevens has disobeyed the Prophet's teachings. Her husband tells us that she has neglected her household duties. She burned his dinner three times in the last month alone." The elder lifted his calfskin-bound book and shook it with theatrical outrage. "Three times!"

"Oh, yeah," a dry female voice drawled at Trinity's elbow. "There's a whipping offense right there."

Startled, Trin jerked around to see one of the mercenaries standing behind her. She relaxed. She'd thought for a moment one of the female colonists was trying to tempt her into heresy, a trap Trin had no intention of falling into again.

But this woman was obviously not local. Almost as tall as the sheriff himself, she was dressed in black half-armor that sheathed her shoulders, chest and upper thighs in plates of beamer-resistant Cylar. Twin beamer pistols rode her slim hips, and there was a dirk thrust in the sheath around one arm. Her blond hair was woven into a set of tight, intricate braids probably designed to accommodate a helmet. She looked tough, capable, and exotic, and Trin felt a twinge of bitter envy at her freedom.

It was said the mercs had nanotech implants that gave them inhuman strength. Elder Jones had preached a sermon on that topic just last Friday, ranting that female mercenaries were an offense against the Maker's Order.

Trin permitted herself a brief, pleasant fantasy of what she'd do with a set of implants. Giving the elder a punch in the nose sounded like a good place to start.

For somebody headed for hell, the merc looked pleasant enough. Her gaze was good natured rather than grim, and there was nothing at all masculine in her delicately angular face. She lifted a brow, her expression appraising and amused. "You don't seem to be buying into all this kak-shit."

"Not particularly," Trin murmured, careful to keep her voice low. "But since I'm stuck here, I don't exactly advertise my opinions."

A woman turned to glare at them. Evidently they hadn't spoken softly enough after all. Trin sighed, knowing their eavesdropper would run to some elder the first chance she got.

At that realization, a daring thought sent her heartbeat leaping. If she was headed for trouble anyway, why not go all the way? It wasn't as if she had anything to lose.

Trin tilted her head at the merc in a *follow me* gesture and slipped away from the crowd. The mercenary sauntered after her, curiosity evident on her pretty face.

Up on the scaffold the whip landed with a loud slap. Mary yelped. Trin winced.

"I'd be a lot more impressed by everybody's piety," the merc muttered, looking toward the scaffold, "if half the men here didn't have hard-ons. Including the sheriff and the guy with the book."

Despite herself, Trin smiled. "You're not supposed to notice."

"Well, as hard-ons go, these *would* be easy to overlook." The merc grinned wickedly as Trin choked on a scandalized snicker. When she got her breath back, the woman stuck out a hand. "Lieutenant Cassidy Vika, *Starrunner*. You're not from around here, are you?"

"Trinity Yeager. And no, we immigrated when I was fourteen."

"Figured. You're not nearly tight-assed enough to be a native." Vika gave her an appraising look. "Mind if I ask why you moved to this world to start with? It sure wouldn't be at the top of *my* list."

Trin laughed shortly. "I doubt Dad was thinking all that clearly when he made the decision." An old, familiar pain stabbed her heart with such force, she had to look away. "He and my mother were mercenaries. Mom was killed in battle out around NeoGenesis, and he decided it was time to get out of the business before I ended up an orphan. He evidently felt Orville's Paradise would be a good place to raise a kid." The sherif landed a particularly hard blow, and Mary screamed. "Maker knows why."

Cassidy rested a hand on one of her beamers and frowned, looking toward the scaffold. "How long is he going to do that? Because if he keeps it up much longer, he's going to start inflicting real damage, and I'm going to have to kick his ass."

"Actually, that's . . ."

"Fifteen!" the sheriff shouted.

". . . all," Trinity finished as the woman slumped, panting, against the post. Her satisfied husband swaggered over to untie her and lead her off.

"Good thing," Cassidy grunted. "My patience was wearing thin."

"Mine ran out a long time ago." This was her chance. Her stomach coiled into a sick knot of hope and fear. "I figure it'll be about a week and a half, tops, before it's my turn for the strap."

The mercenary frowned. "You? Why?"

She hesitated. If the Temple elders got wind of what she was attempting . . . But the risk was worth it, and she was already in trouble just for talking to the merc. "The elders are holding a bride auction for me next week on my twenty-fifth birthday. I figure my new husband will invent an excuse to send me to the Sinner's Post as soon as he possibly can, just to prove he's in charge."

Cassidy's blond brows flew upward. "They're auctioning you off? Like a slave?"

"Afraid so." It felt good to talk about it. Trin had learned years ago that complaining about Orvillian dogma to anybody else only bought her a session at the Sinner's Post. "All the bachelors of Rectitude are expected to turn out for the bid. I'm supposed to marry the winner."

"Why the hell doesn't one of them just propose?"

"They have. I keep saying no." Remembering her parade of suitors, Trin grimaced. "None of them is anybody's idea of Prince Charming."

The mercenary shook her head. "Hell of a birthday present."

"You're not kidding." Trin glanced around for more eavesdroppers. The square was emptying out, colonists heading back to work in the surrounding shops and businesses. Some of them gave Trinity disapproving looks as they passed. She lowered her voice. "I've got to get off this planet. Is there any way I can talk to your captain, arrange for passage? I don't have many credchits, but I'm more than willing to join the crew and work."

Cassidy frowned, her expression doubtful. "Well, we did loose a couple of guys at Dyson's Hole, but . . . I don't know, Trin. My sensors tell me you don't have any nanotech implants. We're a merc company—we fight people that eat unenhanced humans for lunch. Sometimes literally."

"I could get the implants." In fact, she'd like nothing better. It would feel good to finally have the muscle to defend herself against people like the sheriff and his son. "Look, yours is the first ship we've seen in Rectitude in three years. The Maker only knows how long it'll be before we get another one, and by then I'll be married. The elders won't be happy about my trying to leave now, but once I've got a husband, he's not going to let me anywhere near another ship." In her desperation she grabbed the other woman's forearm. "I've got to get out of here *now*, Cassidy."

The mercenary glanced down at her hand, stiffening. Embarrassed, Trin hastily released her. Cassidy sighed. "I don't blame you. I've visited my share of nutball colonies, but Orville's Paradise seems even nuttier than most." She hesitated a moment. "You'll find the captain in the Spacer's Tavern by that pitiful excuse for a shuttleport. His name is Nathan August. But I'll tell you right now, you're going to have to talk fast. He's not going to want to take an unenhanced human on, no matter how shorthanded we are."

Trin set her jaw. "I'll convince him."

"Yeah, well, good luck with that. You're going to need it."

✦ ✦ ✦

TRIN headed for the shuttleport at a pace just short of a run. The port was located on the outskirts of town, and she had to move fast if she was going to make it before the captain left.

Moving in long strides, she ducked between two shops, her boot heels clicking fast on the pavement. But as she reached the end of the alley, a tall male figure suddenly stepped out in front of her. "Hello, Trinity."

"Andy." Trin drew up in dismay.

Andrew Makerson wore the uniform of a sheriff's enforcer, its brown fabric snug across his bull shoulders, black boots gleaming. His white-blond hair was cut in a tight pelt. Like his father, the sheriff, he had a broad, beefy face that would have been handsome if not for the malice in his pale eyes. "Where you headed, Trin?"

Of all her suitors, she feared Andy the most. Still, she was damned if she'd cower. "No place illegal, so I don't see that it's any concern of yours."

Andy's eyes narrowed. "Since we'll be getting married next

week, I think it is. What were you doing talking to that infidel trash?"

Trin bit back her instinctive protest—*We're not getting married, Andrew*—and shrugged. "She said hello, so I spoke."

"You don't talk to mongrels, Trinity. She didn't look genetically pure to me. Not with those eyes."

Trin had no idea what it was about Cassidy's eyes that had struck Andrew as nonwhite. Probably some tiny detail only an Orvillian would have noticed. "Next time I'll ask for a DNA scan before I say hello."

Andrew drew himself up to his full height, squaring his shoulders to emphasize their width. "I don't like your tone, Trinity Yeager." He took a menacing step closer. "You really need to learn your place. And I'm looking forward to teaching it to you."

Anger made her reckless. " 'Fraid the lesson'll have to wait, Andy. You're not my husband yet, and I'm not breaking the law." Lifting her chin, Trin stalked past him. From the corner of one eye, she saw him lift a fist. She tensed, but he didn't hit her.

If he won the auction next week, that would change.

Chapter Two

FIVE minutes later Trin reached the Outworld Quarter. It was like stepping back into the space-faring life she'd known as a child. Unlike the nineteenth-century-style town square, the buildings of the OQ were prefabricated, with curving lines that had probably looked racy and sensual when the structures were new.

Unfortunately, it had been too long since anyone had landed at Rectitude. The cluster of warehouses, restaurants, and hostels were in dire need of a fresh coat of mag paint. Even the computer-run shuttle-control center was starting to look distinctly run-down.

The Spacer's Tavern stood off to one side of the others, as if ostracized by its more respectable peers. Its lines were dumpy rather than sleek, and the air of seediness around it was even thicker.

Trin didn't care. She'd have walked into hell for a chance to get off Orville's Paradise.

"Trinity!" A damp, pudgy hand clamped around her wrist and dragged her to a stop before she could step through the tavern's bat doors. "You're not going into that infidel den of depravity dressed like that! I forbid it!"

God, not another one. Trin shot a cold look at her captor. She was wearing a black unisuit that wouldn't incite a passion-starved trillite miner, but she wasn't surprised at his reaction. Gordon Pureblood made a point of being a prig. "You don't have the authority to forbid me anything, Gordon."

He glowered at her, his round face petulant. His scalp showed pink through his thinning hair in a sunburn he'd probably acquired watching Mary's punishment. Knowing Gordon, he'd showed up early. "We're getting married next week, Trinity. And I don't think it's appropriate for my wife to—"

"We are *not* getting married," Trin interrupted, sick of hearing that particular song.

"Yes, we are." He tilted both his chins. "I've been saving my money for months. I'm going to be the high bidder."

She gritted her teeth and twisted her wrist free of his sweaty hold. "Well, you haven't bought me yet, so you don't have the right to manhandle me."

Gordon's cold, black-pebble eyes narrowed between folds of fat. "Once we're married, you're going to learn your place."

The men of this town really needed to come up with a new threat. "My place," Trin growled, "is where I say it is. And right now it's in there." She pivoted on her heel and stalked through the door of the bar, knowing her tormenter would never set foot inside.

"You come out this minute, Trinity Yeager, or you'll be sorry!" he yelled after her, his voice spiraling into a squeal. "Trin! I'll tell the elders, see if I don't!"

Trin eyed the door, waiting for him to barrel through, wrapped in sanctimonious outrage. Instead his boots rang on the sidewalk as he stomped off. She'd been right; he didn't have the guts to risk being seen going into the tavern.

This had damn well better work, because if she was still here when they held the auction, she was finished. She could handle Gordon—though she'd probably end up tied to the Sinner's Post afterward. But if she married good ol' Andy, she knew the chances were very good he'd eventually beat her to death.

Trin had a strong suspicion that if he did kill her, all the men in town would just shake their heads and say, "Well, she never did know her place." Hell, they'd probably put it on her headstone.

The mercs were the only chance she had of avoiding that auction. She had to get them to take her with them. One way or another.

Taking a deep breath, Trin turned and surveyed the bar's dark interior. She'd never been inside, since it was strictly for infidels. The elders only allowed it to exist at all because they didn't want rowdy foreigners starting brawls in local restaurants. Trin was courting a week in a prayer cell just by stepping through the door.

"Oh, fuck me!" a female voice purred.

Startled, Trin's gaze shot to the central trid globe hovering over the bar. To her astonishment, it depicted a huge ruddy shaft sliding slowly between a woman's glistening vaginal lips.

They were showing a pornographic trid. Right there in the bar. Did the elders know?

Trin stared at the image in scandalized fascination. She'd lost her virginity in a furtive encounter with another teenager five years before, but it had been so painful and they'd come so close to getting caught, she hadn't dared try again. The penalty for fornication was thirty lashes at the Sinner's Post and five years in a prayer cell, and it hadn't seemed worth it. Not for so little pleasure.

But Maker's Beard, she didn't remember Jimmy's cock being that big. . . .

Focus, Trin, she told herself sternly, dragging her eyes away from the globe. *You're not here for the porn.*

"Ohhhh!" the actress moaned. "Deeeperrrr!"

Trin's cheeks flamed. Slinking to the bar, she edged her hip onto the nearest stool, trying to keep her eyes averted from the amazing things the handsome, very naked man was doing to his partner.

"May I take your order?" the bar asked as a trid menu appeared before her eyes. Like the other businesses in the OQ, the tavern was automated. It got too few customers to maintain a human staff.

Trin blinked at the selection. It had been ten years since she'd been in a place like this. She hoped she remembered how to order.

Too, she'd never had alcohol in her life. Orville taught that drinking spirits was sinful, so nobody in Rectitude served liquor. On the other hand, she didn't want to look like a prig to the captain, so . . .

"I'll have a Star Mead, please," Trin decided finally, managing a matter-of-fact tone as she placed her palm on the bar's surface. A blue light flashed around her hand, signaling that the computer had recorded her palm print and would debit her account. She thought she had enough credchits to cover it. Barely.

An opening appeared in the bar's surface, and a curving bottle thrust upward, filled with something blue and faintly phosphorescent. Trin accepted it and took a wary sip. The cold, bitter liquid bit into her tongue and burned its way down her esophagus. Gamely she forced herself to swallow another foaming mouthful, hoping she wouldn't get drunk on one bottle. She needed her wits about her.

"Oh, God, your cunt is so *tight* and *wet!*"

Trin shot a glance at the trid. Jimmy definitely hadn't been that big. Or flexible. Or imaginative.

As she swallowed and looked away, she saw the mercenaries. Two of them, both male, sat at a small table rimmed in glowtubes that cast the only illumination in the room. One was a big, handsome blond, the other equally big, but dark-haired. They were the only other patrons in the tavern. She hoped one of them was Captain August.

Eyeing the pair cautiously, Trin tried to decide on her approach. A small forest of bottles stood on the table between them; they must be well and truly launched. She wasn't sure if that was good or bad.

Either way, they were an intimidating—and attractive—pair. Matte-black half-armor and holstered pistols gave them an air of exotic danger enhanced by broad shoulders and brawny arms. Trin felt a wickedly sensual interest steal through her. *Stop that!* she told her stirring libido. Sex was a distraction she didn't need right now.

As she watched, the blond threw back his head and boomed out a laugh. His hair was as long as a woman's. It flowed halfway down his back in a stream of molten gold that matched the short goatee framing his mouth.

As Trin gazed at him in scandalized fascination, she realized the thick mane actually enhanced his masculinity rather than detracted from it. Otherwise, his broad, angular face and square jaw would have seemed too hard, too aggressive. As it was, he reminded her somehow of an archangel, one of the martial kind who carried swords.

Then his full mouth curled into a smile so wicked and knowing, Trin changed her mind. If the man looked like an angel, it was one the Maker had kicked out of Paradise. And that carnal grin made it clear why He'd done it. The man was a menace to anything female, saints and angels included.

The other mercenary sat back in his chair, drawing Trin's attention with the way he settled into a long-legged, arrogantly male sprawl. He was as dark as his partner was blond, and his hair was cropped ruthlessly short, emphasizing the stark lines of his face.

He wasn't anywhere near as pretty as his friend, either. His face was narrow, the bone structure a little rougher and less refined, with a long nose and thick brows that drew low over deepset blue eyes.

But it was his mouth that made Trin feel downright uneasy. The upper lip was narrow and curving, while the lower was full, sensual. He looked cruel, she decided. Yet there was an air about him, an indefinable something that made her acutely aware of being female.

"Oh, God," the trid actress breathed, "you're so hard, so thiiiick. . . ."

Trin blinked and licked her lips. Chances were good one of the men was Captain August. She had to approach them. Convince him to give her a chance.

Unfortunately, she had a feeling the captain wasn't the handsome, laughing blond. It was the dark one. The cruel one.

She wasn't sure what scared her more: the idea that he'd turn her down, or the thought that he just might take her on. She wasn't at all sure she could handle him.

But he looked like he was more than capable of handling her.

✦✦✦

CAPTAIN Nathan August took another sip of his Star Mead as he sprawled at his table listening to his internal com unit.

"We won't have any trouble filling the order for the 10,000 crates of meat and produce," the Paradise broker said through his communications implant. *"A ground transport will deliver them to the Rectitude shuttleport at 1500 today."*

They'd have to shuttle the cargo up themselves, then process it into ration packs. Apparently the locals thought even orbital flight was sinful. Idiots. Space travel had gotten them to this mudball, hadn't it? *"Sounds good,"* Nathan commed back, the implant transmitting his mental reply to the other man. *"We'll be looking for it. I'll have the other half of the payment ready for you."*

"The Maker's blessings on you, Captain. And may Orville himself guide you away from the path of sin and death you now follow."

Nathan gritted his teeth and reminded himself again just how low the *Starrunner*'s rations were. *"August out."* His com disconnected. Looking over at his executive officer, he glowered. "You do realize all these people are bugshit crazy? What the hell kind of religion is Orvility, anyway?"

Sebastian Cole grinned and picked up his bottle of mead for a slow sip. "I'm not sure *religion* is the right word. I think the actual term is *scam*. As in, 'Hand over all your earthly possessions to me, and I will lead you to a promised land where I will enjoy the fruits of your labor.' "

"And they fell for that?"

"Like the saying goes, there's one born every nanosecond." He curled his lip. "Hell, one of the local bigwigs even tried to talk *me* into immigrating."

Nathan hooted, rocking his chair onto its back legs. "You? Live on a planet where sex is a sin?"

"I was a little surprised myself, but evidently I look 'genetically pure,' whatever the fuck that means." Sebastian's smile went sly. "The elder told me I needed to assume my proper place, instead of serving under a mongrel so obviously my inferior."

"A mongrel?" Nathan glowered. "Me? What the hell did he mean by that?"

"I'm not sure, but I don't think he likes your nose."

"My nose? What's wrong with my nose?"

Sebastian widened his eyes in exaggerated innocence. "I don't know, Captain. It's a very nice nose. Really."

Nathan snorted and picked up his own bottle. "Kiss my ass."

"Sorry, you're not my type." He glanced toward the bar and lifted a brow, attention evidently caught. "Now, she, on the other hand . . ."

Nathan followed his friend's gaze to the little redhead colonist perched on a barstool across the room. She was staring at them as if afraid they'd eat her. Which wasn't a bad idea, come to think of it.

She looked delicious.

Chapter Three

THE black unisuit the little colonist wore was snug enough to display a long, lean, lightly muscled body. Her breasts mounded beneath it in deliciously ample handfuls. Nathan found himself wondering whether her nipples were the same pretty pink he'd seen on other redheads. He wouldn't mind finding out.

Normally that thought would be his cue to wander over for a seduction, but there was something about her that kept him in his seat.

Maybe it was the innocence in those big green eyes. They made her look younger than the twenty-four his computer estimated. The effect was only heightened by her pretty, gently rounded face with its pointed chin and slim, straight nose.

There was nothing little girl about her mouth, though. It was full-lipped, pouting. Starkly carnal. He'd love to watch his cock ease between those red lips as she slowly suckled him.

Then there was all that hair, shimmering copper shot with gold highlights, neatly coiled in an intricate arrangement on top of her head. Nathan could almost see her, lush, tanned, and naked, spread out on top of that fiery mane as it spilled across his bed.

Except—there was that damned innocence. Something about her shouted *Keep off the virgin!* On any other world he'd assume the impression was an illusion created by those big, soft eyes. But given the zealotry of the Orville cult, it was entirely possible Red was as untouched as she looked.

Nathan shifted uncomfortably in his seat, feeling heat spin into his groin as that thought aroused a certain predatory protectiveness, a yen to guard her from every other man while simultaneously corrupting the hell out of her himself. *Down boy,* he told himself sternly. *You don't play your kind of games with an innocent.*

Now, an experienced redheaded submissive with innocent green eyes and a taste for bondage . . . God, there was an arousing thought.

"*Mmm,*" Sebastian commed, eyeing her with lecherous interest. "*Captain, mind if we invade this tight-assed colony? I see somebody I want to take captive.*"

Nathan grinned, not even remotely surprised his friend was thinking the same thing he was. "*She'd probably just lie there and pray the entire time you were trying to seduce her.*"

"*Not if I gagged her first.*" Sebastian dipped one lid in a lascivious wink. "*Preferably with my dick.*"

"*Asshole.*"

"*Look me in the eye and tell me you weren't imagining the same thing.*"

Nathan's gaze slid to the redhead again. "*It's a thought,*" he admitted. "*But she's not exactly in our weight class.*"

Just as he was feeling virtuous, she slid off her stool and started toward them. Head up, shoulders back, pretty breasts leading the way.

"Maybe not," Sebastian commed, *"But does she know that?"*

Nathan blinked. That stiff-legged march should have looked awkward as hell. Instead, it gave her lush body a sweet little feminine jiggle that made him want to beg for mercy.

Even through the fog of alcohol and lust that surrounded him, he felt a flicker of wariness. What the hell did she want, anyway?

Unless . . . Nathan's imagination instantly went into overdrive. Maybe she wasn't a virgin. Maybe she was one of those women whose fantasies centered around bondage and wicked male mercenaries. There was nothing he loved more than obliging that particular kink.

If Red turned out to be a closet submissive, he'd have her naked, bound, and stuffed full of cock before she had time to get the come-on out of her mouth. It had been way, *way* too long since he'd played "seduce the captive" with a pretty sub.

Red stopped beside the table and looked down at them, her green eyes wide and wary. She licked those lush lips as if trying to work up the guts for whatever kinky request she had in mind. Nathan watched her tongue and went hard and hot as a cheap beamer pistol.

"Maker's blessings on you," she said at last. "I'm Trinity Yeager."

He nodded, trying to paste a polite, professional expression on his face—at least until he knew what she wanted. "Captain Nathan August of the *Starrunner*." Gesturing at his friend, he ignored the blond's knowing grin. "My executive officer, Sebastian Cole. What can we do for you?" And would it, please God, happen to involve cable restraints and a fantasy about vicious, well-hung mercenaries?

He probably shouldn't have had that last mead.

"Honored." Red lifted her chin and braced her feet apart like a trooper in parade rest. "I have a proposal of sorts. A request."

"Yes?" Nathan prompted, and was faintly embarrassed at the hot purr of anticipation in his own voice. He ordinarily had more subtlety.

"I want to be a mercenary. I'm interested in joining your crew."

Stunned, he stared at her, his alcohol-fuzzed brain struggling to follow the abrupt conversational detour.

Sebastian roared with laughter. The smile faded from Trinity's face as she looked over at him, a hint of hurt in her green eyes. "Oh, Ms. Yeager, I'm sorry," he gasped. "I'm not laughing at *you*."

Nathan, knowing exactly who his friend was laughing at, kicked him viciously under the table. Sebastian only hooted louder.

When his executive officer's howls finally subsided into wheezes, Nathan said coolly, "I'm sorry, but I'm afraid that's out of the question."

He expected her to instantly back down from his chill, forbidding tone. Instead she straightened even more. She probably had no idea what squaring those shoulders did to her luscious breasts. Nathan clenched his teeth and tried to ignore them.

"I'm in good physical shape, Captain," Trinity said. "I really am stronger than I look."

"*Oh, yeah,*" Sebastian commed. "*I'll bet she has a real tight grip.*"

"*If she does, you won't be finding out.*" Nathan shot his

second-in-command a glare that made him go poker-faced. Sebastian quelled, he returned his attention to Trinity. "Whatever your physical abilities, you're not a cyborg, Ms. Yeager. The rest of the crew have nanotech enhancements that make them far stronger than a human could ever hope to be." He hoped she hadn't noticed the slight slur in "nanotech." That last mead really had been a bad idea.

She leaned forward to rest her palms on the table. Nathan struggled to keep his gaze from drifting to the tight bodice of her unisuit. "I realize that. I plan to get the implants myself as soon as I can save the funds."

Damn, he was not in the mood for this. "Why—so you can kill people? That's what mercenaries do, Ms. Yeager. We're killers. We hire out our ships and our bodies to the highest bidder. Is that what you want?"

"And if so, can I make a bid?" Sebastian commed.

"I," Nathan told him, thoroughly out of patience, "am going to kick your ass the minute we get back to the ship."

". . . father was a mercenary before we immigrated here," Trinity was saying, unable to overhear the silent byplay without a com implant. "I heard his stories, I know what it's like. I want that lifestyle, Captain August. I want to travel to other planets, and I'm willing to fight—even kill—to help people defend themselves against aggressors. . . ."

"Sometimes, Ms. Yeager, we are the aggressors." The idealism shining in those green eyes was rapidly eating away at what little patience he had left. "Being a merc is a violent, bloody ride that often ends in violent, bloody ways. This is a nice planet. Stay here, do whatever it is you do, raise babies and die of old age. I assure you, you'll be much happier."

"Captain, I'm well aware of the risks of being a mercenary. My mother died in combat." Her curvy upper lip lifted, exposing small white teeth in a snarl. "As for this being a 'nice planet,' next week the bigots who run this colony are going to auction me off to the highest bidder. He'll marry me whether I like it or not, and the laws of Orville's Paradise will give him the right to beat or even rape me whenever he wants. And if I complain, if I don't obey him in every last detail, he could kill me without having to answer too many difficult questions. Your life may be hard and violent and bloody, but so is mine. And at least you're *free*!"

"Damn," Sebastian transmitted in an awed tone, *"there's a lot more in that fluffy package than meets the eye."*

Nathan stared at her, caught flat-footed for one of the few times in his life. The situation she was describing was appalling, assuming she wasn't exaggerating. Yet every instinct told him he had no business exposing such an innocent to a mercenary's life, no matter what her alternatives were.

It wasn't simply that she was female. Women made up half his crew, and he'd have no hesitation about kicking down a door with any of them. But an upbringing on a religious colony, extreme or not, did not equip anyone for the hard, violent life of a merc.

It was one thing to fuck the little redhead. It was another to take her into a situation that could get her crippled or killed. "If that's true . . ."

"It is."

". . . I'm doubly sorry. But we just don't take passengers. Everybody on my ship works, and I don't have any openings." He winced and waited for Sebastian to com, *"But wouldn't you love to fill one of hers?"* For once, though, his executive officer remained wisely silent.

"There's got to be something," Trinity insisted, her voice edged with desperation. "Cook. I'm a good cook. . . ."

"We don't need a cook. We eat prepackaged rations, like every other military company." He waved a hand in dismissal. "I appreciate your willingness to—"

"Any job at all, no matter how menial," she said, fiercely demanding. "Anything."

Frustrated, uncomfortable, and more than a little horny, Nathan lost his temper. "I need a fuck toy," he snarled. "How's that?"

She stared at him, her soft, pink mouth curving into an O that looked entirely too dick-ready for the peace of his libido. Sebastian raised a hand as if shielding his eyes. Grimly Nathan waited for her to explode in outrage.

"All right," she said.

"I'm sorry I can't . . . What?" The room revolved slowly. He *really* shouldn't have had that last mead.

"I said I accept your offer." Her gaze was cool, steady, and surprisingly cynical.

What offer? Nathan wondered in mild panic. *When did I make an offer?*

"Now what, genius?" Sebastian commed, his mental voice dripping sarcasm.

Inspired, Nathan added, "You'll also be required to service my executive officer." That should make her think twice.

"What a pal."

Her gaze slid to Sebastian. Nervousness flickered across her expressive face, but her voice was brisk when she replied, "That won't be a problem. Not if you get me off this planet. How long would you expect me to . . . ah . . ."

Nathan's lips twisted. "Serve under us?"

She didn't flinch. "Yes."

He pulled a number out of the air. "Six months."

The colonist considered the figure, then nodded. "That's acceptable."

Oh, God. It was?

Chapter Four

SHE hadn't even blinked.

It was tough to believe a virgin would be willing to take on both of them, but she had, and she hadn't blinked.

So did that mean she wasn't a virgin? Nathan wondered, suddenly intrigued. If not, he could satisfy his randy hunger with a clear conscience. Then he'd send her home where nobody would shoot her.

Trinity stared back at him, a stubborn angle to her pointed chin. There was no pleading in her gaze, but there was definitely a trace of desperation.

Could she be telling the truth? Would the cult's elders force her into an abusive marriage? Or was she simply playing a role, trying to free herself from the stultifying religious strictures of her culture?

If the situation she described was real, he had no problem giving her transport off-world. It wasn't necessary for her to actually join the crew, after all. He could help her land a berth on a vessel captained by one of the merchants he knew. Plenty of them owed him favors, and it would be a safer life for her than a merc's.

But he refused to be the victim of a scam. Was she lying?

There was one way to find out—one very delicious way he'd no doubt thoroughly enjoy. Nathan felt his cock harden.

"Before we make any agreements, I want a test-drive," he drawled, giving her his best menacing smile. If she were lying, she'd back down when they started playing hardball. "Let's see you take on the two of us first."

She only shrugged. "I have no objection to that."

His cock grew even harder at her assent. He reminded it she'd probably back out.

"Then if you'll accompany us to the ship . . ." Testing her resolve, Nathan rose from his chair; that alone had been known to make some challengers back off. Not Red, though her green eyes widened. He started toward the door, placing his feet more carefully than he ordinarily did.

"*Nate, what the fuck do you think you're doing?*" Sebastian commed as he and the colonist followed.

"*I'm drunk, I've got a hard-on, and I want to see what she's made of,*" Nathan replied. "*And you're going to help.*"

"*You don't really mean to make this fluffy little virgin one of the crew?*" Sebastian sounded scandalized.

"*Of course not. But I do want to know if she's as determined to leave this planet as she claims. If she's really in trouble, she'll stick it out. Otherwise, she'll go running home to Mommy where she belongs.*"

"*So this is a test.*"

"Exactly."

Sebastian eyed him. *"Sure it's not just the fit of her tight little cunt you want to investigate?"*

Nathan gestured at her to proceed them. As she strode out the door, he grinned wolfishly, watching the feminine sway of her lovely backside. *"Well, that, too. Assuming she doesn't run for home before I get around to it."*

The three of them stepped from the bar's dim confines into the bright, hard glare of the afternoon. Nathan's head instantly produced a protesting throb. He ignored it, intent on getting Red back to the ship and into his bed. She probably wouldn't stay there, but he suspected she'd be thoroughly entertaining while she was.

In the meantime, he ordered his computer implants to sober him up for the flight. Almost instantly, the throbbing in his temples faded as his thoughts slid into focus.

He shot another glance at Trinity's butt. Damn, it was as luscious as he'd thought. He'd hoped alcohol had made her more appealing than she really was. As it was, satisfying his aching hard-on was going to take a while.

Which reminded him. *"Lieutenant Vika?"*

Cassidy Vika's voice responded in his mind. *"Yes, Captain?"* Vika was one of the *Starrunner's* fighter pilots, but she also did double duty as a security officer. Tough, capable, and skilled, she always rose to any challenge he cared to throw at her.

"The supplier is supposed to deliver that shipment of food at 1500. Meet the driver at the port and accept it, then give me a call."

"Will do, Captain. Ah—did a colonist named Trinity Yeager find you?"

"Yes. Do I have you to thank for that, Lieutenant?"

" 'Fraid so, sir. She seemed genuinely in need of a ride off-world. And based on what I've seen this morning, I wouldn't want to live here, either." She paused. *"Did I screw up?"*

"Don't worry about it, Vika. I plan to investigate the situation." His gaze tracked to Trinity's back. *"Thoroughly."*

"Aye, Captain." There was a note of knowing laughter in Cassidy's voice. *"Vika out."*

Sebastian by his side, Nathan followed Trinity down the narrow sidewalk toward the gates of the landing pad. She seemed to radiate a combination of nerves and determination that perversely intensified his appetite. He couldn't wait to . . .

"Trinity! Trinity Yeager, where are you going?" a man called in a grating nasal whine.

Trin didn't even break step, even when a short, fat little male scurried around Nathan to grab her by one wrist. She sent the intruder a coldly contemptuous look he totally ignored.

"I demand to know where you're going with this infidel trash!"

"None of your business, Gordon." She tried to jerk free, but he clamped down on her wrist so hard, the skin dimpled under his sausage fingers.

Nathan's temper began to steam. He took a step forward.

"You can't leave with them!" the man stormed. "I forbid it!"

Before Nathan could put the fat bastard into orbit, Trinity lifted her lip in a snarl. "You can't forbid me *anything*, Gordon. You're not my father, and you're not my husband. And you never will be."

"The auction . . ."

"Is next week!" In a surprisingly skillful move, she hooked one foot behind the colonist's ankle and drove a shoulder into his pudgy chest, sending him sprawling. She danced clear as he hit the ground with an outraged *whoof.*

Trinity leaned over him, bracing both hands on her knees as he blinked at her in shocked outrage. "And in the meantime, do you know what I'm going to do?" she growled, her voice low and deadly. "I'm going to *fuck* these mercenaries, Gordon. I'm going to fuck both of them! And I'm going to enjoy it a great deal more than I'd ever enjoy *anything* having to do with you!"

Straightening, she whirled and stalked toward the landing strip gate.

"You . . . You . . . I'll call the sheriff!" the little man howled as Nathan and Sebastian followed her.

"Call him!" she snarled back.

"That muffled explosion you just heard," Sebastian commed as they followed her, *"was the sound of our little friend blowing all her bridges to quarks."*

"Did sound that way, didn't it?" She'd handled that well. *"The question is, will she want to rebuild them after she finds out what she's in for?"*

✦ ✦ ✦

TRINITY'S outrage sustained her all the way across the landing pad to the mercs' shuttle, a long, low-slung predator of a craft bristling with gun ports. Several faint burn marks along her sides suggested she'd seen recent combat. The sight of her brought reality crashing home.

Trin was about to sleep with men who had a battleship. *Two* men who had a battleship.

Oh, Maker's Beard, what have I gotten myself into?

Though her thoughts skittered wildly, Trin kept her face expressionless. She couldn't afford to show her fear. Who'd want to go into battle with somebody scared out of her wits at the thought of just having sex with a couple of mercs?

A couple of very large, very muscular, very exotic mercs. One of whom was watching her like he'd like to eat her.

In one big bite.

Nathan August was the most intimidating human being she'd ever met, including the sheriff and Andrew. It had been all she could do to hang on to her wits while he'd been giving her that *look* back in the bar.

His eyes were truly beautiful—a shimmering, cobalt blue—but they alternated between hot and predatory and cold and dismissive. Either expression unnerved the hell out of her.

On the other hand Sebastian seemed perpetually amused, though there was a shimmer of amorous interest in his gaze, too.

They wanted to have sex with her. Not only that, but the captain wanted to make her their pleasure toy for the next six months. It was a humiliating offer, but it wasn't as if she could afford to stand on pride.

Despite the dictates of common sense, Trin was disappointed in him, if not particularly surprised. She should have known a mercenary wouldn't be willing to save her out of the goodness of his heart.

There was also the troubling possibility she was leaping straight from the frying pan into the fire. Still, August had specified six months. Six months as sex toy for two mercs was infinitely preferable to a lifetime of abuse with Andy Makerson. For one thing, she doubted the mercs would beat her to death. She was pretty sure she could take whatever else they could dish out.

Paradise had taught her to be tough.

Whatever he had in mind, the captain was eager to get started. As soon as they boarded the shuttle, August dropped into the pilot's seat and powered systems up. Trin settled into one of the passenger seats while Sebastian took the copilot's spot. He and August started drawling techspeak at each other; she caught one word in five.

As she watched, August stroked his hands through the glowing trid control displays, ticking through his takeoff checklist with the ease and rapidity of long practice. The shuttle's engines began to rumble, a low, subsonic growl felt more in the bones than anything else. The craft didn't even rock as it lifted off its wheels, slipping skyward as weightlessly as a plume of smoke.

Then what felt like a fist crushed down on Trinity's chest, and they blasted for orbit so hard and fast, she barely had time to gasp.

August flew the shuttle like the combat pilot he probably was—all skillful, reckless insouciance. Trin managed not to shut her eyes and pray.

To distract herself from her fear, she stared out the viewport, watching the pink sky darken to purple with the shuttle's rapid ascent. In minutes it was a deep, flat black. The curve of Paradise spread below, its seas a shining blue, the land red everywhere it wasn't purple with vegetation.

A white, shining point rose over the horizon. As she watched, half-hypnotized, it zoomed toward them like a meteor.

"The *Starrunner*," Nathan said over his shoulder, pride in his voice.

She was an impressive vessel, Trinity saw as they approached. Lean and sleek, the battleship was designed to withstand the stresses of slipping into the alternate universe where faster-than-light travel was possible.

Judging by all those weapons' ports, she could have reduced Orville's Paradise to chunks of rubble in about an hour and a half.

As Trin watched, a black opening appeared in the *Starrunner*'s gleaming side—one of its landing bays. August ran through the docking procedure, his hands playing over the trid controls, creating a symphony of grav and antigrav forces that skillfully deposited the shuttle on the deck. The great double doors closed behind them.

Trin's heart was still pounding from the ride when the captain rose from the pilot's seat to give her a feral male grin. "Welcome to the *Starrunner*," he purred, in the exact same tone of menacing anticipation the devil might have used greeting a sinner in hell.

Trin gave him her best undaunted smile. "Why, thank you, Captain August."

"Believe me," he said, his eyes dropping to her breasts, "the pleasure's all mine."

Sebastian's grin was equally wicked. "Well, not *all* his."

What have I gotten myself into? moaned a sane fragment of her mind. She ignored it.

This was one test she had no intention of failing.

Chapter Five

WHATEVER Trin had expected a battleship to be, the *Starrunner* wasn't it. The gently curving corridors were wide and bright, filled with bustling, determined people who looked more like the trids she'd seen of corporate professionals than the hardened killers she knew them to be.

As they walked, the captain played genial tour guide, pointing out the ship's mess, sickbay, and crew quarters. He didn't mention the bridge or the ship's weapons systems. Either they were on another deck, or it was information he didn't want her to have. Probably both.

But as they turned off one particular corridor, she noticed both men losing the geniality in dark anticipation. Finally the captain stopped before one of the doors and murmured, "August."

The door obediently opened. He turned and stepped back, extending a hand to gesture her through. "Home, sweet home." His smile seem to sizzle down her spine as she entered.

Nathan's quarters were just as welcoming as the rest of the ship—a spacious suite filled with colorful artwork and intriguing souvenirs of his travels. There was an office with an imposing cyberconsole that looked as if he could have piloted the *Starrunner* from its massive chair. Adjoining the office was a sitting area with a couch and chairs on one side and a breakfast nook on the other. It was all surprisingly homey.

At least, until Nathan ushered them to his bedroom.

A huge tridscreen surrounded a bed more than big enough for all three of them. Dry-mouthed, she stared at the gently undulating gel mattress, wondering if he threw orgies often.

Before her overstimulated brain could produce any really Byzantine fantasies, Nathan turned to her and drawled, "Strip."

"Now?" She blinked, startled.

"Now." He bared his teeth in that white wolf grin. "I want to see what I'm getting."

Sebastian looked surprised, as if the obnoxious snap in the captain's voice was unusual.

Whether it was or not, though, the hot blue glitter of Nathan's eyes made it clear he'd meant every word. Trin licked her lips. Could she really do this?

"Backing out already?" His challenging gaze cooled.

"No, of course not." She reached for buttons of her unisuit.

It was tricky managing the tiny disks with her nervous fingers, and Trin silently cursed the Orvillian dogma that insisted modern suit seals would lead the faithful into sin. You could sin just as much with buttons. It just took longer.

When she finally had the suit open to the crotch, Trin looked up to find both men staring at her with molten anticipation.

"What are you waiting for?" August demanded, his voice a low, rasping growl. "I want you naked."

Trin wanted to get angry, but the hunger in the captain's eyes made outrage impossible. She grabbed the shoulders of her suit and started wiggling out of it. Her breasts bounced as she bared them, nipples hardened to tight, pink buds.

One of the men made a low sound, rumbling, male and ravenous.

Her gaze flew to the captain. He was standing in an elaborately casual pose, brawny arms folded, one powerful shoulder propped against one bulkhead. But below his half-armor, his tight uniform pants bulged around the outline of a massive erection.

Beside him, his handsome second-in-command watched her with a lupine half-smile. Meeting her gaze, Sebastian wet his full lower lip with his tongue and dipped an eyelid in a wink. His cock was just as hard as August's.

Her heart in her throat, Trin pushed the suit down her legs.

✦ ✦ ✦

"OH, God," Sebastian moaned into his com unit, *"she's a natural redhead."*

And she was. Her bush was as fiery as the mane on her head. Her deliciously full, up-tilted breasts bounced as she kicked her unisuit aside with one slender foot. She was blushing so brightly, Nathan half expected her to grab the suit and dive for the door.

Instead she braced her fists on her hips and lifted her chin with a cool smile that made him want to applaud. "I hope I meet with your approval."

Nathan pasted on a suitably mocking smile. "Not bad. I've had better. . . ."

"Not lately," Sebastian commed.

". . . But not bad. I don't suppose you're a virgin?" He displayed his teeth. "I like virgins."

"A little over the top, boss."

Trin didn't think so; she paled. Still, she gave him that confident smile again, and her voice quavered only slightly when she said, "Sorry, I'm afraid not."

"Too bad. I was really in the mood to pop your cherry."

"Definitely over the top."

"Fuck off." Nathan contemplated that lush little body with a twinge of regret. As much as he'd love to just screw her brains out, he didn't quite buy her denial of virginity.

He needed a test just uncomfortable enough to make her think twice, but which wouldn't do permanent damage to her hymen in case she did decide to back out. The loons on Orville's Paradise probably attached a lot of significance to that little bit of flesh. He didn't want her to end up paying the price for her escapade.

Wicked inspiration struck. "Ever had your mouth fucked?"

Trinity rocked back. "Uh, no."

"Good." He gave her a toothy, deliberately menacing grin. "That'll do."

"God, I'm horny as hell, and you're trying to run her off," Sebastian complained. *"What do we do when she leaves us literally high and dry?"*

"Actually," Nathan drawled back, *"I thought I'd fuck you up the ass."*

There was a long, long silence. *"So what are we going to do until I have to shoot you?"*

Nathan turned the nasty grin on him. *"Well, first,"* he said, *"we tie her up."*

Sebastian moved toward her like a big cat stalking something small and tasty. Trin instinctively backed up a pace, but he grabbed her by the waist. Before she could do more than yelp in surprise, he tossed her effortlessly through the air. She landed on the gel mattress with a soft plop.

Trin strangled another yelp as the blond merc pounced on her and flipped her onto her stomach, then grabbed her right wrist and pulled it behind her. "What are you doing?"

"Tying you up." There was laughter in Sebastian's voice as he caught her right foot with the other hand, then bent her leg until ankle met wrist.

"Why?" Frightened, she tried to kick free, only to discover she couldn't break his grip. "I told you I agreed! I'm not going to fight!"

"We have no intention of hurting you." As he looked down at her, the wicked humor faded from Sebastian's face. "It's a game. Haven't you ever heard of bondage?"

"Let her up," August ordered.

Instantly the blond released her, but Trin didn't scramble to her feet. If this was another test, she was determined not to fail.

Rolling onto her side, she looked up at the captain. He held a length of something gold and metallic. She recognized it as the same kind of magnetic cable she used to hobble goats.

"Some people enjoy being bound during sex," Nathan told her. "They like the sense of helplessness. But if the idea frightens you, we won't do it."

Trin's heart was pounding, but she lifted her chin. "I'm not afraid of you. Any game you want to play, I'll play."

The captain lifted a dark brow. "A rash statement. And one I'm not sure I trust." He studied her face. She fought to hide her instinctive nervousness. "If you decide at any time that we're going too far for you, say *'Starrunner,'* " he said at last. "That's your safe word. We'll end it then."

"And I'll have failed your test."

"No," Nathan said instantly. "I don't want you hurt because you're trying to prove a point. If you use the safe word, I won't hold it against you. So I expect you to use it. Is that clear?"

"Perfectly." She rolled back onto her stomach and stretched her arms back until she could grab her ankles. "I'm ready to play your game."

Nathan looked down at her face for a long moment. Then his blue gaze traveled over her naked body, and heat gathered in his eyes. He smiled. "Good."

He reached for her.

✦✦✦

NATHAN'S erection surged to its full length as he used the two restraint cables to tie Red's delicate ankles to her slender wrists. By the time he stepped back, she was bound, naked, and thoroughly helpless, and he was hard as a neutronium rod. Gazing at her delicious ass, he began stripping out of his armor.

"You know," Sebastian said, following suit, *"it occurs to me if she's never given a blow job, she's probably never had her pussy eaten, either."*

Nathan watched her thighs flex as she twisted to watch them, fine muscle rippling all up and down her body. Between her long, smooth legs, he could see the delicate flesh of her sex, furred in bright copper curls. He smiled slowly as he dropped his armor on the deck, imagining how she'd react to a male tongue flicking over wet flesh. *"I suspect you're right,"* he commed. *"Let's expand her . . . horizons."*

He slid a knee on the bed and grabbed Trin by one slim shoulder, flipping her onto her back again. Her breasts bounced temptingly. Big green eyes watched as he spread her legs wide.

The unease in her gaze touched him. Nathan hesitated, realizing she needed reassurance in this moment of profound vulnerability.

So instead of sliding between her legs, he tilted up her chin. "Don't be afraid, Trinity."

"I'm not."

"Good." He bent his head and took her mouth. Her lips were velvet soft, damp and sweet, and he explored them thoroughly in a slow, sweet kiss. By the time he finished, she looked dazed.

It probably wasn't her first kiss—but not by much.

Nathan badly wanted to discover what additional pleasure he could introduce her to before her nerve broke. Need growling through him, he slid down to settle between her silken thighs. Glancing up, he saw Sebastian taking her mouth in a lazy kiss of his own.

A pang of surprising jealousy made Nathan frown. As a rule, he didn't have a possessive streak. He wasn't sure he liked the idea that little Red could arouse it.

Determined to ignore the lapse, Nathan lowered his head between her thighs and inhaled, breathing deeply of the rich, salty musk of her sex.

Trinity looked down at him as Sebastian broke the kiss. "What are you . . . ?" she began as Nathan caught her vaginal lips between two fingers and parted them. He gave her a long, slow lick, and she gasped in surprise. As he settled down to feast in earnest, he heard Sebastian purr, "Has anybody ever told you what pretty nipples you have? I wonder if they're as delicious as they look?"

She whimpered. His friend laughed. "Ah. They are. Isn't this my lucky night?"

+ + +

TRINITY had never in her life experienced anything as hot as the feeling of two men moving over her body, sucking here, biting there, teasing her most delicate flesh until it was wet and aching. She moaned helplessly.

She'd never even heard of half the things they were doing.

Yet arousing as all this was, none of it touched her quite the way Nathan's kiss had. There'd been such tenderness in the touch of his mouth, as though he actually cared. . . .

No, she told herself firmly. *Forget it, Trin. That's just asking for trouble.*

"Is her pussy as delicious as her tits, boss?" Sebastian asked between gentle, nibbling bites at one hard nipple. His erect cock rested against her hip as he snuggled against her side. The shaft was long, with a slight upward bow to it, as if it could reach in deep. The captain's wasn't quite as long, but nearly twice as thick. She remembered that much from the moment he'd stood looking down at her after he'd stripped, tall and brawny and built for combat.

What would it be like when he began working all that hard flesh into her scarcely used sex? Would it feel as incredible as what he was doing with that impossibly clever mouth?

Would it affect her like his kiss?

Maker, she hoped not. She was far too vulnerable to these two as it was.

Chapter Six

Nathan's strong hands clamped over Trinity's thighs, pinning her against her impulse to writhe as he suckled her clit. The sensations he created stormed her nervous system with such savagery, she could only lie there and quiver. "What are you doing?" Trin groaned finally, clit and labia burning from the beamer-hot pleasure.

Sebastian lifted his head from her peaked pink nipple. "He's eating your creamy little pussy, Trin."

"Eating my . . . ? Ahhh!" The captain drew his tongue in a long wet stroke between her lips, making her shiver as pleasure snaked and burned along her nerves.

Presenting a forefinger to her opening, Nathan began working it inside. She writhed helplessly at the feeling of being stretched for the first time in years. The protest was out of her mouth before she could call it back. "Don't!"

"Oh, yes," Sebastian chuckled in her ear. "We like our victims nice and wet before we start using them." As his captain feasted, he cupped one of her breasts until the stiff nipple pointed upward. He leaned forward, the raw silk of his hair stroking over her skin, and trapped the little peak between his teeth. Gently, relentlessly, he began alternately sucking and raking it with his teeth, creating delicious little pleasure zings.

It was all too much—too intense, too savagely arousing, too delicious. Yet bound hand and foot, there was nothing Trin could do to escape as the two warriors pleasured her.

"You like being helpless, Trin?" Sebastian asked, twisting one of her nipples with slow, hot skill. "I hope so, because we like helpless little submissives."

He leaned closer until he could whisper into her ear. "There's something about the look in a woman's eyes when she's all tied up, staring at your cock. You can see her wondering how it's going to feel when you slide it inside her." He palmed her other breast and started teasing its erect, longing tip. "Meanwhile you're looking at her, trying to decide how you're going to fuck her first. 'Cause when she's bound like that, she's all yours. Any way you want her, you can take her. Slow and sweet, or rough and hard. And God, that's soooo hot."

At those darkly arousing words, heat lashed through Trinity like a whip. She could feel something huge growing inside, swelling as if it would burst wide any moment.

Maddened with a dazzled lust that was so much more intense than anything she'd ever known, Trin lost control of her fear. This was going too far, too fast. "Stop! God, please stop!"

"You want us to stop, use the safe word," Nathan rumbled from between her legs. "That's what it's for."

The sound of his voice instantly reassured her. Trin sucked in a breath, realizing she didn't really want the mercy she was about to plead for. She snapped her teeth shut.

"Oh, yeah—you love it," Sebastian said in a voice as rich and wicked as sin. "Beg some more, sweetheart. Beg the nasty mercenaries not to suck your pretty pink nipples and your stiff little clit. Beg us not to fuck you. Makes me so *hard*. . . ."

Then Nathan closed his mouth over her clit and sucked just as Sebastian raked his teeth over her nipple again. Fire exploded behind her eyes like a sun going nova.

Trinity screamed from the sheer, terrifying glory as pleasure pulsed through her in long, rolling waves.

+ + +

SHE was lying limp and boneless, wrung out from the force of the first orgasm she'd ever had in her life, when Nathan scooped her off the bed and deposited her on her knees beside it.

Dazed, Trin watched as he turned to a cabinet and bent, digging around until he produced an arrangement of straps. He dropped the thing over her head, and Sebastian rose to buckle it into place. Meanwhile the captain took the round ring attached to the straps and held it up to her mouth. "Open up," he ordered roughly.

She blinked at the ring. "What is it?"

"It's a ring gag," he told her. "We use it when we want to fuck a submissive's mouth."

Submissive? When the elders used that phrase, they were talking about a woman's duty to her husband. Trin wasn't really sure what that term meant in this context, but somehow it sounded . . . wicked. So much so, in fact, that she was more than willing to experience whatever it was he meant to do to her now.

Maker knew she'd enjoyed it all so far.

Trin licked her lips and obeyed. The captain inserted the ring between her jaws, forcing her lips into an O. The ring was covered in something soft that tasted faintly of mint. She swallowed around it and looked up at the two men.

"What about the safe word?" Sebastian asked his captain.

Nathan grimaced. "Good point." He contemplated the problem, then returned to the cabinet. A moment later he came back and displayed a long, violently blue object. It was shaped exactly like a male cock. "Hold on to this," he said, tucking it into one bound hand. "If you decide you want to call this off, drop it. It'll make a nice thump when it hits the deck, and we'll stop."

Trin clutched the artificial phallus anxiously. She didn't want this to end until she found out what was going on.

Particularly not when they were both grinning at her, wearing identical expressions of male anticipation, their flushed shafts violently hard. Trinity's mouth began to water helplessly around the gag.

Nathan threw a glittering look at Sebastian. "Go get the clamps."

She swallowed.

Clamps?

✦ ✦ ✦

SLOWLY Nathan allowed the stim-clamp to close around one of Trin's hard nipples. She jerked with a low, desperate moan. He looked up quickly, but the expression in her dazed green eyes was one of arousal more than pain. The clamp had a bite, but it also stimulated pleasure receptors in her skin. He checked her hand. She still had that death grip on the dildo. She obviously had no intention of calling things off any time soon.

Testing, he reached between her wide-spread thighs as she knelt before him. She was so richly creamy, his cock jerked.

God, he burned to fuck her. He knew from his careful exploration of her deliciously tight cunt that she wasn't the virgin he'd suspected. And that made her fair game.

Assuming she didn't change her mind.

And he was beginning to suspect she wouldn't back out after all. Whenever she met his gaze, he saw a combination of innocence, awakening desire, and determined courage in those clear green eyes. That blend fascinated and aroused him until he burned to pull her beneath him and take her so hard they'd both detonate like a pair of plasma grenades.

When he lifted his eyes to her panting breasts again, it was just in time to see Sebastian clamp the other nipple. She jolted back against his friend, groaning behind her gag in a voice rich with arousal.

Sebastian, holding her from behind, lowered his mouth to her ear. "Like that?"

She nodded vigorously. Unable to resist, Nathan slid a second finger into her juicy sex. She felt incredibly tight, just begging for his cock.

"*Damn, Nathan,*" Sebastian commed, "*can we keep her?*"

It was an intriguing thought. He brushed his thumb over her clit and watched her twist in her bonds, her green eyes dazed with passion. He'd assumed that a young female raised on a planet of religious zealots would be as emotionally frigid and repressed as her culture. Trin had proved him wrong with a surprising combination of reckless courage and delicious eroticism.

She made him hotter than hell.

For a moment Nathan let himself imagine what it would be like to make her his full-time submissive, his to take whenever he wanted. . . . *"It's a tempting thought."*

"Oh, yeah." Sebastian opened the clamp and let it close again while rotating his wrist, gently twisting her nipple. *"Sweet sub to the core."*

"The question is, would she really want to play the game?"

"She certainly seems to be enjoying it at the moment."

Nathan pumped his hand, feeling her slick interior muscles gripping his fingers. She was sò damn wet, so hot. So tight. *"But we haven't really started playing yet. Let's see what happens when we do. Fuck her mouth."*

"I thought you'd never ask." To Trin, Sebastian said aloud, "It's time for you to discover the joys of sucking cock, Red." Grinning wickedly, he rose to his feet.

Nathan watched the little colonist's eyes widen. He gave her a dark smile and moved back, giving his friend room.

✦ ✦ ✦

TRINITY drew in a breath as the blond mercenary caught the back of her head in one big palm and pulled her closer to his jutting cock. Even if she'd wanted to resist, the gag's ring held her jaws open and ready. She quivered, impossibly aroused.

Then he slid the flushed head between her lips. It felt like velvet, tasted of salt and man, and taking it into her mouth made her hotter than she'd ever been in her life.

He moved in deeper. She could feel the tiny folds just after the head, then the smooth, stretched-tight skin that covered his long erection. Eagerly she began to suck. Sebastian groaned in decadent pleasure as his hand curled into a fist in her hair. "God," he groaned, "her mouth is so hot . . ." He rolled his hips in short, slow thrusts, fucking her face through the gag.

Trin's gaze slid to Nathan, who watched with feral masculine interest. Reaching down with one big hand, he caressed his own tight balls as he wrapped the other around his thick, jutting cock. Slowly the captain began to stroke. "Suck it, Red," he ordered in a deep growl. "Suck it hard. I want to see those cheeks hollow."

Maker's Beard! Cream pooled between her thighs as, closing her eyes, she obeyed.

Trin had learned about blow jobs back in high school—furtive whispered conversation between teenage boys, overheard with desperate interest. But she'd never performed one, and she wondered nervously how to go about it.

"Use your tongue," Nathan ordered in his arousing rasp. "Lick his shaft while he fucks your mouth."

Tentatively she rolled her tongue over the underside of Sebastian's rod. He groaned, his fist tightening in her hair. Encouraged, she angled her head, rocking it from side to side so she could caress him. With her hands bound to her ankles, there wasn't much else she could do.

"That's right," Nathan said. Though her mouth was full of Sebastian's thick shaft, she was intensely aware of the mercenary captain as he moved around behind her. He stepped in so close she felt the brush of his thighs against her back. Trin quivered.

Sebastian drove in a particularly deep thrust. She choked a little on his length and he moderated his thrust, murmuring a soft apology.

Nathan crouched and slid his powerful arms around her torso, one hand claiming her breast, the other slipping between her spread thighs. She closed her eyes and moaned around his second's cock as it steadily stroked in and out.

"You look hot having your mouth fucked, Red," the captain breathed in her ear. A long finger brushed over her clit once, then circled the erect nub. Pleasure rolled over her in a dark, sweet wave. "Helpless and bound, ready for whatever we want." He slid his hand deeper between her legs, found the creaming opening of her cunt. She whimpered as he eased one finger in all the way to the knuckle. "Ahhh. And you like it, too. Don't you? Being a sex toy for a pair of horny mercs." He reached up to the clamp that was still attached to her nipple, began opening and closing it. Every time it moved, it sent a new jolt of sensation into her nipple, unpredictably stinging or pleasurable. Shivering, she opened her legs even more and watched Sebastian's muscled belly work as he used her. Her hand was sweating around the blue phallus.

"You have no idea what we could do to you," Nathan continued in that dark, menacing rumble. "I'm thinking about what it would feel like to slide my cock between your soft pink lips, or maybe inside this juicy cunt." His finger thrust in deeper as his voice dropped again. "Listening to your arousing little whimpers. Feeling you so tight and slick and helpless while I fuck you. Even if we didn't have you tied up, you wouldn't be able to stop us from doing whatever the hell we want with you." He slowly twisted the clamp until she gasped around Sebastian's cock. Nathan chuckled wickedly, then added another finger to the one stroking inside her cunt. "After all, we're big, nasty cyborgs, and you're soft and female and tiiiny." He stretched the word out, packing a shipload of nasty innuendo into its two syllables. "My favorite kind of victim."

Trinity closed her eyes and whimpered helplessly, Sebastian's cock shuttling in and out of her mouth. She really shouldn't find this so damn arousing.

But she did. Maker help her, she did.

Chapter Seven

TRIN groaned in guilty pleasure as Nathan's long fingers went right on tormenting her juicing sex. She could feel another searing climax floating just out of reach. Concentrating ferociously on the sensations flooding her, she almost dropped the blue dildo and had to fumble for it frantically.

"God, yes!" Sebastian groaned as his broad shaft rode faster and faster in and out of her mouth. "Damn, Red's a natural-born cocksucker. Let's put a collar on her and keep her."

Trin shivered at the rough eroticism behind the mock threat. She didn't understand why it made her so hot. A decent woman might endure all this with stoicism if she had to, but she certainly wouldn't feel such feral arousal.

Apparently Trin wasn't a decent woman.

Sebastian stiffened, his back arching. "I'm coming!" he

gasped. She felt his cock jerk in her mouth. Something bitter flooded over her tongue.

"Swallow, Red," Nathan growled. "Swallow every last drop. Because next"—he leaned closer until his whisper gusted against her ear—"it's my turn."

Her eyes drifting closed, Trin obeyed, swallowing greedily even as her Orville training screeched in righteous indignation.

At last Sebastian pulled free of the ring gag and collapsed back on the bed, panting, a sated smile on his face. She knelt on the floor and watched him, feeling a certain dark pride she'd reduced him to such boneless pleasure.

"God, that was good," he groaned.

"And I want to find out just how good." Nathan stepped in front of Trin. She straightened eagerly as he slid his thick rod right into the ring and her waiting mouth.

Trin began to suck, feeling every bit the wanton they'd call her back home.

As hot as it had been when Sebastian had taken her this way, it was even more outrageously arousing when Nathan did it. Her sex went slicker with every oral stroke.

She shouldn't feel this way, shouldn't revel in the sheer wicked kink of it all. Even if she cared nothing for morality, the whole idea of approaching Nathan had been to get away from a bunch of men who wanted to dominate her.

But somehow this submission was different. For one thing, though they demanded her obedience, she sensed Nathan and Sebastian had no interest in hurting her. They weren't abusers. They wanted her willing—not to mention enthusiastic—participation.

When the sheriff had tied her to the Sinner's Post, it might have been a sexual game to him, but the last thing he was interested in was her pleasure. She was an object to him, not a partner. And the rest of the colony's men felt no different.

Nathan's big hands rose to cup the sides of her face, cradling her tenderly as she suckled him. Something in that gesture drained away the last of her shame. Even dominating the hell out of her, the captain treated her with affection.

That was what made this all so seductive, Trin realized. Affection had been in very short supply in her life for a very long time.

Suddenly Nathan pulled free of her mouth and rocked back. The slick head of his cock brushed her cheek as she glanced up, questioning. He stared intently down at her, probing her eyes with his. "Do you want me to come in your mouth, Trinity?" the captain asked, almost gently.

Looking up into his brutally handsome face, she swallowed. And nodded.

Nathan's eyes blazed, and he plunged his cock inside her mouth again. Trin welcomed his silken length with hard suction and a stroking tongue, dying to taste him as she had Sebastian. Wanting to render him helpless with her mouth.

The velvet rod jerked against her tongue, began to pulse salt and heat. "Yes!" His growl was low and fierce. "Take me!"

On the verge of climax herself, she hungrily obeyed.

The dildo dropped from her hands unnoticed.

✦ ✦ ✦

FOR a long moment the only sound in the room was the rasping gasps of spent breathing.

Finally Nathan stepped back a little so that his cock slipped free of Trin's mouth. She tried to suck it back in again, but he forced himself to pull away. "Nice," he rasped, reaching up to un-buckle the ring gag from around her head. "Very, very nice."

And it had been. His knees were still shaking. She might be in-experienced, but she more than made up for it with enthusiasm.

As the gag fell away from her mouth, Trinity licked her lips and worked her jaw. He knew it was probably aching after the vigorous oral use she'd just received.

He took her head in his hands and began to massage the hinge of her jaw. Trin sagged against him, her eyes closing in pleasure.

"Damn," Sebastian commed as he rolled off the bunk to untie her hands, *"it's not just an act, boss. The girl is really sensual. And if she's not a genuine submissive, I'll eat these restraints."*

"Oh, definitely. But we're going to keep our distance anyway," he replied. Ignoring Sebastian's commed protest, he told her, "You've won your transport off-world, Trinity."

Big green eyes lifted to his and lit in relief. Then, as he watched, heat gathered in her gaze, a sweet female anticipation. "So you'll accept me as your . . ." She hesitated and licked her lips. "As your fuck toy?"

"That's not necessary."

Nathan was watching closely enough to catch the disappoint-ment that flashed across her mobile face. "But why not? I thought . . . Did I . . . ?" She clamped her teeth shut and winced, as if she'd committed some erotic *faux pas*.

"You were incredible," he assured her. "But I'd never require a woman's sexual submission as the price of helping her."

Confusion drew her brows into a frown. "But you said . . ."

He shrugged, suddenly uncomfortable. "I was drunk, I was horny, and I wanted to see how far you'd go. I also wondered if you were exaggerating your desperation."

"I wouldn't do that!" Trin protested, glowering.

"The captain," Sebastian said dryly, tossing the restraints aside, "is not in the habit of taking anybody or anything at face value. It's a good way to get people killed."

"Which brings up a point," Nathan said. "I'll be more than happy to give you transport anywhere you want to go, but I think you might want to reconsider becoming a mercenary."

Trin frowned. "What? Why?"

"I meant what I said. It's a tough, bloody life. I won't deny you have courage—it took guts to come here, much less let us tie you up and fuck you—but there's a long jump between that and getting shot at. Or shooting somebody else."

✦ ✦ ✦

IRRITATION banished the last of Trinity's afterglow. After years of having her abilities belittled by the men of Rectitude, hearing a similar song from August stung. "You might be surprised at what I can do."

He held up both hands as if to ward off her anger. "I'm just suggesting you consider your options. There are a number of worlds we'll be visiting that might make a good home for you. Or I can get you a berth on a merchant ship, since several traders owe me favors. I'll tell you right now, crewing a civilian vessel would be safer." His concern seemed genuine.

Trinity frowned. There had to be a catch. She'd met plenty of men on Rectitude who talked a very good game, only to reveal themselves as self-serving in the end. "No," she said slowly. "I want to be a merc." More to the point, she was tired of being a victim.

"You don't have to make the decision right away. Give it time.

But if you do decide that's what you want to do, there are women aboard who'd be happy to take you on as an apprentice. . . ."

"Note, he said 'women,' " Sebastian interrupted, shooting his captain a look that blended affection and amusement. "We men would be, too, but the captain's the jealous type."

Jealous? What did he mean by that?

Before she could explore that thought further, Nathan stiffened, his eyes narrowing. "Oh, hell."

"That's not good." Sebastian frowned. "Oh, fuck, not good at all!"

"What's not good?" Trinity asked, confused. Nathan shushed her and seemed to listen to something she couldn't hear.

Oh, that's right, she realized suddenly, remembering her father's old stories. Mercenaries had communications implants.

Someone was talking to them.

✦✦✦

"THE colonists are refusing to let me take delivery of the shipment, Captain," Cassidy Vika said over Nathan's com.

"Dammit, they can't do that! The contracts are signed. We've already paid half the fee up front."

"I told them that, but there's a hundred of them here, and they won't let the transport onto the landing pad. One of their elders claims you kidnapped that colonist, Trinity Yeager. For . . . ah . . . immoral purposes. They demand to see her."

"That's bullshit. I didn't kidnap her, she went with us willingly."

"Maybe you should let her tell them that. They might actually believe it."

"Send the elder to go to the port communications center, and I'll explain it to him."

"*I tried that. He said he wouldn't use that 'instrument of the devil.' He said he wants to see her in the flesh.*"

"*Bloody hell.*" Nathan dragged a hand through his short hair in frustration. They had to have those rations. The *Starrunner* had just evacuated a shipload of refugees from Dyson's Hole to another planet after the war there made Dyson's uninhabitable. Feeding more than a thousand colonists had put such a dent in the stores, the *Starrunner* would run out of food in another week. And the nearest planet was three weeks away at top speed.

The bastards had them over a barrel. "*All right, tell the elder we're coming down.*"

With plenty of reinforcements.

Cassidy hesitated a moment. "*Captain, I think I should warn you—these people are nuts. I saw this same elder presiding over the beating of a woman in the town square. The excuse was she burned her husband's dinner, but I think the whipping was actually for the sexual entertainment of the male colonists. You'd better watch your back.*"

Which explained why Trinity was so determined to leave. "*I'll keep that in mind, Lieutenant.*" His computer broke the connection as he moved to get a clean uniform from his closet. "Get dressed," he told Trin. Sebastian had heard the com message and was already half into his uniform. "We've got a problem."

Alarm flickered in her green eyes as she hurried to scoop up her unisuit. "What kind of problem?"

Tersely he briefed her as they pulled on their clothing. "So we're going to show them you're all right," he concluded. "While we're at it, we can swing by your place and you can pack. Be thinking about what you absolutely have to have, because you won't be able to take anything but the bare essentials."

"There's nothing on that rock I want to take with me." Trinity was so white, even her lips were pale. Her hands shook as she buttoned her unisuit. "They're going to insist I stay, Captain."

From the pained resignation in her gaze, she expected him to go back on his word. Nathan gritted his teeth. "Tough," he snapped. "You're coming with us."

"But what if they won't let you have those stores?" Her green eyes were emerald-bright with fear. It made him wonder what they'd do to her for trying to defect from their wretched little colony.

"Then we'll take the stores by force," Nathan told her. "This is a warship, Trinity. I'm damned if I'm going to be blackmailed by a bunch of dirtsuckers."

"It'd be better to settle this without bloodshed, though," Sebastian pointed out.

He sighed, reining in his temper. "Yeah, I'd rather not have to kill anybody over this." Trinity gave him a worried blink, and he sealed his uniform with a jerk. "But I'm not giving up you *or* that food, so I'll do what I have to."

She didn't look convinced. It made him wonder how many men had betrayed her.

Chapter Eight

DISAPPOINTMENT rode Trinity's shoulders like a lead cloak, galling and bitter.

Dammit, she'd come so close.

She shot the captain a look as he prepared the cargo vessel for takeoff from one of the *Starrunner*'s many landing bays. His hands were skilled and sure as he ticked through the procedure, but his jaw was tight with simmering anger.

Next to Trinity, a big, heavily armed mercenary shifted in his seat, obviously more than ready for a fight. Another twenty mercs filled the craft, all of them equally grim-faced and eager.

Alongside the cargo craft, a troop transport also waited for takeoff. It was fully loaded with another eighty mercs.

Nathan obviously did not intend to let the colonists take him off-guard.

Trin had no delusions, though. Elder Jones would give him the choice between those stores and her, and he'd hand her over. Not that she could blame him. Why risk the lives of his own people when he could get what he wanted without bloodshed? It wasn't as if they'd kill her, after all.

At least not right away.

Well, at least Trin had one good memory to cherish out of all this, though she figured the elder would make her pay for it. She only wished she'd had time to ride Nathan's magnificent cock. Even if he let her down in the end, the sex had been fantastic. And it was worth it, just to thumb her nose at the elders.

The big transport's engines began to growl, a low rumble she could feel in her bones. Ahead of her, the massive airlock door opened, revealing a bright spill of stars against the blackness.

The cargo vessel lifted off *Starrunner*'s deck, rocked from side to side before it stabilized, then shot forward like an arrow from a bow. Acceleration pushed Trin back in her seat as the pink curve of Orville's Paradise spilled below. Grimly she watched it swell larger and larger as the cargo craft swooped down.

She'd come so close to getting away.

+ + +

DAMN, Trin thought in dismay as she stepped out of the cargo craft behind Nathan and Sebastian. *Every man in town is here.*

The crowd of a hundred that Nathan had described had swelled to well over a thousand, all of them male. At least they'd left the women and children at home.

The entire mob marched across the paved landing pad toward the two *Starrunner* craft, faces grim, obviously ready for a fight. She saw with dismay that every one of them was armed with the projectile weapons that were all the Prophet allowed.

Of course, guns wouldn't do much good against the mercenaries, who wore body armor and helmets. Trin, on the other
hand, felt like a sitting duck in her unisuit.

Nathan swore and turned to Sebastian. "Get her back inside
and give her somebody's armor. These bastards look like they're
ready to start shooting."

The blond nodded and caught Trin by the arm. "Come on,
kid," he said to her. "Let's find you something else to wear." Sebastian turned to the female trooper standing by the door, waiting
to move out with the rest. "Hey, Shamilin—looks like you're
going to be sitting this one out. We need to borrow your suit."

+ + +

FIVE minutes later, Trin adjusted her new chest plate while the
trooper knelt in front of her, tightening the borrowed greaves over
her boots. "It's a little big," Corporal Shamilin told her, a cheerful smile on her dark face, "but it'll do."

Sebastian clapped Trin on the shoulder. His gaze was steady as he
told her, "You'll be fine, kiddo. And no, Nathan is not going to hand
you over to those people. When he gives his word, he keeps it."

"Sure." She'd believe it when she was back onboard the *Starrunner*. The situation was just too dangerous, and giving her back
would be too easy.

Hell, maybe it was the right thing to do. Was her freedom worth
the lives of Nathan's crew—or even the lives of the colonists themselves? How many people would die if shooting broke out?

But if she went back, Trin knew she was dead herself. Maybe
not now, but within the year. Maybe two, tops. Or less, if that
abusive bastard Andy Makerson bought her.

As she and Sebastian walked down the transport's ramp, her

knees were shaking, but Trin managed to keep her face expressionless. She hadn't walked to the Sinner's Post all those times for nothing.

Nathan was standing several meters from the transport, locked in argument with Elder Jones. Just behind Jones stood a phalanx of colony elders, along with the sheriff and Andy Makerson. Nathan himself was flanked by a hundred hard-faced troopers who scanned the massed colonists with wary eyes.

They were outnumbered ten-to-one. True, the mercs were armed with beamers, and their nanotech implants made them more than a match for anything human. It still wasn't a good situation. Trin's heart sank even more.

"There you are!" As they joined the group, Sheriff Makerson stepped forward, grabbed her by the forearm, and jerked her toward him. "Come here, you little slut!"

Sebastian's beamer appeared an inch from the sheriff's face. He'd moved so fast, Trin hadn't even seen him draw the weapon. "Let her go or die, dirtsucker."

Fear widened the sheriff's eyes before he recovered enough to sputter, "Now, look, this isn't your affair. She's one of our flock and—"

"No," Trinity gritted, jerking free of his hold. "I'm not. I never was."

"Ms. Yeager, if you'll join us?" Nathan had turned to watch the byplay.

Trin moved to his side, Sebastian at her shoulder like a blond angel of vengeance.

"I was just explaining to the elders that you have applied to join my crew," Nathan told her steadily. "And I've accepted your application."

Jones's face flushed with rage.

Trin took a certain wicked pleasure in smiling sweetly up at her lover. Might as well enjoy this while it lasted. "Yes, Captain. I look forward to serving with you."

"From what we hear, you've already been serving him, you little whore," Andy Makerson snarled.

Nathan's blue gaze whipped to his. "That's enough." He didn't draw his weapon, but there was cold death in his eyes. Andy swallowed and looked away. "In any case," the captain continued, after an icy pause, "you can see she's leaving of her own free will."

"No!" Jones turned toward her, his expression a blend of outrage and a surprising desperation. "Trinity, you can't mean to defile yourself with this mongrel! Just look at him! It's obvious—"

"No, actually, it's not obvious," Trin interrupted, taking a grim joy in finally telling an elder what she thought. "I have no idea what you're talking about. And I don't particularly care. I'm joining Captain August's crew, and I'm getting as far away from you and this bigot's paradise as I possibly can."

"You can't!"

"She can," Nathan snapped, his voice dropping to a tone of chilling menace that had the elder shooting him an intimidated glance. Trin smiled at him in gratitude.

"You don't understand," Jones tried again, raising his voice in entreaty. "Trinity, we never told you this, because, well—" He broke off, obviously at a loss.

Trin folded her arms and lifted a brow, beginning to enjoy herself. It was petty of her, she knew, but having the upper hand over the elder was a rare, sweet pleasure. "Yes?"

"You're a direct descendent of Prophet Orville himself!"

✦ ✦ ✦

NATHAN lifted his brows in surprise. Here was a twist he hadn't seen coming.

Trinity's jaw dropped. *"What?"*

"That's why your father applied to immigrate here. Why we accepted you. He provided a gene scan proving he was a direct descendent of the Prophet." Jones extended a pleading hand, but she stepped warily back. "And so are you, Trinity."

Confusion and disbelief flashed over her mobile face. "I thought the Prophet was a celibate."

"He was, but he had a wife. She divorced him when he announced he had been Touched by the Maker. They had two children. You're the great-great-great"—Jones waved a hand, obviously not sure how many *greats* there were—"granddaughter of the Prophet's eldest son."

Nathan frowned, surprised at the stab of disappointment he felt. That obviously put a different spin on things. If Trinity was some kind of hereditary prophet, she had an excellent reason to stay.

"So?" Trin propped her fists on her hips. "Assuming you're even telling the truth, what difference does that make?"

The crowd gasped in outrage. Nathan rocked back in surprise at her cold dismissal of the idea.

Jones spread his hands. "Child, you could be the *mother* of the next Prophet."

Her gaze was flat and steady. "But you don't believe I could become a prophet myself."

The elder blinked. "Well, no, of course not. You're female."

"Riiiiight."

Sensing he was losing her, he started talking again. "But your son could be a prophet. Think of it, Trinity! You'll be honored above all women. . . ."

"That's not saying much." As Jones sputtered, Trin stepped closer to him until they were almost nose to nose. He was several inches taller than she was, but she didn't look intimidated. "Tell me something, Elder. Did you know I was the Prophet's descendent the last time you tied me to the Sinner's Post and ordered me whipped?"

He shifted under her cold stare. "You were in error, child. You needed to be shown the Way."

"Yeah, sure. Tell the truth, Elder—you enjoyed ordering the Prophet's offspring whipped, didn't you? I thought at the time you were even more excited than usual before a beating, but I didn't know why. Now I do."

The beefy blond in the uniform stepped closer, ignoring Nathan's warning glare. "This is why the elders never told you. We knew you'd take on airs!"

"Yeah, there's nothing as uppity as a woman who doesn't think you've got a right to beat her." Trin's lips thinned as she looked the blond over. Nathan tensed, sensing how close the bastard was to exploding. "I wondered why you were so hot to marry me. You're hoping you sire the next Prophet!"

The blond sneered. "I certainly wouldn't want an arrogant little whore like you for any other reason."

"Yeah, well, no son of mine is going to grow up to be a con man," Trin snapped. She lifted her voice until it rang over the crowd. "Which is exactly what Orville was. His so-called 'prophesies' are just a mishmash of thefts from a dozen other religions, from Christianity to—"

Jones huffed in outrage. "How dare you imply our Prophet was influenced by a false faith started by a Jew!"

"Try reading a Bible sometime, Elder. Oh, that's right—you can't get one here, can you? They're forbidden. Ever wonder why?"

"Harlot!" somebody in the crowd screamed.

"Heretic!"

Nathan had heard enough. "Okay, that's it." He turned to his troopers. "Clear a path for the ground transport to bring in the food. Anybody gives you trouble, shoot 'em." To Trinity, he added, "Come along, Ms. Yeager. We're heading back to the ship."

The elder looked horrified. "No! Trinity, you can't mean to pollute the Prophet's bloodline by fornicating with this mongrel. . . ."

Trin shot him a glittering look. "Actually—yeah. Every chance I get. In fact, I was giving the captain a blow job when this grandstand act of yours interrupted. I plan to take up where we left off the minute we get back to the ship." As the elder gaped at her, she added in a clear, carrying voice, "You know, Nathan's got a *really* big dick. Which, God knows, is something I'd never get the chance to experience if I stayed here." She curled her lip. "I mean, judging from the erections I see whenever you guys beat somebody."

Nathan had to bite his lip to stifle his bellow of laughter.

"Bitch!" Behind her, the one she called Andy jerked a knife from his belt. "I'll see you in hell!"

Before the colonist could ram the blade into a gap in Trin's borrowed armor, Nathan's hand clamped over his fist. Bone crunched. The man howled.

"You son of a bitch!" Snarling, Nathan seized him by the throat with his free hand and jerked him off his feet. A red haze descended over his vision as he stared up into the blond's purpling face. *The bastard had tried to kill Trin!*

The knife fell from the colonist's ruined hand as he used the other to claw at Nathan's fingers.

"Andrew!" the sheriff yelled, grabbing for his weapon.

"Touch it and he dies!" Nathan roared, giving the blond a shake as, behind him, his troopers aimed their weapons at the sheriff. For an instant the only sound was the colonist's choked gasps.

"As much as I'm enjoying this, you'd better let him go before you kill him," Sebastian commed. *"I think you've made your point, Nate."*

Knowing his second was right, Nathan dropped the man with a growl of disgust. The blond hit the pavement on his ass, gasping for breath. The sheriff went to his knees beside him.

"Sebastian, take half the men and load the stores on the transport," Nathan ordered. *"I'm going to get Trin out of here before one of these bastards tries anything else stupid."* To Trin he added, "Let's get out of here."

The remainder of the troopers fell in around him and Trinity as they started toward the second shuttle. The colonists watched them, muttering in anger, but not quite willing to risk the mercenaries' beamers after all.

Until Andy lifted his voice. "You'll pay for this, Trinity Yeager!"

Nathan whirled. "No, by God, she won't. In fact, you idiots had better start praying Trin has a long and happy life. Because if she encounters any would-be assassins, I'll be back—with an invasion force." He let an artistic pause develop. "And her blood-line will be the least of your problems."

"And by then," Trinity added, "I'll have nanotech implants of my own." Her smile was chilling. "We'll see how *you* like being at the mercy of somebody stronger than you are."

Nathan snorted. "Trinity, you don't need implants to be stronger than this bunch."

Her smile was blinding.

Looking down into her pretty face, he strongly suspected he was falling in love.

Chapter Nine

THE flight back to the *Starrunner* was a long, dizzy pleasure for Trin.

I did it, she thought as Nathan murmured to his copilot. *I'm free! No more beatings! No auction. No Andy! Yes!*

Best of all, she'd finally told Elder Jones exactly what she thought of him and his con man's cult. Everything she'd been biting back for years. The vague sense of shame she'd always felt at her own cowardice was gone.

She had a new life.

Lost in her own delight, Trin barely noticed when the shuttle slid into its berth. Even the roar and hiss of atmosphere being pumped in around it scarcely penetrated her joy. When the troopers rose to file out, it was all she could do not to dance as she followed them.

"Ms. Yeager?"

She looked around with a happy smile as Nathan appeared at her elbow, tall and dark and looking very professional. "Yes, Captain?"

He gave her a short, stiff nod. "If you'll come with me, please." Pivoting, he strode off down the corridor.

Trin followed his broad back happily, unconcerned about where he was leading her. For the first time in her life, a man had actually come through for her. He hadn't betrayed her. Hell, he'd been willing to start a battle with the men of Rectitude to protect her. She was glad it hadn't come to that, but she couldn't help but be delighted.

When she'd whirled around to find Andy dangling from Nathan's grip with a knife in his crushed hand, she'd been stunned. The sheriff's son had been willing to murder her in cold blood in front of more than a thousand witnesses.

But Nathan had saved her life.

She was still struggling to take the idea in when she followed him into his quarters. The door slid shut behind her.

Nathan turned toward her, his eyes so hungry she instinctively took a step back. Yet his hands were unspeakably gentle as he brushed the hair back from her face.

Something tight in her melted, and she gave him a smile that trembled. "Thank you. Oh, thank you . . ."

Which was apparently the signal he'd been waiting for. He stepped full against her, his big, hard body pressing hers against the door. She moaned in welcome the instant before his mouth came down to claim her lips in a kiss so searing, she lost her breath.

Trin's own hunger flared, and she kissed him back, licking and sucking at his lips the way he'd taught her. With a growl of need and impatience, he began plucking at the straps of her armor. The chestplate dropped with a thud. "Let me have you," Nathan whispered against her mouth. "Please, Trin!"

"Yes!" she moaned, tilting her head up.

He took the gesture for the invitation it was and began to bite and suckle his way along her jaw. Meanwhile, his impatient hands plucked at straps and pulled at armor. She did the same to his, hungry to uncover his magnificent body. The tough plates landed at their feet with a series of thumps.

Until, as if he just couldn't stand any more, he stood back, grabbed the neckline of her unisuit, and ripped the tough fabric ruthlessly down the front. Her breasts spilled free.

Nathan hastily shucked out of what remained of his armor, then pulled her into his arms. Cupping one big hand under her ass, he lifted her, bending her over his arm so he could suck the nearest nipple into his mouth. Trin groaned in helpless pleasure at the intense sensation of wet heat and gentle, nibbling teeth. Wrapping her legs around his waist, she clung to his strong shoulders. "You saved my life. He was going to kill me, and you saved my life."

He lifted his head from her breast just long enough to growl, "You were magnificent. When you told that elder what you thought of his idiot cult, it was all I could do not to cheer."

She grinned. "It did feel good."

"I'm sure it did." Bracing her as she wrapped around him, Nathan turned and walked toward his bed, grinning into her eyes. "By the way, thanks for announcing to everybody—including my crew—that I've got a big dick."

Trin felt her cheeks heat. She'd been so far gone in reckless indignation, she hadn't even considered her audience. "Oh—I'm sorry!"

"I'm not." The grin broadened. "That's the kind of rumor no guy minds." He spilled her back onto the bed, following her down to cover her in a warm blanket of male sensuality.

"It's more than a rumor, Captain." She drew her legs tighter around his backside and rolled her hips, enjoying the way his thick erection pressed against her stomach. "Much, much more."

"Glad to hear it." He reached between their bodies to find the join of her thighs, then slipped a finger into her core. She sighed at the sensation. "Now, if you'd said I had a needle dick, then I'd have had to punish you."

Something in the dark, seductive thrum of his voice made inner muscles clench in greed. "Yeah? How?"

He must have seen the leap of lust in her eyes. His own widened, then narrowed in sudden speculation. "I'd have warmed this pretty little butt with my hand. And then I'd have tied you up and fucked you. Hard."

It had always infuriated her when the males of Rectitude punished her for some infraction, particularly when she suspected hurting her aroused them. But coming from Nathan, the threat was altogether different—an erotic game, meant to stoke her hunger as much as his.

And it did. The thought of being draped bare-assed across his lap for a spanking struck her as deliciously kinky. The elders would have been shocked.

Trin smirked. "Needledick."

A delighted grin bloomed across his face the instant before he assumed a threatening glare. "Are you talking to me?" His growl was so deep and menacing, hot little muscles clenched in her sex.

Trin licked dry lips. "Yeah. What are you going to do about it?"

"Well, for starters," Nathan rumbled as his cock lengthened and throbbed, "I'm going to watch those cheeks turn a pretty pink under my hand. Then I'm going to fuck you." Heat gathered in his balls as he looked down at her lush, vulnerable curves. "Hard."

She stared up at him. Her smile sent a bolt of lust right into his groin. "Good. I want to be fucked." Pausing, she licked her lips. "Hard."

With a rough growl of hunger, Nathan rolled off the bed, then bent and scooped her into his arms. She yelped and pretended to struggle, but he dropped down on the mattress and hauled her facedown over his knee.

"Brute!" Her attempt at outrage was spoiled by a giggle.

"That's me." Nathan inserted a finger into her delicious sex. She was even hotter than she'd been the last time he'd probed her. God, he couldn't wait to slide inside.

Withdrawing his fingers, he cupped the sweet, round curves of her butt, savoring the smooth skin. "Mmmm," he purred, "what a perfect pair of cheeks. I'm going to enjoy heating them up."

Trin moaned, the sound a purr of excitement as she squirmed over his knees, her ass flexing and lifting in blatant invitation.

Sebastian had speculated she had a submissive streak. It looked as if he was right. And Nathan planned to take full advantage of it.

Then he paused, frowning. Cassidy Vika had said the men of

the colony enjoyed seeing the female colonists beaten. He did not want Trin to think he was cut from the same cloth—hurting her solely because he enjoyed it, without any concern for her at all.

"You remember your safe word, right?"

"Starrunner," she replied, a hint of impatience in her voice.

"Are you sure this is—"

She shot him a glittering glare over her shoulder. "Needledick!"

Well, that answered that question. "You asked for it." He lifted his hand.

✦ ✦ ✦

TRINITY took a deep breath as the mercenary's muscled thighs flexed under her body. His erect cock rested against her hip, long and hard and eager. She could feel her own slick heat increasing.

Whap.

The first slap was loud, but barely even stung. It was more a hard pat than anything else.

A measured interval went by as she waited for the next spank. She squirmed against Nathan's thigh as her arousal grew.

Whap. That one was no harder. *Whap!* The one that followed came a little faster, but with that same ruthless control.

He picked up speed, inflicting a constant patter of light slaps that didn't really hurt. *Whap, whapwhapwhap!*

Heat spread across her butt with each impact of Nathan's broad palm. Slowly the slaps started getting harder, then harder still until she found herself squirming, as much with sheer arousal as from the gathering sting.

Bucking against his powerful thighs, she felt a hum of pleasure burning under her skin like a low-level electric charge. And every time Trin writhed under a smack, the silken hair on Nathan's thighs teased her nipples, sending another zing of pleasure through her.

Her ass was really beginning to burn now. She pictured herself draped butt-up across the mercenary's lap, bound and helpless, cheeks reddening steadily under his lustful paddling.

Nathan's hand paused in its rise and fall. For a moment there was silence except for their gasps. He was breathing just as hard as she was. She knew it wasn't from exertion.

"Ready to beg for mercy?" Nathan asked, his voice rough with arousal.

Her ass felt hot and inflamed. So did her pussy and the tips of her aching breasts. She clenched her fists, feeling the rise of a reckless heat. "I can take anything you can dish out—Needledick."

"Ohhhh," Nathan growled. "We'll see about that."

✛ ✛ ✛

TRINITY squirmed and bucked and screeched under the next half-dozen swats, unconsciously rubbing her satin hip against his rock-hard, aching cock. Watching her struggle in an erotic symphony of quivering female curves, Nathan couldn't remember the last time a spanking had turned him on more.

And he wasn't alone. According to his sensors, Trin loved it just as much as he did.

He was so hot, it took him a moment to realize she'd stopped yelping under his smacks. Until she groaned, *"Starrunner!"*

Nathan froze as she voiced the safe word, ice stealing over him. He snatched her off his lap and put her on her feet so he could examine her flushed backside. "Did I hurt you?"

But though he'd paddled her thoroughly, he'd been careful. There was no sign of any bruising at all.

"I can't take it any more." She turned in his hold to meet his gaze in stark demand. "Fuck me! I'm going insane!"

Nathan nearly melted into a puddle of relief. "Shit! Don't do that to me! You're only supposed to use the safe word if you're in distress."

She shot him a mock glare. "Believe me, I'm in distress. In fact, I'm going to die in the next five minutes if you don't bang my brains out. Right now."

He laughed in sheer relief. "As my lady commands." Scooping her into his arms, Nathan surged to his feet, turned, and tossed her down across the bed before grabbing her delicate ankles.

Her face was flushed as red as her well-spanked ass, but her gaze was bright with laughing hunger. Lust surged high in him as he eagerly spread her long, slim thighs. Looking between them, he saw that her lips were swollen from a combination of arousal and his careful spanking. Her bush, red as a fox's pelt, was damp and matted with arousal. Her breasts quivered with every panting breath she took, nipples hard and flushed red.

Sliding a knee onto the bed, Nathan shifted his grip to the backs of her knees, rolling her onto her shoulders. And, in the process, angling that ripe, wet cunt up for his cock. Her delicate little hands found his biceps, curled around them in a grip that spoke of need and desperation.

Almost shaking with the force of his lust, Nathan draped her calves over his shoulders and took his cock in one hand. The thick head brushed red, springy curls, then velvet lips, then began working its way into slick, deliciously snug flesh.

He didn't think he'd ever had anything wetter or tighter.

"Maker's Beard!" Trinity gasped. "You're . . . Aahhh!"

Nathan echoed her cry with a long groan of his own as he

arched his buttocks, forcing his way deeper into her silken heat. She clamped around him, unbelievably tempting. He could feel a pulse throbbing hard in his balls.

He only hoped he could hang on long enough to make her come before he blew like a sonic grenade.

Chapter Ten

SHE was never calling him Needledick again, even as a joke. He was huge.

Trinity whimpered in need as he forced still more of his cock into her cunt, filling her by relentless millimeters. Her ass stung and burned from the spanking, but she really didn't care. She'd never felt like this before. Had never known such pleasure or such desire. It made her entire life until now seem as pallid and bland as milk.

Nathan fed another centimeter of cock into her, and she felt the huge, glittering wave of her approaching orgasm swell even brighter, hotter.

Finally he was all the way inside. Her legs draped over his shoulders, he came down over her, bracing his hands on the mattress. He searched her eyes. "Are you all right?" His voice was deep and strained.

"Yeah." Need clawed at her. She wanted to feel him riding her. "Maker's Beard, what are you waiting for? Fuck me!" She'd never said the words before today, but in the last couple of hours, she'd lost track of how many times she'd used them.

And she'd meant it each and every time.

He gave her a flashing white grin. "Don't mind if I do." The long, long shaft began sliding from her, the friction of its movement maddening and delicious.

"Oohh, that's good!"

His grin widened. "It certainly is." He reversed the stroke. In. And out. And *innnn*. And *outtt*. Slowly. So slowly.

She found herself squirming, trying to hurry him, to get more of that magnificent cock. But pinned under his big body, held in those big hands, she was helpless. Nathan would use her just the way he wanted, at just the speed he wanted, and there was nothing she could do about it.

Goaded, she tossed her head on the mattress. "Please, Nathan," she heard herself begging. "I can't take any more of this!"

His gaze flickered. "Want me to stop?"

"No!" It was a scream of frustration. "I want you to fuck me faster!"

Nathan laughed in dark male satisfaction—and obeyed. He rode her as hard as he'd spanked her ass earlier, shafting her in short, delicious thrusts that ground his pelvis against her clit. With every stroke, ribbons of hot pleasure snaked around her spine and jerked her tight. Her thigh muscles began to jerk and spasm.

Trin could feel the orgasm building, getting bigger and hotter and fiercer with every thrust. Ready to break free. "Yes!" she gritted, half-insane with anticipation. "Yes, Nathan! More!"

He gave her exactly that, jolting his cock in and out of her, sweat flying from his face. "God," he gasped. "You feel so damn good. . . ."

Dazed, she looked up to meet his wild gaze. The muscles of his chest stood in hard relief with effort. His cock felt like a length of fire as he ground deep, his pelvis jolting against hers.

Detonation. A sweet fireball flooded her in a soundless explosion of ecstasy, pleasure whipping like a storm through her battered nervous system.

As she convulsed, she heard Nathan bellow. "Yes! God, Trinity!"

Then the heat drowned out everything else.

✛ ✛ ✛

TRINITY lay in a damp, exhausted heap, sprawled across Nathan's brawny torso. After that last explosive climax, he'd rolled over and pulled her on top of him. Now she listened to his thundering heartbeat. It felt so damn good, being in his arms.

Maybe a little too good.

Oh, God. Was she falling in love with him?

The thought filled her with a blend of elation and terror. She'd never been in love before. Never known anybody she respected and desired enough.

Until Nathan.

But he was the captain of the *Starrunner*. And she wasn't sure *what* she was. He'd implied she was a *Starrunner* crewmember to the elders, but for all she knew, he'd just been trying to warn them off.

Even if he did let her join the crew, what then? True, he'd been damned hungry for her, but she'd heard that didn't mean much with men.

Trinity could already tell her own need for him ran much deeper than that.

As her heart began to sink, a big, warm hand tangled in her hair. She lifted her head to look at him, startled.

And then his mouth was on hers again, as tender as it was demanding. With a groan he rolled her beneath him.

✦✦✦

SEVERAL delightful hours passed before they finally emerged from Nathan's quarters, driven more by hunger than anything else.

He took Trin to the ship's mess and settled her into a seat she had trouble sitting in—and not just because of that spanking. Her embarrassment was mitigated by the fact that the captain's knees seemed no more steady than her own.

"Looks like the crew's finished processing the new food stores," he told her, handing over a heated package.

"So they didn't have any more trouble with the colonists?" Cautiously she examined the meal, trying to figure out how to open it.

With a smile, Nathan reached over and did something to the box. It popped open, revealing a steaming dish of food. Trin picked up the enclosed fork and took a bite. It was surprisingly good.

"No." He went to work on his own box. "Seems we did a pretty good job of shutting them up."

"So what's next? For me, I mean."

Nathan looked up at her. His eyes were very blue. "That depends. What do you want to do?"

"I want to get the implants and join your crew, Captain."

She thought she saw a flicker of relief in his eyes. "Done. I'll get you a copy of the standard crew contract."

Something deep in her relaxed. "What? No more questions about whether I've got the courage to be a mercenary?"

"After the way you faced down the elder and his band of idiots? Not likely."

Before she could reply, a male voice interrupted. "Oh, look—it's Trinity Yeager and the man with the big dick." Sebastian plopped down opposite them.

Trin choked on a bite of alien vegetable. Sebastian gave her a helpful thump on the back that almost dislodged a rib.

"Smooth, Commander," Nathan said dryly. "Very smooth."

"I do try." As Trin caught her breath, he leaned back in his seat and eyed them both. "Well, you two seem in one piece. More or less."

Nathan's smile was openly smug. "More or less."

"Uh-huh." Sebastian eyed his captain speculatively.

Obviously attempting to ignore his friend, Nathan started telling Trin about their next mission. She listened eagerly.

He'd segued into a discussion of the politics of that particular star system when Sebastian suddenly announced, "I give it a month."

Trin frowned, unable to follow his conversational detour. "You give what a month?"

"Him." Sebastian tilted his head at his captain. "Before he begs you to put him out of his misery and marry him."

Trin stared at the blond in flabbergasted astonishment, trying to ignore the leap of her heart at the thought. "Don't be ridiculous. We've only known each other a few hours."

Sebastian's lips quirked in a half-smile. "And I've known him twenty years, and I've never seen him so besotted."

"Besotted?" Nathan glowered, dark brows drawing low. "I am not besotted."

Sebastian's grin was sly and knowing. "In that case, you won't mind sharing." He turned toward Trin. "I'm really looking forward to taking up where we left off, sweet. I never did get a chance to . . ."

"Forget it." That steely, menacing growl left no room for doubt.

"Why, Captain!" Green eyes widened in mock innocence. "Are you developing a possessive streak?"

"You bet your ass." Nathan bared his teeth at his friend. "Lay one finger on her—or anything else—and I'll cut it off."

Satisfied, Sebastian sat back in his chair. "That's what I thought. Fifty credchits says you're on your knees before the month's out."

Epilogue

Starrunner's gym
Three weeks later

✦ ✦ ✦

"KEEP up your guard, Trin," Nathan called. "That left hand is dropping."

Her expression fierce with concentration, Trinity raised her left fist into position as she and the sparring robot circled.

Nathan watched, his sensors doing a running evaluation. He wanted to make damn sure she was ready before he took her into her first battle as a member of the *Starrunner*'s crew. So far, everything looked damn good.

So did Trinity, on a lot of levels. She wore the brand-new suit of combat armor he'd ordered for her, its sleek lines emphasizing her lean grace. And she had plenty of strength to back up the look, too, because Nathan had advanced her the money for the nanotech implants soon after they'd left Orville's Paradise. He'd wanted her to feel safe in the knowledge she'd never be vulnerable to bullying bastards again.

Now the implants were fully grown at last, extending through her body in a network designed to strengthen her bones and muscles. All she needed was practice in how to use them.

That was the tricky part. Since she was still getting her body under control, Nathan had her working with the sparring robot. It was safer for everybody; only an idiot stepped onto the practice mat with a fledgling cyborg who didn't know her own strength.

Just looking at them, though, you'd think the robot had the edge. The thing towered over Trinity, an intimidating armored colossus designed to get new recruits used to fighting things that were big and nasty.

The *Starrunner* encountered a lot of things that were big and nasty.

Trin, however, didn't seem the least bit intimidated. She called the thing Andy. Nathan strongly suspected it wasn't short for *android*.

The 'bot swung at her, its massive metal fist a blur. Trin ducked just as fast and thrust a forearm up to block the strike, exactly as Nathan had taught her.

He concealed a smile. Coming along nicely. "Little slow on that block, Trin!" There was always room for improvement.

Her green eyes narrowed in icy determination.

Oops. Seems he'd fired up that redhead's temper.

With a snarl on her pretty face, Trinity went after her hulking opponent, throwing punches and kicks in a sizzling assault that had the robot backpedaling as it blocked her blows. Just as its long arms were spread wide for one of those blocks, she powered a kick straight up into its metal jaw.

Backed by every erg of her new strength, the ferocious blow sent the robot's head flying off its shoulders. It hit the deck and bounced, clanging.

Nathan winced. Yeah, she definitely wasn't ready to practice with humans yet.

"Take that, Andy!" Trin crowed, bouncing on her toes, as the robot's headless body toppled slowly backward.

"Nice shot," Nathan drawled, walking across the combat ring's padded floor toward her. "But you've really got to work on your control. Sometimes we don't want to tear the bad guy's head off."

She smirked and sauntered over to meet him, mischief bright on her pretty face. "Depends on the bad guy." The impish grin widened. "Speaking of which, Captain—I don't suppose we could make a little trip to Orville's Paradise?"

Nathan thrust his tongue into his cheek. "Now, why, I wonder, would you want to do a thing like that?"

"Ummmm . . ." Trin pretended to consider as she rose on her toes and looped her arms around his neck. "I'm homesick? No? Ummmm . . . I want to thank them for all their years of kind instruction in the Way of Orville?"

"How about"—he tilted his head back and pretended to think—"you want to kick their fat asses all the way into orbit."

Green eyes widened with mock innocence. "Me? Engage in petty revenge?"

"You. Engage in petty revenge."

Trinity smirked. "Okay, you've talked me into it."

"Bloodthirsty little wench." He took her mouth in a long, sweet kiss.

No matter how many times Nathan had kissed her—and he'd done that a lot over the past three weeks—he never got tired of the taste of her lips, or the way her body melted into his.

Though he had to admit, it didn't melt half so comfortably in fifteen kilos of combat armor.

Still, they made the best of it. The kiss went on and on, an intoxicating duel of licking tongues and gentle bites. By the time Nathan drew back, they were both panting.

"You know, all of a sudden this armor isn't as comfortable as it was a minute ago," she told him in a husky voice. "Want to go back to your quarters and get naked?"

"I love you." There. He'd finally said the three words he'd been thinking since he watched her confront Elder Jones and the rest of the Orvillian lunatics.

Trin's green eyes widened. She looked utterly stunned. "What?"

"I love you." Saying it felt so good, Nathan suspected he'd be repeating it a lot. He threaded his hands through her silken red hair and caressed her delicate cheekbones with his thumbs. "Marry me."

She blinked rapidly, searching his eyes, as if trying to determined if he was playing some kind of cruel joke. Slowly he watched the belief grow as she read the truth in his face. "You mean it."

"I've never meant anything more." Resting his forehead against hers, he looked into her eyes. "Put me out of my misery, Trin. Please."

"I love you." The words were a faint whisper. Then she, too, said it again. "I love you!"

Obviously forgetting her strength, Trin threw herself against

Nathan so hard both of them tumbled to the floor. Unabashed, she started pressing kisses against his mouth, his cheek, his eyebrows.

Chuckling, he grabbed her shoulders and managed to pry her off. "Does this mean you'll marry me?"

"Yes! Maker's Beard, yes!"

Relief made him close his eyes. He'd thought she cared for him, too, but he hadn't been sure. Now he was. The joy and love on her face was unmistakable.

Long fingers clamped over each of his wrists. Startled, Nathan looked up at her as she straddled him and forced his hands to the deck. "Hey, what's this?"

"I was just thinking," Trinity drawled, her green eyes bright with laughter and wicked passion, "that it's past time I tied *you* up."

After a startled moment he grinned. "You know, I guess it is at that."

✦ ✦ ✦

THEY were married a week later in the *Starrunner*'s primary landing bay, the ship's chaplain doing the honors as the entire crew watched.

Nathan wore his dark blue dress uniform, his tall boots gleaming as brightly as the medals on his chest. Trinity, too, wore brand-new dress blues, and was much prouder of them than the frilly wedding gown she'd have donned back on Orville's Paradise.

Later, as the bride and groom danced the first dance, they saw Sebastian working the crowd. "What's he up to?" Trin asked as Nathan whirled her around in dizzy circles.

The captain glanced over her shoulder as his friend counted a stack of credchits. "I think he's collecting from everybody dumb enough to take his bet." He grinned at her. "After all, it only took you three weeks to get me on my knees."

She shuttered her lashes at him. "Actually, I think that's the one position I haven't had you in."

Nathan's grin broadened. "Believe me, darling—I'm looking forward to it."

The Thrall

Chapter One

STEPPING out of the *Starrunner*'s shuttle onto the soil of Bedesem Colony was like traveling back in time.

A long, long way back.

Sebastian Cole stopped on the ramp to stare, taking in the horse-drawn wagons rolling past the field where the shuttle had landed. Picturesque stone cottages stood just across the rutted dirt road, surrounded by neat beds of vegetation and flocks of geese and chickens. Each of the cottages seemed to have a dog out front, every one of them barking in hysterical chorus at the the shuttle's arrival.

Somewhere in the middle of the canine hysterics, a shout went up. A gaggle of kids poured out of one of the larger buildings, headed for the shuttle at a dead run. The whole crowd pelted across the road to stop at what they evidently considered a safe distance, eyes wide in wonder as they stared at their starfaring visitors.

Like everything else in sight, they all looked distinctly medieval in their bright tunics, tights, and ankle-length boots. One young lad had what appeared to be strawberry jam on his face and a wooden sword thrust in his belt.

"Damn," Sebastian commed, using the computer implant that allowed him to communicate silently with his *Starrunner* crewmates. *"Did this colony just blow off the past fifteen hundred years, or what?"*

Beside Sebastian, Captain Nathan August frowned as he looked out over the scene. He was a big, hard-faced man, good to follow into battle, bad to meet in combat. *"They do seem to be a lot more primitive than I expected,"* he admitted. *"They evidently lost a lot during the Time of Isolation."*

"Maybe, but I wonder why they haven't started upgrading yet. You'd think they'd have started importing tech from off-world by now." Nathan's wife, Trinity, stepped from the shuttle to gaze around them. *"This place makes Orville's Paradise look high-tech."*

The thud of hoofbeats had the three looking around. A troop of men on big, muscular horses galloped up with a rattle of swords and a jangle of tack, sending the children scattering like geese. The whole bunch was kitted out in leather breastplates, loincloths, and thigh-high boots, a rig Sebastian would have hated to wear into battle. It wouldn't have stopped a beamer, a bullet, or even a sword stroke worth a damn.

On the other hand, he could see how the same costume might be fun in the bedroom, given a kinky partner with a sense of humor. Sebastian the Barbarian? He smirked.

"Which one of you is Captain Nathan August of the *Starrunner?"* the leader of the troop called.

"I'm August," the captain replied warily.

The man nodded his helmeted head. "Greetings. We're your escort to the palace of His Dominance."

"Oh, this is going to be good," Sebastian commed as the three of them started down the ramp toward the horsemen. *"Nothing says, 'I've got balls' like making people call you 'His Dominance.'"*

✛ ✛ ✛

THE palace was a dark, towering structure built of brooding gray stone, embellished with gothic spires and stained-glass windows.

That churchlike impression was instantly shattered when Nathan, Sebastian, and Trinity walked into the gleaming white foyer. Dead center under the vaulted ceiling stood a towering black marble statue of a naked woman kneeling before an armored man. Her wrists were bound behind her back, and she was sucking her conqueror's cock with submissive enthusiasm.

"You've got to admit, it makes a statement," Sebastian commed finally, after a two-minute gape.

"Yeah, but a statement of what?" Nathan folded his arms and rocked back on his heels, looking the statue over with a raised brow and a grin.

"How about, 'We've got more kinks than a corkscrew'?" As he glanced at his captain, Sebastian caught the gaze of a hard-eyed palace guard watching them suspiciously. He was unable to resist giving the man a taunting wink. Without an implant of his own, the guard couldn't hear the conversation no matter how hard he tried to eavesdrop.

"I can't believe they put that thing out where anybody can see it." Trinity sounded so scandalized, Sebastian had to grin.

He wasn't surprised at her reaction, though. Trin had spent her teenage years on Orville's Paradise, a planet colonized by a rabid religious cult. Nathan had expanded her horizons considerably, but even after a year of marriage and her new life as a mercenary, she was still easy to shock.

Frowning, Trinity added out loud, "I hope they don't let children in here."

"Children," a stuffy male voice announced, "are not permitted in this section of the palace."

The three pivoted to see a man striding toward them. In contrast to their own conservative blue dress uniforms, he wore a pair of tight leather pants with thigh-high black boots. Black buckled straps circled his flabby biceps, and a leather breastplate covered his chest. It was sculpted to look a lot more muscular than he was. A leather codpiece completed the ensemble, draped with gold chains that jingled musically as he walked.

"*Either he's way too happy to see us,*" Sebastian quipped, "*or he stuffs that codpiece.*"

"*He'd have to, or he'd get calluses on his dick,*" Nathan commed. "*All that leather's got to chafe.*" Spotting Trinity's wicked smile, he added, "*And what are you grinning at?*"

"*Actually, I was wondering if I could get the name of his tailor,*" she purred. "*You'd look a lot better in that rig than he does.*"

Sebastian bit the inside of his cheek to control a bark of laughter. Maybe Nathan had done a better job at expanding Trin's horizons than he'd thought.

Leather Man came to a jingling halt a pace in front of them, shoulders drawn back, both chins lifted. "Welcome to the Dominality of Rabican," he announced. "I am Dom Javier Grosvenor Bayard, adviser to the Dominor—"

"Not on matters of fashion, I hope," Sebastian commed, keeping his face straight with an effort.

Trin made a strangled sound. *"Sebastian, if you make me laugh at this self-important clod, I'm going to spank you."*

"Oh, would you?"

Trin's snicker at his mock plea had Bayard peering at them in puzzlement.

Nathan, ignoring the byplay, introduced the three of them in grave, rolling phrases. Sebastian had no idea how his captain always managed to treat Bayard's ilk as if he took them seriously. Sebastian himself didn't have the patience, which was how he knew he had no business captaining a ship.

Oh, he might have the knowledge of strategy and tactics, even the necessary leadership skills, but he was just no damn good with idiots.

When Nathan finished his spiel, Bayard gave them all a short, stiff bow. "Very good. If you will accompany me, I will take you to His Dominance." Turning on one high, booted heel, he marched off down the corridor, right past a wall-length mural of a naked woman writhing in a particularly uncomfortable arrangement of ropes.

"You know, we've been to some really strange Forgotten Worlds," Sebastian commed, eyeing the mural as they passed, *"but this one is headed for the top of the 'stories-I-like-to-tell-when-I'm-drunk' list."*

"Good," Nathan shot back. *"You needed new material."*

"Only because you've known me twenty years," Sebastian replied loftily. *"Others are riveted."*

"No, dear," Trinity said sweetly. *"They're just appalled."*

He eyed her. *"On second thought, I think* you're *the one who needs the spanking."*

His captain turned to give him a long, long look.

"And Nathan's just the guy to give it to you," Sebastian added quickly.

"He's brighter than he looks," Nathan told his wife.

She smiled. *"He'd have to be."*

+ + +

AGONIZING protocol notwithstanding, Sebastian decided as he followed the others through the palace, this should be one of their more enjoyable missions. At least, judging from the file Trin had compiled in preparation for their meeting with the Dominor.

According to her research, Bedesem Colony had been lost for a full two hundred years after being caught on the wrong side of the Tormod Front. Which pretty much explained the feudal technology. Even after being reunited with the rest of the human empire for the five years, the colonists still clung to their old ways.

In any case, two centuries was an awfully long time to be cut off from the rest of the human race—and plenty of time to develop interesting kinks. Particularly for a colony that was already pretty kinky to begin with.

When humankind began its first major colonization push after discovering the secret of interstellar travel three hundred years ago, all kinds of groups decided to try their hands at creating Utopia. There were religious cults like the ones who'd founded Orville's Paradise—bigots who hated anybody with a different skin color, language, and/or religion; neosocialists, neofascists, and assorted other neoists.

There had also been lots of people who wanted to enjoy their various sexual kinks undisturbed, including one shipload with a taste for Bondage, Discipline, and Sadomasochism—BDSM.

Which acronym had morphed over the past two hundred years into the word Bedesem, as in Bedesem Colony.

According to Trin's research, thousands of people with a yen to experience full-time dominant/submissive relationships had shipped off to found this colony. Unfortunately, no sooner did they have their fantasy world up and running than war broke out with the alien Tormod, who had taken violent exception to human incursion into their space.

Nobody was entirely sure how many colonies found themselves on the wrong side of the Tormod Front, but estimates ranged anywhere from twenty to one hundred separate worlds. Millions of people, all completely cut off from the rest of humankind.

Luckily, however, the Tormod were methane breathers with no interest in human-habitable planets, or things could have gotten even uglier for the Forgotten Worlds. As it was, the Tormod only objected to alien spacecraft crossing their space; they hadn't bothered to wipe out the colonies themselves.

Two decades ago the Humans and the Tormod had finally signed a treaty. Since then, humankind had started reestablishing contact with the Forgotten Worlds. Bedesem was only the latest, having been rediscovered just five years past.

Now one of Bedesem's ruling Dominors wanted to hire the crew of the *Starrunner* for some kind of mission. The question was, what did the leader of a kinky feudal society want with a bunch of twenty-fourth century cyborg mercenaries?

And would it by any chance involve big-breasted submissives who loved to suck cock?

Sebastian hastily wiped off the grin that thought inspired as Bayard stopped before a massive set of soaring double doors. The adviser nodded regally to one of the guards standing at attention. The guard stepped forward to open the door, and Bayard sailed through to the strains of drums and flutes.

Sebastian gave the hem of his dress uniform a straightening tug and followed the others as they filed in after him.

"Captain Nathan August of the interstellar mercenary warship *Starrunner,* and two crew members," Bayard announced with a grand gesture in their general direction.

Sebastian blinked.

A naked and very flexible girl was doing a slow bump and grind in the center of the room. Scarlet wall hangings set off her creamy curves and waist-length blond hair, and the polished marble floor reflected her full breasts as she bent and jiggled temptingly. Her evident intent was to display her no-doubt outstanding ass to the man sprawled in the golden throne behind her.

But if she was trying to get his attention, she had her work cut out for her; two more women crouched at his feet. As one of them moved her head, Sebastian realized the pair was paying loving lip service to the erection the man had liberated from his jeweled codpiece.

Without turning a hair, Bayard stepped back and made a sweeping gesture at the fellatio recipient. "His Dominance, Xarles Ferrau, Dominor of Rabican."

"Ah, you're here!" the Dominor said, straightening belatedly. One of the girls made a protesting sound and moved her head as though trying to recapture whatever portion of his anatomy had escaped her mouth.

Ferrau looked down at the dick-sucking duo and made a shooing gesture as he scooped his softening cock back into his codpiece. "Enough! Take yourselves off!"

The girls, including the dancer, instantly scampered in different directions, jiggling deliciously. Sebastian watched them go with longing until Trin jabbed an elbow in his side. *"Pig,"* she commed.

Rubbing his ribs, he grinned down at her fondly. Marrying Trin was the smartest thing Nathan had ever done. *"Oink,"* he agreed.

While he'd been distracted, Nathan and the Dominor had begun the obligatory protocol mating dance.

They kept it up so long even Nathan's patience began to fray. "You said in your message that you were in need of our assistance, but you couldn't discuss the details over the com," the captain said finally, spreading both arms in a *Well, we're here* gesture. "How may we be of service?"

The Dominor sat back on his throne and eyed them. He was not a tall man, and his round face was as blandly ordinary as his thinning brown hair. Still, there was something about him that drew the eye—some impression of intelligence and authority. "I have heard a great deal about the power of your . . . what's the phrase?"

"Nanotech implants," Nathan supplied. Then, just in case the Dominor hadn't already heard the lecture, he added, "Cybernetic structures no bigger than molecules. They graft themselves to our muscles, bones, and nervous systems to perform different tasks, ranging from strength enhancement to computation to detecting infrared radiation."

"Nanotech implants. Yes, that's it." Ferrau gave him an intense, narrow-eyed look. "I'm told these things make supermen of you—that you're stronger, faster, and more clever than ordinary men. Is this true?"

"Yes."

Damn, Nathan did that well. Just that flat "yes," without elaboration. It made the statement all the more believable. As it should be, since it was the simple truth.

"Show me." The Dominor gestured, and another naked lovely appeared, carrying a long object wrapped in a length of black velvet.

Sebastian contained a sigh. They always wanted demonstrations.

The girl started to hand the package to Nathan, but Ferrau said, "No, not him. The blond one."

Sebastian raised a brow but accepted the package anyway. Unwrapping the fabric, he found it did indeed contain the expected steel bar.

Bored, he caught the bar by either end and twisted it neatly into a loop. With his implants, he barely had to expend any effort at all.

"Yes!" The Dominor sat forward in his throne, his eyes gleaming. "You'll do nicely."

"We're delighted to hear it," Nathan said patiently. "But again, for what?"

"Rescuing my son." Ferrau's mouth drew tight, and a hint of desolation flickered in his pale eyes. "He's been abducted, and I'm afraid he's in great danger."

Chapter Two

"SOMEONE kidnapped your child?" Trinity asked. "That's terrible! How old is he?"

The Dominor sat back in his seat with a sigh. "Actually, Arnoux is twenty-six. He was out with a hunting party when he was set upon by agents of Ila Orva, the Dominess of the neighboring dominality of Corvo." He rubbed the spot between his brows with the fingers of one hand, as if trying to ease a headache. "He's been Ila's prisoner for the past month."

"So you want to hire the *Starrunner* to attack Corvo?" Nathan asked.

Ferrau's head jerked up. "Sweet Goddess of Pain, no! You might kill him. Assuming Ila did not slay him herself, as she's threatened to do if I dare mobilize my forces. Arnoux is my only son, and my wife . . ." He trailed off. "No, I can't risk that. This

must be done subtly, but with great speed. Before the Dominess . . ." Ferrau stopped, and his mouth tightened.

"Before the Dominess what?" Nathan demanded.

The Dominor rose from his throne and began to pace. Despite
his height—or lack of it—there was enough muscle on his frame
to indicate he did more than lounge on a throne and enjoy the oc-
casional blow job. "Ila has sworn to break him to the collar," he
said, worry and outrage lacing his voice.

Trin frowned. "What does that mean?"

Ferrau glanced up at her and made an impatient gesture.
"Make him a Thrall, a member of our submissive class. It's a huge
insult. Those of my family have been dominants since the colony
was established. To imply any of us would willingly submit . . ."
He clenched his fist. "I'd declare war on her for that alone, if she
didn't hold Arnoux."

"What'd you do to torch her cargo?" Sebastian asked, idly
wrapping the bar around his wrist. Catching the Dominor's be-
wildered expression, he translated, "Make her angry enough to
insult you."

"Ah." He sighed. "I backed out of negotiations to wed
Arnoux to the Dominess's eldest daughter, Marcelle. I had discovered . . . things about that girl that put a bad taste in my mouth.
She's hard on her Thralls. Very hard." His expression grew grim.
"It's said she's only satisfied when blood has been spilled." The
Dominor shook his head and began to pace in front of his throne
again. "If Ila had offered her youngest child, Zaria, I might have
considered it. Indeed, had she offered to wed her son, Brys, to my
daughter, Seva . . . but she did not. And I did not want such a one
as Marcelle raising my grandchildren."

"I don't blame you, but it sounds as though you've managed

to offend Ila's royal ego," Trinity said. "Which means she's not going to want to give him up."

"No." Ferrau sank onto his throne and slumped. "She's sworn she will force my son to embrace submission. But I know him. He's a stubborn one, and proud with it. She won't break him." He looked up at them. "I have warned Ila if she gives him to that vicious bitch Marcelle, I will have my revenge, even if I must reduce both our dominalities to ash. But I fear she will run out of patience and let her daughter have her way. You must free him first."

"We could launch a clandestine raid," Nathan said, his gaze taking on the distant, calculating expression Sebastian had learned to respect. "Something stealthy and fast. Liberate him and—"

"No." The Dominor made a slashing gesture with one hand. "There is too much risk. I've been unable to discover where in the palace Arnoux is being held. If you try to find him during a raid attempt, they could kill him before you could pinpoint his location."

Nathan inclined his head, conceding the point. "I assume you've thought of an alterative."

The Dominor straightened eagerly. "Indeed. I have made contact with the Thralldealer who provides Ila with her stock. If you could place a man with him . . ."

"An undercover mission," Sebastian said, looking up from the rod he'd absently twisted into a corkscrew. "Send somebody in posing as one of these Thralls. He could find out where Arnoux is and spirit him out before they even know what hit them."

A fierce grin lit Ferrau's face. "Exactly," he said, rising from his throne and approaching Sebastian to stare up into his face. "And you would be perfect for it!"

Sebastian blinked. "Me?" *Play submissive to some vicious female dominant? Not likely.*

"Yes," Ferrau insisted. "Ila would jump at the chance to buy you. The face, the hair . . ." He gestured from Sebastian's goatee to his waist-length blond mane. "I knew you were the man for the job the moment I saw the combat recordings your captain sent me after I contacted him."

"Sounds risky," Trinity said, a frown on her pretty face.

"Extremely," Nathan agreed. "Sending him in alone, without backup . . ."

Ferrau gestured at the piece of steel Sebastian had absently mangled. "A man who could do that would be more than a match for the Dominess's entire palace guard." His eyes glittered. "And I will pay you. Very, very well."

Sebastian lifted a brow, though Nathan still looked dubious. "Just how well are we talking?"

Ferrau told him.

✦ ✦ ✦

THE next day Sebastian found himself riding in a Thrallwagon on the way to the dominality of Corvo. Where he was supposed to rescue Arnoux Ferrau after submitting to some bad-tempered female dominant with pretensions of royalty.

Oh, well, he thought philosophically, staring out through the bars of his cage at the passing landscape, *It's not like I ever minded eating a little pussy. . . .*

✦ ✦ ✦

ZARIA Orva looked at the naked man who lay sprawled on the thin pallet. She felt her gorge rise. His back was a bloody mess, scoured to raw meat by blow after blow of a whip.

"Marcelle really was in a mood last night, wasn't she?" she

said grimly to the guard who fidgeted by her side. Dom Searle had bitterly protested her plan to enter Marcelle's pleasure quarters and rescue the Thrall, but she'd insisted anyway. "Mother warned her about using that steel-tipped cat on her submissives. She's going to kill one of them one of these days. Assuming she hasn't already."

Sighing, she crouched to look into the man's pain-dulled eyes. At least the poor bastard wasn't Ferrau. When she'd learned Marcelle had beaten one of her Thralls again, Zaria had been terrified her mother had finally handed the Domince over. But no, this time the victim was a member of Marcelle's long-suffering stable.

"Domina, you shouldn't be here," Searle told her. "If the Domina hears—"

"And who's going to tell her?" Zaria asked, glancing up in time to catch the narrow glare the guardsman aimed at her handmaid. "And don't give Gemma that look. I ordered her to keep me informed whenever Marcelle goes too far. I don't want my mother put in the position of having to charge her own daughter with the murder of a Thrall."

Or worse, of covering that murder up to spare her favorite. Zaria wasn't sure which way her mother would jump, and would rather not find out.

"Milady," Searle said, sounding worried, "if your sister ever learns you've interfered—" He broke off. Dominant and warrior though he was, he couldn't quite bring himself to say that the next target of Marcelle's murderous rage might be her own sister.

Zaria felt her stomach twist in dread at the thought. But glancing down at the Thrall's bloody back, she felt her determination harden. She couldn't let this man die. And he would, if he wasn't removed from the palace tonight.

Marcelle was fully capable of torturing him again whenever another rage took her, whether he'd healed or not. And that could be the death of him.

Zaria sighed. It had all been so much easier before Brys left. Her brother was only a year younger than Marcelle, and he'd grown into a big, strapping man. He'd kept a rein on the worst of their sister's rages when their mother had not.

But five years ago there had been some kind of confrontation between Marcelle, Brys, and Ila, and he'd bought a commission in the army. Since then, he'd paid only brief visits, primarily to see Zaria.

Meanwhile, Marcelle had grown steadily more violent and out of control.

Well, Brys was gone now, and if anybody was going to save Marcelle's Thralls, it would have to be Zaria herself.

"Run and get hot water and clean rags," she ordered Gemma, rising to her feet to glance around the small, narrow cell. "We'll clean him up here and bandage him." To Searle she added, "Have the stable Thralls prepare a wagon with fresh bedding. I'll drive him to the Outworlder's clinic myself." Zaria returned her attention to the Thrall's savaged back. "I fear only their doctors will be able to save him."

Gemma was already heading out the door like the good Thralline she was, but Searle hesitated. "Milady . . ."

"Stop worrying, Searle," Zaria told him. "She'll never suspect me." Her mouth took on a bitter twist. "She doesn't think I have the courage."

✦ ✦ ✦

THE rescue went as smoothly as Zaria could have wished. The guards looked the other way as she, Gemma, and Searle carried the Thrall out and loaded him into a wagon parked in the palace courtyard. She had no fear any of them would tell her sister. They might not respect her—they knew too much about her tastes for that—but they loved her too much to let her suffer the brunt of Marcelle's rage. Besides, they had a duty to protect the royal family.

Even from each other.

She, Gemma, and Searle returned to the palace several hours later, the Thrall having been left in the Outworlders' care. The doctors at the clinic had promised to transport him to Rabican once he was healed. He could seek out a kinder mistress there.

Wearily she climbed down from the wagon. It had been a long drive to the clinic, and her shoulders ached from the reins. But as she stared across the courtyard, she heard Searle growl to Gemma, "As for you, Thralline, you will meet me at dawn in the dungeon. I feel the need to . . . deal with you."

"Yes, Dom Searle," Gemma said. Her breathless voice sounded more eager than frightened.

Despite herself, Zaria felt a little kick of heat of her own at the thought of Searle's discipline. With a sense of shamed anticipation, she knew she, too, would be getting up at dawn to see what the Dom intended for Gemma.

Chapter Three

THE next morning Zaria rose before the sun and rolled from her warm, comfortable bed. In the dark of her room she dressed quickly in her Domina's leathers, hands shaking with eagerness and furtive shame.

She knew she shouldn't be doing this. She should get back in her bed and go to sleep while Dom Searle disciplined his lover in whatever way pleased them both.

Instead, she lit a candle and padded out into the corridor in the wavering circle of its light. The echoing marble halls of the palace were silent this early, though she thought she could hear the faint sound of voices from the kitchens. The Thralls were already at work.

Hurrying toward the dungeon entrance, she found the massive wooden door she sought and swung it open. It creaked loudly as it revealed the stone steps leading down into the darkness. Lifting her candle, her heart pounding hard, she descended.

When she finally reached the echoing chamber far beneath the palace, Zaria could hear Searle's voice rumbling somewhere in the darkness. She threw a glance in that direction as she stepped behind the decorative screen that stood across the back of the room.

"Such pretty nipples," the guardsman said, stroking big, blunt fingers over Gemma's small breasts. He was naked, his brawny body gleaming in the torchlight as he stood over his helpless lover.

The Thralline, equally nude, was draped on her back over a punishment bench that held her torso arched and her legs spread wide. He'd chained her down until she could barely move, but judging by her expression, she didn't mind at all.

"So pink and hard," Searle purred, "so delicately responsive." His voice dropped to a suggestive rumble. "I think they need to be punished."

The girl gasped.

Zaria licked her dry lips as she took her accustomed place behind the screen. It was designed for the Dominess's use, for those times when she wanted to watch a Thrall's punishment without taking a direct role. In reality, however, Zaria used the screen far more often than her mother ever had, especially since Gemma and Searle had become lovers.

As she settled into a thickly padded chair behind the grate, the guard's gaze flicked toward her, tracking the movement of her candle. Searle knew she watched them, of course, just as she'd done so many times before. Yet he had never given her away to the Dominess.

Zaria was grateful. Her mother would have been outraged, not because Zaria loved to watch the guard take Gemma, but because her need to do so hinted she hungered for a man to dominate her the same way.

Now Zaria watched in longing as Searle turned to a nearby table and selected one of the erotic toys there.

It wasn't only the couple's passion she envied, though she yearned to experience that kind of heat for herself. No, what she envied most was their acceptance of the roles they'd been born to—Searle as dominant, Gemma as submissive. Neither longed to be anything else.

While Zaria herself dreamed of a submission she shouldn't want and never dared experience.

Searle let the padded clamp close over Gemma's nipple. The girl arched in her bonds, whimpering at the pleasurable sting.

Behind her screen Zaria shivered with a combination of need and self-disgust. Not for the first time a thought ran through her mind: *I should have been born a Thralline.*

But she hadn't been. She'd been born a Domina of the house of Orva, and this hunger she felt was wrong. She should take as much joy in dominating a man as her mother did. She should yearn to watch Searle writhe under her boot and beg to serve her pleasure.

But when Searle applied a second clamp to Gemma's other breast, her body leaped in need.

The Thralline whimpered, a long, voluptuous sound of mingled pleasure and pain, as he flicked and twisted and tormented her stiff nipples. His delicious ruthlessness had Zaria squirming in her chair, her fingers slipping under her armored bodice to tease her own tight peaks. By the time he rasped, "Are you ready to suck my cock?" she was shamelessly wet.

Gemma twisted in the wooden rack that held her body arched in a graceful bow, her clamp-adorned nipples pointing stiffly at the ceiling. "Yes," she groaned. "Oh, now! Take my mouth, Master—pump your cock down my throat!"

Searle strolled around to the head of the rack, where Gemma's head hung exactly at the height of a man's groin. She opened her mouth eagerly, and the warrior slid his thick erection between her lips. He let his head fall back with a groan of pleasure, dark hair swirling down his broad back. As he slowly began to thrust, Gemma suckled him eagerly.

Zaria opened her mouth in a soundless moan. Of all the sex acts, this was one she was utterly forbidden to indulge in. No royal Domina would ever willingly suck a man's cock.

Yet watching Searle stroke his width in and out of Gemma's lips, she ached. One hand slid between her thighs as the other teased her nipple. Shuddering, she imagined herself bound and helpless in just such a rack, feeling the velvet heat of a warrior's erection sliding seductively over her tongue. She could almost hear his rough commands as he ordered her to suck him, almost smell the masculine musk of his scent as she obeyed.

Letting her head fall back, Zaria imagined herself utterly at the mercy of her handsome dominant—secure in the knowledge he loved her, as Searle loved his Thralline. Gasping, she tightened her grip on her nipple, pulling and tugging as she stroked between her thighs. "Oh, Gods."

Her need growing, she closed her eyes and pretended the fingers caressing her belonged to the dark erotic conqueror of her dreams. The one who took her a willing captive, who stripped and bound her and made rough, tender love to her while she begged him for a mercy she didn't want.

The dominant lover she could never have.

"Enough," Searle said at last. Looking up, Zaria saw his grin flash in the darkness, very male, very knowing. "It's not your mouth I want to spill my seed into this morn." He pulled his ruddy cock tenderly from Gemma's lips and stepped between her splayed thighs. Zaria stood on her toes for a better view as he parted Gemma's nether lips and began working the thick shaft inside. His low groan of pleasure blended with the Thralline's whimper of delight.

"Oh, fuck me, Master!" Gemma cried, straining to grind herself deeper onto his shaft. "Give me no mercy!"

"Oh, sweet, you'll get none!" he growled, and began to pump. "Especially after that trick with the Domina yestereve!"

Zaria slipped her fingers under her leather loinband. She was very wet, very ready. Resting her forehead against the grate, she stroked herself deeply as the guard rode Gemma in hard, grinding lunges.

At last he bellowed out his climax, his cry blending with the Thralline's scream of pleasure. Zaria, hidden behind her grate, allowed herself no more than a gasp as she came in a flood of forbidden sweetness.

+ + +

MINUTES later she crept back up the stairs to the palace's main floor, dogged by the guilt she never failed to feel.

Zaria knew she dishonored her house every time she indulged her unnatural desires. And yet, she could not stay away, though she regularly swore to herself she'd never return to the dungeon again.

Her mother would be outraged.

And how Marcelle would taunt her. Even Brys would be disappointed that his cherished baby sister was a deviant.

Well, she simply wouldn't let them find out. She'd go on hiding her dreams of handsome dominants, just as she'd always done. Her family would never discover the truth.

And maybe someday she could resign herself to her proper place. Maybe someday she would finally discover the joy in forcing a man to bend to her will. All she needed was the right man.

"Domina Zaria!" a male voice hissed.

Zaria blinked and looked around. One of the Thralls stood in the corridor, wearing only the scrap of silk wrapped around his hips that was all her mother allowed her submissives. His body was muscled and beautiful, and Zaria thought instantly of painting him. "The Dominess requests your attendance, Domina," he said. "The Thralldealer is here."

She contained a sigh. Her mother never lost hope some handsome submissive would finally move her to truly dominate him. Apparently Ila found Zaria's mechanical efforts in that direction less than convincing.

But perhaps today Ila would get her wish. Maybe today Zaria would finally meet that perfect Thrall.

Fired by that hope—and more than a little guilt over her foray into the dungeon—Zaria strode off down the corridor toward her mother's audience chamber.

But even as she walked along the palace's winding corridors, her mind drifted back to the scene she'd just witnessed. She'd love to sketch Searle with Gemma, but she didn't dare leave a record of her wicked obsession. If Marcelle ever got her hands on such a thing, she'd use it at the most humiliating possible moment to discredit Zaria as publicly as she could.

But if she dared sketch the couple anyway . . . for a moment Zaria let herself dream of capturing the lines of Searle's strong, muscled body rising over Gemma's slim, soft one . . .

She was still imagining the pleasure of that sketch when a

guard opened the doorway to her mother's chamber. With an acknowledging nod, Zaria stepped inside.

And stopped dead, gaping at the most beautiful man she'd ever seen.

He stood naked in the audience chamber, his head raised in a pose of unconscious male arrogance despite the silver shackles he wore on corded wrists. His hair was a long, silken waterfall of gold down his back, matching the neatly trimmed beard that framed his sternly beautiful mouth. His face was made for the fall of light and shadow, elegant planes and angles forming cheekbones, chin, and broad, high forehead. His deep-set eyes were a color she'd never seen before, a vivid shade of dark green, as pure and sharp as gemstones. Looking at him, Zaria felt her chest ache with the need to capture the amazing color of those defiant eyes.

His body was a powerful match for his face, all chiseled muscle lying in great slabs across his broad chest, bulging arms, and thick, powerful thighs. The only soft thing about him was the cock hanging impressively between those brawny thighs.

I'll paint him as a warrior, Zaria thought, half-hypnotized. He met her eyes with a curl of amusement in the line of his lips. She realized suddenly that she had crossed the room without being aware of it, drawn irresistibly to his arrogant beauty.

Perhaps he'd sensed her fascination. Perhaps that was why he met her stare with a boldness she'd never seen in a Thrall facing those who would buy him. Usually such men kept their eyes submissively lowered, but not this one. Indeed, his gaze flicked down from her face to brazenly focus on the cleavage revealed by her armored top.

Ten Gods, he was *ogling* her! As if she were a Thralline presented for his purchase!

Goddess help her, she wished she were. . . .

Chapter Four

Z ARIA stared up at the Thrall, caught halfway between outrage and a feminine frisson of pleasure. He didn't seem to notice. A distinct heat grew in his eyes, and she felt something nudge her thighs. Looking down, she realized his cock had risen, growing quickly into a long, thick erection with an intriguing upward curve. Despite her offended dignity, she felt her nipples peak.

"Oh, he is impressive," Dominess Ila Orva purred.

Zaria started and looked toward her mother. With all her attention focused on the fascinating Thrall, she hadn't even noticed the Dominess was in the room.

Ila sprawled on her throne, wrapped in an elegant red silk robe shot with gold, her jeweled coronet glittering against her graying chestnut hair. Though nearly fifty, her long, elegant face still held the beauty that had once brought even dominants to their knees.

Now, as she watched Zaria, her dark, intelligent eyes gleamed with satisfied amusement. "I see the Thralldealer's merchandise has won your interest." Her gaze flicked toward the big male. "He's an arrogant one, isn't he? Wouldn't you like to tame him?"

No. The thought flashed across Zaria's mind. *Actually I'd like him to tame me.* Her cheeks heated in embarrassment at her own wanton thoughts. "He does need discipline," she managed.

The Thrall's gaze lifted lazily to hers, and his lips twitched as if suppressing a laugh. His lifted gold brow communicated a silent message: *Do you honestly think you're up to the job?*

Stung, she opened her mouth to snap out a reprimand, only to be interrupted by the ring of boots on marble.

Marcelle strode into the room, slapping her quirt against the top of her boot. A tall, powerful woman, she had the same strong features and curling chestnut hair as their mother, yet she lacked Ila's beauty. Zaria had once been puzzled about that, until she realized the tight lines of cruelty around Marcelle's mouth poisoned her looks.

"Ten hells!" her sister raged, slinging her quirt across the chamber. "It's as though he vanished off the very planet!"

"Who has, dear?" the Dominess asked, the lazy humor vanishing from her face.

"My Thrall. The new one. And I'd barely broken him in!"

Oh, to the contrary, Zaria thought, even as long practice kept her face impassive. *You'd broken him quite thoroughly.*

For a moment she considered telling her mother what Marcelle had done to the Thrall, perhaps even admitting her own role in his rescue.

No, best not. Her mother wouldn't believe the extent of the man's injuries, and the Outworlders had already healed the worst of them with their advanced technology. Marcelle would reclaim her Thrall, and Zaria would be unable to rescue the next man her sister abused to the brink of death.

"Ahhh, but what's this?" Marcelle purred.

Zaria looked up in alarm as her sister sauntered over, eyes fixed on the big, naked Thrall.

No! She'll want him, and if Mother gives him to her . . .

The blond Thrall, not realizing his danger, gave Marcelle the same lazy smile he'd given Zaria. Before she could step between them, her sister's hand flashed out, wrapped around his cock, and gave it a vicious twist.

The Thrall roared in startled pain. To Zaria's shock, he dared to grab Marcelle's hand and throw it off. Guards lunged toward him, and the Thralldealer made a sound of involuntary protest. The man and woman standing with him took a step forward, probably to beat down their recalcitrant captive.

"No!" Zaria cried, stepping between the Thrall and her sister's lifted fist. "He's mine! You will not touch him!"

An unholy light flooded Marcelle's eyes. She took a step forward as an ugly smile curled her lips. "Oh, won't I?"

As Zaria looked up at her taller, brawnier sister, something inside her cringed. Then she remembered the bloody back of Marcelle's last Thrall, and fury stormed in to replace the fear. "No," she gritted. "Not this one. I saw him first. I want him."

Marcelle laughed, a disbelieving shout of contempt. She lowered her head until she was nose to nose with Zaria. "You wouldn't even know what to do with him!"

"I'd know not to leave him a bloody ruin," Zaria snapped, refusing to back down from the frenzy she could see growing in her sister's dark eyes.

"That's enough." Ila's voice slashed through the atmosphere of violence swirling over the room. "Marcelle, your sister gets the Thrall."

Forgetting her fury, Marcelle swung around to gape. "Mother, look at him. She can't handle—"

"At least she's never had a Thrall disappear," Ila said. "How many have you lost this year alone?"

Six, since Zaria had grown sick of watching her sister's submissives suffer under Marcelle's brutal hand.

"He touched me!" Marcelle raged. "He should be punished!"

"Dear, when you twist a man's cock when he's not expecting it, these things happen." The Dominess's eyes flickered. "Besides, it's past time your sister developed a . . . suitable interest in a man." She turned to the Thralldealer. "How much?"

As the dealer diffidently named a price that was probably far less than he'd originally intended, Marcelle turned toward her again. The killing light in those black eyes made Zaria step back a pace. "You. Will. Pay." Whirling, Marcelle stalked out.

✛ ✛ ✛

"YOU know," Sebastian commed as Marcelle slammed the door behind her, *"I don't believe I've ever wanted to kick a woman's ass quite that bad."*

"Yeah, well, it's a good thing you controlled yourself," Nathan replied. He, Trin, Cassidy Vika, and another crewman were posing as the Thralldealer's assistants. Which meant they, at least, weren't standing around with their dicks hanging out for any passing lunatic to grab. *"We damn near ended up in a battle with the entire palace guard."*

"Bloody hell, we should have gone for it," Sebastian growled, his abused cock still throbbing. *"We could have taken the queen*

bitch hostage, and I could have given that vicious little lunatic the ass warming she so desperately needs."

"*We still don't know where the Domince is,*" Vika pointed out. "*They may be holding him somewhere else altogether. We can't take the chance.*"

"*Which means we're going to have to do this the way we originally planned,*" Nathan said, fixing a stern gaze on Sebastian. "*And that means you can't let yourself be taken off guard like that again. These women are sadists—and that includes your new owner. One of them will probably go after you again. Don't lose your temper next time.*"

"*Actually, I'm not so sure the other girl is quite that nasty,*" Trin said thoughtfully, eyeing the little Domina who still stood protectively at Sebastian's side. "*She was willing to step in front of him and defuse the entire situation. And judging from the look in Bitch Sister's eyes, she took a chance to do it.*"

Trin had a point, Sebastian decided, looking down at his new "owner."

Of course, he'd hoped to be bought by the mother, which would have simplified things considerably. Still, this girl had all the potential of being a much better alternative, from a personal standpoint if nothing else. She might be short, but she had a luscious little body. He was particularly looking forward to getting his hands—among other things—on those magnificent tits.

Besides, the girl had spine. She had to be a good fifteen centimeters shorter than Bitch Sister, and at least fifteen kilos lighter. She was also curved where the bitch was all wiry muscle. Yet she'd been willing to tackle Marcelle on his behalf.

All of which couldn't help but give a guy a warm, fuzzy feeling. Especially since there was a chance he'd get to sample her before he had to spring Ferrau. Particularly those galactic-class tits.

Hiding a grin, Sebastian started making plans.

+ + +

AT last Zaria was able to escape back to her quarters with her new prize, Searle at their heels. She was itching to sketch the thrall. . . .

Among other things, whispered a wicked little voice.

Striding into the wide, airy room that was her studio, Zaria headed straight for the cabinet that held her supplies. Glancing automatically back at the Thrall—he had the unusual name of Sebastian, according to the Thralldealer—she saw he'd stopped to look around. His gaze was distinctly calculating, which might explain why Searle watched every move he made with narrow attention. Her guardsman plainly didn't trust him.

Perhaps with good reason. Perhaps she should tie the Thrall up, just to be safe. Her mind flashed to the image of Gemma, her body arched into a bow in the rack that morning. She pictured Sebastian's brawny form curved in the same dramatic pose and licked her lips.

Even her mother would approve of that composition.

"Lock him in the mounting block," Zaria ordered Searle over her shoulder as she opened the supply cupboard and contemplated its contents. She decided she'd start out with a charcoal sketch. There'd be time for oils later.

"Mounting block?" she heard Sebastian mutter. "What do I look like, a horse?"

"You look like whatever the Ten Hells the Domina wants you to be," Searle growled. "Now get into position."

By the time Zaria had her easel set up with a thick sheet of paper affixed to the clip, Searle had manacled the Thrall to the block. The female superior position had never done that much for her, but when she turned and saw Sebastian bent in a bow over the mounting block's padded curve, she felt heat spin into her core.

The block was made like a wooden half circle standing on the floor. He lay draped over it on his back with ankles and wrists shackled to either side. Afternoon sunlight poured over his muscled contours, gleaming among the strands of his long hair as it spilled to the floor in a pool of golden silk.

Zaria had never seen a Thrall look more beautiful—or more pissed off. The green of his eyes had gone positively icy, and there was a distinct snarl in the line of his handsome mouth.

And unfortunately, his impressive cock was completely limp. Not at all the effect she was looking for.

Zaria crossed the room to him, barely aware of Searle closing the door behind him now that the Thrall was safely secured.

Sebastian lifted his head and glared up at her. "This is damned uncomfortable."

"Oh, don't be a nig," she said, bending over him and taking his cock in hand. "I know you've ridden a mounting block before."

He watched warily as she began to handle him, as though afraid she was going to give his cock the same nasty jerk Marcelle had. "What's a nig?"

Zaria lifted a brow. It was a common expression. "A Thrall who whines at every little command." Keeping her touch light and tender, she caressed his cock lovingly.

He swallowed. "You do realize that doesn't detach? I mean,

you can borrow it, but only if the rest of me comes along for the ride."

Zaria chuckled. "Don't worry, Sebastian. I have no intention of doing any damage to your magnificent anatomy."

He gave her a flashing, roguish grin that made his goatee tilt up and something turn over in her chest. "Magnificent, huh?"

She smiled and cupped his balls. They were heavy, deliciously full in her palm. His cock filled, swelling to equally impressive proportions. "Oh, yes. Definitely magnificent." Releasing him, she turned back toward her easel. "Now hold that pose."

"What?"

Zaria grinned at the outrage in his voice. Her sister had never realized that you didn't need a whip to instill discipline.

"A good Thrall doesn't ogle the Domina in public, Sebastian," she purred as she stepped behind her easel and picked up a piece of charcoal.

Chapter Five

SHE was going to *draw* him?

Sebastian stared at Zaria in disbelief as she stood behind her easel, sketching in long, confident strokes with some kind of black stick. He'd assumed she'd bought him for kinky sex, especially when she'd had that guard chain him to this . . . whatever it was. And he'd been perfectly willing to play along, as long as she didn't intend to yank any tender portions of his anatomy.

He hadn't realized she'd intended to torture him.

Look at her, standing over there with those incredible tits just barely contained in two leather cups that weren't nearly big enough for the job. She wore some kind of narrow leather thong thing that passed between her legs and left most of her pretty ass bare, while thick leather straps circled her legs from small booted feet all the way up to her crotch. The whole rig was obviously going for the I'll-kick-your-ass-and-make-you-beg-for-more look, but on her, it didn't quite come off.

That failure might have something to do with the softening effect of the lush sable curls tumbling over her shoulders. But more than likely it was her eyes—soft, brown, and damn near too big for her heart-shaped little face. Add the straight, delicate nose and the full lips that just begged for cock, and any pretensions of being a vicious dominatrix were simply doomed.

However, he could easily picture her all tied up and ready to take his dick in the orifice of his choice.

Damn, now there was a thought. He felt his cock twitch in lecherous appreciation.

Since there didn't seem to be much else he could do at the moment, Sebastian let himself sink into wicked daydreams in which she was the one shackled to the mounting block.

Only he sure as hell wouldn't be messing around with any little black sticks.

✦ ✦ ✦

"THERE'S a term for women like you," Sebastian growled after she'd spent a half hour sketching him. His cock had gotten longer and harder with every minute that passed. Zaria wasn't sure she wanted to know why.

She gave him a grin around her easel anyway. "Domina?"

"Tease," he growled. "You know what happens to teases?"

Something inside Zaria gave a hot little kick of excitement. A Thrall had never looked at her like that, with feral masculine heat in his eyes, as if imagining all the ways he'd like to take revenge for her taunting.

New Thralls more typically wore expressions of breathless anticipation, as if eager to see what wicked thing she would do to them. Those familiar with her, however, only looked slightly bored. After all, they wanted a dominant as much as she did, and she simply wasn't convincing in the role.

But as she looked at Sebastian's powerful body bound in a muscular arch, his thick cock pointing stiffly at his chin, his vivid eyes locked hungrily on her body, she felt a flood of heat. It was easy to imagine what he'd do to her if he got loose. The thought made her nipples rise to hard, tingling peaks.

Suddenly she wanted to tease him in truth. Wanted to watch all that male fury steam.

Slowly she lifted her hands and reached for the laces between the cups of her armored bodice. Sebastian's gaze sharpened. "What?" she asked, her voice a throaty purr even to her own ears.

"Yes?" He licked his lips, watching her fingers pluck at the laces. "Did you ask a question?"

"You asked if I knew what happens to women who tease." Slowly she pulled the lace out of another eyelet. Her breasts bulged, on the verge of escaping the tight leather bodice. "I'm asking . . . what?"

He shifted in his bonds as his eyes flared hot. If anything, his cock hardened even more. "Somebody makes them pay." The words were a low, velvet-edged growl.

She gave the lace another slow tug, pulling it out of the last eyelet. Her top sprang apart, liberating her breasts. The air felt cool on their hard, puckered peaks. "How?"

"With clamps," he rumbled, his gaze locked on her breasts. "Attached to stiff little nipples."

"Oh, I don't think so." She swaggered—and she'd never swaggered in her life—over to the nearest chair. Swinging a booted foot up on the seat, she bent to unlace her leggings. "Nobody would dare torment a Domina's breasts." Deliberately she began unwinding the straps of her leggings until the soft leather fell away from her thighs. She tossed the straps aside and threw a look at Sebastian just in time to see him roll his hips upward. His cock bobbed hungrily. She licked her lips.

So this is what it's like to dominate a man, Zaria thought, and went to work on her other leg, conscious of his burning gaze. "Nipple punishment is the kind of thing reserved for lowly Thrallines."

"Or pretty little Domina teases who find themselves kidnapped."

She caught her breath and looked up at him, startled that he'd dare voice her secret fantasy.

For a moment, as she looked into his hot male gaze, it didn't sound like an empty threat at all.

+ + +

SEBASTIAN watched, all but drooling as the Domina stripped off the rest of that ridiculous armor, baring the soft, intensely female body he'd spent the last half hour fantasizing about.

As she moved, the cloud of sable curls slid around her slim shoulders. She threw him a quick, dark look and arched her spine, lifting the full mounds of her breasts. They were pale as cream, crowned with plump pink tips that really did seem to beg. Her legs were equally tempting, slender, long in proportion to her doll-like height, with a fine thatch of soft curls between them.

Sebastian was seriously tempted to pop the chains that held him to this silly bondage rig. He figured it would take him about five seconds to get his "mistress" hogtied with the bullwhip hanging on the wall behind her. Then another hour or so for a highly erotic interrogation, during which he'd both extract the location of Ferrau and get her nicely wet. After that, he could give her the royal fucking they'd both be more than ready for, and then he'd go rescue the kid.

God, it was tempting, particularly when she turned her back on him, set her legs apart, and bent over, displaying glistening pink folds and a perfectly rounded ass that made his dick jerk in lust. She looked over her shoulder at him. "Somehow, I doubt kidnapping a Domina is as easy as you dream," she purred.

Don't bet on it, sweetheart.

Unfortunately, this was no time to go off half-cocked . . . so to speak. Sebastian knew he needed to get a better sense of the guards' locations and patrols, not to mention where they had Ferrau stashed and what condition he was in.

So, like it or not, the little Domina's punishment was going to have to wait. But looking at that luscious butt, he could only hope it wouldn't be for long.

Zaria straightened up slowly, giving him plenty of time to consider her delicious, wide-spread legs and utterly fuckable ass before she turned around and sauntered back over to him. Sebastian gave her his best menacing look, but she just lowered her lashes over chocolate brown eyes as one corner of her full mouth quirked upward in a taunting smile.

He was so hard, his cock throbbed.

Her gaze dropped to the aching shaft, and that wicked smile widened. Casually, with elaborate disinterest, she reached down to run the tip of one long nail along the length of his prick, which jerked lustfully as his balls drew tight "Oh, that looks . . . painful."

"Climb on and see," he growled, eyeing her erect pink nipples. He badly wanted to find out if they were as sweet as they looked.

"I could," Zaria mused, contemplating the drop of pre-cum clinging to the head of his cock. "Or I could just"—she scooped up the drop with one long finger—"let you suffer." She licked it from her fingertip with a flick of her pointed pink tongue.

He went still as he fought to contain the impulse to break his shackles. "Oh, you're living dangerously, little girl."

She gave him an evil grin and bent lower until her head hovered just over one of his nipples. Smiling a dark, wicked smile, she gave the hard little button a lick. The pleasure of that wet tongue made him jolt in his bonds and groan. "I'm not a 'little' anything, Thrall."

"Better be careful." Excitement burned in his veins. "Because neither am I."

She reached down to wrap those cool, tapered fingers around his aching cock. "I noticed. And I wondered"—another slow, taunting lick as her fingers tightened on his cock in a seductive pull—"just how big can you get?"

"If you keep that up, you're going to find out."

"Oh, I hope so." Another taunting lick. He managed not to moan. "I'm so looking forward to it."

"You do realize," he gritted as she licked him again, then lifted one hand to rake her nails gently up his ribs, "one of these days I'm going to have *you* in chains?"

"That, I very much doubt." She laughed softly, tauntingly, and swung a leg over his torso, all but thrusting her butt in his face. Inhaling sharply, he breathed in the hot, musky cream of her arousal. "Now, why don't you use that mouth for something other than silly threats? Eat your Domina's pussy like a good Thrall."

With a low growl of excitement, Sebastian lifted his head and obeyed, licking and biting gently at the wet, tender folds. She was just as delicious as he'd imagined. Flicking her tight little pearl-like clit with his tongue, he imagined her tied up, spread wide, and ready for his raging hard-on.

He suckled and nibbled until she dropped her bitch-goddess pose and backed into his face, grinding her wet cunt against his mouth.

"More!" she whimpered.

"Fuck me!" he growled back, rolling his hips upward in a demand he knew was anything but submissive.

"Ooooh," Zaria moaned. "Yes!" Moving with lithe speed, she swung off him and turned around, her dark eyes meeting his with dazed heat as she mounted him. Grabbing his cock around the base, she pointed it skyward, traced the head of his shaft through her creamy flesh, and found her opening. Slowly she settled her weight back onto his hard length, forcing it inside her sweet, clamping cunt centimeter by luscious centimeter.

He groaned in erotic pleasure. God, she was tight. And wet. And amazing.

+ + +

ZARIA caught her breath in a gasp of pleasure at the feeling of the Thrall's massive cock working its way into her sex. He was damn near too much for her, particularly in this position, arched hard upward, impaling her.

"You're tiny," he growled, rolling his hips upward. She sucked in a breath at the way he stuffed her so completely. "I like that."

For a wicked, forbidden moment, she found herself wondering what it would be like to be at his mercy—bound and helpless, while he fucked her with a ravenous male hunger he didn't bother to control. She shuddered in arousal, rose to her toes, and ground herself down hard.

"Oh, yeaaah," Sebastian rumbled, meeting her thrusts with jarring strength. "That's it!"

The pleasure seared Zaria, maddened her. She began jogging up and down, fucking him hard, taking him deep. She could feel her orgasm gathering like a firestorm, jolted closer to breaking every time she rammed herself onto Sebastian's blade-hard cock.

Grabbing his hips, she forced him still harder, deeper, tossing her head at the blazing pleasure as that big shaft raked her tight inner tissues. "I'm coming!" she cried.

"Yeah!" he bellowed, hunching in and out of her in driving strokes. "Yeah, oh, you hot little bitch, just you wait until I get you—!"

He roared under her, his body bowing, driving his cock impossibly deep. Zaria felt her orgasm tear free in a hot explosion of ecstasy that blasted along her nervous system.

She'd never climaxed more ferociously in her life.

Chapter Six

THE next morning Sebastian found himself trailing after his new "mistress" and trying to keep himself from watching her leather-clad ass with too much lecherous interest. He gathered from the ugly looks he got from the palace guards that Thralls weren't supposed to be quite so open in their admiration.

Not that he particularly gave a damn. There was a lot about Zaria to admire, even aside from the explosive orgasm she'd given him the night before.

Or, for that matter, the equally impressive ride she'd given him that morning. A ride that had done a lot to cool his irritation at being chained to the bed all night.

Evidently she still wasn't inclined to trust her new Thrall yet.

She had no idea how untrustworthy he really was. He'd spent hours last night fantasizing about what he'd do to her once the collar was on the other neck.

But as the morning advanced, he began to suspect he wasn't the only one concealing hidden depths. As he followed the Domina on her rounds, it became obvious who kept the palace operating smoothly. And it wasn't the Dominess.

First came a meeting with the cook to discuss what dishes to serve at the evening meal, how to prepare them, and what wines should accompany each one.

Next came a trip to the laundry, where Zaria inspected the job the Thrallines were doing there. Sebastian was interested to note that despite her merciless nitpicking, the women seemed to accept her criticism without resentment. Evidently his little mistress was well-liked, even by those who didn't fantasize about seeing her in a ball-gag.

After that, she checked each and every bedroom in the sprawling building, making sure all the beds were made and the chamber pots emptied.

Sebastian trailed behind her, trying to look harmless while his battle computer scanned and recorded every centimeter of the place.

She'd ordered him along to fetch and carry—and indeed, he found himself lugging various heavy objects around for her. But he didn't mind, because the tour gave him the perfect chance to count guards, note the movements and schedules of the staff, and generally fill in the blanks of his knowledge of the palace.

He'd already stored a map of the building in his computer implant's database, after generating it from scans the *Starrunner* had made from orbit. Unfortunately, however, though it showed the locations of rooms and the largest concentrations of people, the map didn't tell him who those people were. Or, for that matter, where Ferrau was being held, since there was no way to pick the Domince out from the crowd.

Sebastian was going to have to figure that part out himself, through sheer, old-fashioned surveillance.

Then Zaria led him to just what he was looking for: the guardsmen's barracks. While she conducted a surprise inspection, Sebastian did a rough estimate of guard strength based on the number of bunks he counted.

As he trailed behind her wearing his best guileless expression, Zaria tore through the men's quarters, flipping open lockers, pulling swords from scabbards to check for rust, and generally sending the noncoms into a tizzy.

By the time she finished ripping strips off those who needed it, Sebastian felt much more confident in his manpower estimate, though not particularly pleased with the results. There were three hundred guardsmen altogether, far more than even he cared to take on by himself.

As he meditated on that disconcerting fact, the noncoms vanished to do their own strip-ripping, and he and Zaria headed for the door.

Suddenly she stopped in her tracks and glanced around. Preoccupied with his calculations, it took Sebastian a moment to realize she was reacting to low, feminine moans and male gasps.

Zaria turned and headed down a short corridor, following the soft, intimate sounds. Sebastian grinned and sauntered after her. Obviously, she meant to catch some fornicating guardsmen in the act.

She froze in the next doorway and stood staring inside, so tense she almost vibrated. Curious, Sebastian moved closer and glanced in over her shoulder.

Two guardsman had a pretty blond Thralline bent over a chair, wrapped in an intricate arrangement of ropes. One of them was pumping in and out of her from behind, while the other fucked her mouth.

"Oh, come on, Cherese, you can take more of it than that," the man said, with a low, dark laugh. "Relax your throat."

The blonde made a strangled, moaning sound of submission. He sank another inch deeper.

Grinning, Sebastian waited for Zaria to chew the three out for goldbricking. Instead, she whirled and hurried down the corridor, almost colliding with him in her haste. For a moment, she met his gaze, hers vague with startled arousal. A furious blush flooded her cheekbones before she ducked her head and slipped past him without so much as a snotty command to get out of the way.

Sebastian blinked and used his computer implant to do a quick scan of her retreating back. It confirmed what he'd glimpsed.

Zaria had found something wildly arousing in the sight of the blond being dominated.

I'll be damned, my little mistress has a submissive streak. A hot grin of anticipation rolled over his face. *Well, isn't that interesting?*

✦ ✦ ✦

SEBASTIAN was still mulling the delicious implications of Zaria's erotic tastes when she unwittingly led him right where he most wanted to go.

When they stepped inside the soaring chamber, he first took it for yet another of the palace's pretty sitting rooms. The marble floor was covered in brilliant, jewel-toned rugs, while colorful tapestries depicted naked men writhing in blended agony and pleasure.

The furniture was made of some delicate white wood picked

out in gold leaf and upholstered in the same jewel tones as the rugs. The arching ceilings were supported by the usual thick white columns.

But then he noticed something different about each of those supports—a strange projection sticking out from the base, thrusting upward at an angle. Eyeing one, he realized the projection was a rather intimidating dildo.

For a moment Sebastian thought the false cocks must be intended for female pleasure. Then he noticed the rings embedded in the column's surface, presumably to accommodate shackles. He winced and hoped Zaria wouldn't take it into her head to chain him to one of them.

"Hello, Sister." Sebastian turned at the petulant voice to find Marcelle lounging sullenly in the corner on a pile of thick pillows. A bottle sat on a low table by her elbow.

Great, Bitch Sister had been drinking. This was going to get ugly.

That prediction proved true as she looked up at Zaria with something nasty flickering in her gaze. "What, out of the bedroom already, and you with a new Thrall?" Contempt dripped from Marcelle's voice. "What's the matter—couldn't he get it up?"

Deigning to address Sebastian, she added, "Don't feel bad. Her Thralls usually can't. She's too soft and spineless to get them hard."

"Strange," Sebastian drawled, knowing he should keep his mouth shut. "I didn't have any problem with that."

Zaria shot him a warning look. "In any case, Marcelle . . ."

Before she could get the rest of the sentence out of her mouth, a man bellowed, "I said no! Kill me and be damned—I'll not bend a knee to any Domme bitch!"

Sebastian went still, staring at the closed door the cry had come from. Oh, now, that sounded interesting. Ferrau?

Before he could invent an excuse to investigate, the door opened. The Dominess stalked out and slammed it behind her. "That stubborn, arrogant little—" She broke off and began to pace the chamber.

Sebastian concentrated on doing absolutely nothing to draw attention to himself. He'd already noticed these people had a tendency to treat Thralls as furniture. With any luck, they'd let him spy in peace.

"Let me have him," Marcelle said into the thrumming tension, sipping languidly from her goblet. "I'll bring him to heel for you."

"No, thank you," Ila growled. "You'd have us at war in a fortnight."

"Not if the Dominor doesn't find out about it." Bitch Sister's smile was chilling.

"Do you honestly think you could hide something like that?" Zaria demanded. "The minute he saw the scars you like to leave . . ."

Marcelle shrugged. "We'll just tell him Arnoux liked it."

"And what's Arnoux going to say?"

"Anything I tell him to."

Zaria threw up her hands. "You have no understanding of him at all! He is a Dom, not a Thrall, and you'll never make him anything else no matter how you beat him."

"I will." The Dominess's eyes narrowed and hardened. "That bastard Dominor dared say *my* daughter is unnatural and perverted. Well, we'll see who is unnatural."

"Everyone knows the Dominess has only one perverted daughter," Marcelle murmured into her goblet. "And it's not I."

Zaria stiffened at the dig. Sebastian lifted a brow, waiting for the explosion.

It didn't come. Instead she turned toward the Dominess. "This is madness, Mother, and you know it. Return Arnoux to his father before you plunge us into war."

"No!" Ila slashed her hand through the air. "We've come too far. It's war one way or another. But I'll have that boy's submission, if it's with my dying breath."

"But why?" Zaria demanded hotly. "Why court an unnecessary war simply because Ferrau refused to agree to a wedding between Arnoux and Marcelle? Why risk the destruction of us all?"

"It's not an unnecessary war, Zaria!" Ila whirled on her, a snarl curling her mouth. "Marcelle is my heir! One day she'll be Dominess of Orva. To slight her is to slight our very dominality, our people and our power! If we ignore such a grievous insult, we'll look weak in the eyes of our enemies—enemies I fear far more than Xarles Ferrau. By breaking his son, I will demonstrate to any who doubt that we are a power to be reckoned with."

"Only if we win the war, Mother," Zaria said quietly. "Otherwise, we'll have brought down on our own heads the very destruction you fear."

Marcelle's slurred voice sounded from the corner. "You waste your time, Mother. Zaria will never understand." She lifted her head and curled her lip. "Submission is in her blood."

"And stupid viciousness is in yours!" Zaria snapped, both fists lifted in fury. "If you'd been less bloodthirsty, the Domince would be in your marriage bed instead of a Thrall's chains. And none of us would be in this predicament!"

"Better a little fire than spinelessness." Marcelle threw her goblet aside and rolled to her feet, her gaze suddenly sharp and clear.

Sebastian tensed as she loomed over Zaria. Had her drunkenness been feigned to lure her sister into some kind of duel?

"That's enough, Marcelle!" The snap in Ila's voice brought the Domina up short, eyes glittering with frustration.

Warning gaze fixed on Marcelle, Ila asked, "How went your inspection of the palace this morn, Zaria?"

It seemed Mother Dear wanted to change the subject. Smart woman.

With a savage curse, Marcelle flung herself out of the room. Sebastian relaxed. That was when he realized he'd been willing to blow his own cover to protect Zaria from her lunatic sister.

When had the little Domina gotten under his skin?

Chapter Seven

SEBASTIAN managed to keep his mouth shut as Zaria mechanically reported the results of her inspections to her mother.

He maintained that careful silence at the noon meal that followed. Dutifully, he stood behind her chair like all the other Thralls and Thrallines, stepping forward to eat from her hand when she summoned him. It all would have made him feel like an exceptionally large Pekingese, if he hadn't been so busy trying to decide how to turn this twist to his advantage.

By the time they'd disposed of both the rest of her duties and started on the evening meal, he'd mapped out a plan to secure the Domince's freedom. He'd even pinpointed a couple of potential escape routes.

All he needed now was an opportunity.

As the serving Thralls bustled around with their trays, Sebastian used his internal com to reestablish communications with

Nathan and his party. The mercenaries had withdrawn into the hills just beyond the palace's immediate environs to await his signal.

Nathan listened as Sebastian detailed his plans.

"*Sounds good,*" the captain commed finally. "*I'll transport a combat force down from the* Starrunner *and have them ready to back you up when you give the word.*"

"*Give 'em all the copy of Zaria's vidshot I sent you,*" Sebastian told him. "*I don't want any of them hurting her by mistake.*"

"*You like this girl, don't you?*" Trin asked suddenly.

"*Of course he does,*" Nathan said. "*Did you see that bustline?*"

"*Hey, Zaria's more than the sum of her cleavage,*" Sebastian told them, glowering. "*She's bright, she's got guts, and she actually cares about her people. Which is more than the rest of her family can say. She . . .*"

The com carried Nathan's hoot of astonishment. "*My God, he sounds like he's halfway in love.*"

Heat flooded Sebastian's face for the first time in decades. "*Don't be ridiculous. I'm only interested in the tits.*"

"*I thought you said she was more than cleavage,*" Trin challenged.

"*I lied,*" he said firmly, and stepped forward to accept a bite of fruit from Zaria's slim fingers.

Her smile made something turn over in his chest.

✦ ✦ ✦

ZARIA walked into her quarters rubbing the knots of tension gathered in the base of her neck. She was only vaguely aware that Searle and Sebastian had entered after her. She was far too preoccupied with worry for her mother and the dominality.

Ila stubbornly refused to acknowledge that she'd put them on the road to destruction with her determination to tame the Domince. And Marcelle, vicious bitch that she was, was equally determined to take revenge on Arnoux for his father's rejection.

The two of them are going to be the death of that boy, she thought, pacing the room in long strides. *But, what in the name of the Ten Gods am I going to do about it?*

Suddenly Sebastian stepped up behind her, so close she could feel the heat of his body. "Get rid of your watchdog," he breathed in her ear. "If you dare."

Zaria whirled around, startled by his silken challenge. He smiled at her darkly.

Looking into those green eyes, she found herself aching for the distraction she knew he was more than capable of providing. Her heart began to pound. "Searle, you're dismissed."

The guard looked startled. "But . . ."

"Go find Gemma and punish her for something," Sebastian said without looking around. "I'm sure between the two of you, you can come up with an excuse."

Searle drew himself up to his full height—which, she realized, was still several centimeters shorter than Sebastian. "You forget yourself, Thrall! I could have you—"

"Dismissed," Zaria snapped, suddenly impatient with the posturing.

Searle threw her a glower, but even he didn't quite dare refuse when she used that tone. Grumbling, the guard walked out. Sebastian followed him and bolted the door.

Zaria's mouth went dry.

"You people really don't take Thralls seriously, do you?" Sebastian said, turning to study her with narrow, calculating eyes.

He began stalking her, moving across the room like some big, feral cat pursuing something it could eat in one snap.

Automatically she eased back, nervously aware of his sheer size. "What do you mean?"

"I mean if I were your bodyguard, I wouldn't have left you alone with a man like me."

She managed a casual shrug. "You're only a Thrall," she said, though the erotic menace in his eyes was anything but submissive.

"Actually"—before she could duck away, a big hand clamped over her shoulder, spun her around, and jerked her back against his hard-muscled body—"tonight I'm not. Tonight I'm a warrior who's tricked you all into believing I'm nothing more than a Thrall. Just so I could capture my prize—a pretty Domina, left all alone."

"Wha—?" Her surprised cry cut off as his big palm clamped over her mouth.

"None of that," he whispered roughly. "I don't care to have my pleasure interrupted."

It couldn't be, Zaria thought wildly as he picked her off her feet and bore her backward toward the bed. No Dom would ever stoop to disguising himself as a Thrall.

And yet, he'd never really acted like a submissive, had he?

What if it was true?

As he pushed her lightly down onto the mattress, Sebastian grabbed the whip she'd hung on the wall, more for decoration than anything else. Before she could even muster the will to fight, he straddled her hips and tied her wrists behind her back with the light leather lash. Zaria squirmed, shocked and titillated as he lowered his head to whisper in her ear, "There, now. Just the way I like my Thrallines." He straightened off her.

"I'm not a . . ." But before she manage more of her instinctive protest, he'd ripped a strip of fabric from a sheet, whipped the cloth around her head, and tied it into a gag.

"Now, we really need to get rid of all this armor," he said, and flipped her onto her back as if she weighed no more than a child's doll.

Zaria stared up at him in shock as he went to work on the front lacings of her leathers, his big hands surprisingly deft. She really should be fighting him. And yet . . .

He lifted his head and gave her a smile hot with humor and male hunger. "I'm not going to hurt you, Zaria." His silken purr was so completely devoid of any real malice, she felt the knot of fear in her chest instantly loosen. "Though I just may fuck you until you scream for more."

She didn't quite manage to suppress her helpless moan.

Big fingers peeled the leather cups away from her breasts to fondle the soft mounds possessively. "Oh, yeah," he said, as he squeezed her nipples. "God, I've been dying to get my hands on these." That grin flashed again. "Along with my lips, my tongue, my teeth, and my dick." He rolled the little peaks, watching her face closely as she squirmed. Ten Gods, it felt good. "Mmmm. These are delicious. Ever been tit fucked?"

She blinked at him.

Sebastian laughed. "I'll take that as a no." Lowering his head, he gave one nipple a sampling lick that sent pleasure shivering through her body. "Ooooh, yeah," he said. "That tastes as good as I expected." He watched the peak draw tight and pink with her growing hunger. "I do believe I want more. And I'm going to get it."

Closing his clever mouth over her, he suckled hungrily. Zaria gasped behind her gag as her cunt throbbed with every erotic pull of his lips. Simultaneously his tongue flicked her nipple, pressing it up against his teeth, then raking with gentle bites.

She felt dizzy, overwhelmed, as if she'd fallen into one of her own dark fantasies. She had no idea whether he really was a Dom, or simply a Thrall who yearned to dominate as much as she longed to submit.

And she realized she didn't care, because she was more aroused than she'd ever been in her life. He was giving her exactly what she'd always wanted. Exactly what she'd always dreamed of.

Need surged through her, hot and reckless. She knew she might never again get a chance to experience what it was like to yield to a man. And she meant to enjoy ever second of it.

Besides, she was thoroughly sick of obeying the rules and ignoring her own needs. Ten Hells, her mother was willing to plunge the dominality into war, simply out of pride. Her sister didn't hesitate to maim men to serve her own lust. Why shouldn't Zaria let herself enjoy an experience straight out of her hottest dreams? Why did she always have to be the one who denied her needs?

"You want it, don't you?" Sebastian asked darkly, his heated gaze locked on her face as he lifted his head from her wet, hard nipple. "You want to be taken. Fucked."

God, yes, she thought helplessly. *Take me. Give me what I need.*

His hands drifted down her bare torso, straight to her cleft. One long, strong finger slid between her lips and found her opening to slip inside. She whimpered behind her gag at the sensation.

"Mmmmm," Sebastian purred. "Just the way I like my captives. Nice and slick and ready for cock." A second finger joined the first, and she writhed. "Unfortunately for you, sweetheart, I'm not prepared to give it to you yet. You need a lesson in what happens to pretty little girls who try to dominate men much, much too big for them." His smile was deliberately sinister. "And I'll bet you've got all kinds of toys that would be just perfect for the job."

✦ ✦ ✦

THE way Zaria's eyes widened over her gag made Sebastian's dick twitch in anticipation. He rose from the bed and looked down at her, letting her get a good look at the erection behind the ridiculous loincloth she'd given him. Baring his teeth at her, he reached down and ripped it off, freeing his cock to stand straight and straining with eagerness.

If anything, her eyes widened even more. He rocked back on his heels, grinning, to enjoy the view.

The way he'd tied her with her hands behind her back thrust those round, gorgeous breasts upward and emphasized the white curve of her hips against the dark coverlet.

He tilted his head, letting his blond hair slide over his shoulder. Reaching down, he stroked his cock with one hand and caressed his balls with the other. "Oh, yeah," he told her. "I'm going to enjoy making you pay."

His sensors picked up her answering leap of heat at the threat, and he concealed a grin. Subs always loved it when he played sadistic villain.

Leaving her bound and ready, Sebastian sauntered toward the big wooden box that stood at the foot of the bed. He'd noticed a stylized whip carved into the lid earlier, and he had a good idea what it contained.

Flipping it open, he discovered he was right. There was an

array of dildos—including one in a harness arrangement he was instantly glad she'd never tried to use on him—cock rings, various cuffs, jars of what appeared to be lubricants, and several wicked-looking paddles.

Finally he found what he'd been looking for—a small box containing a selection of clamps. Grinning in anticipation, he tried several of them out on his pinkie until he found two that had just the right bite; enough to sting without inflicting actual pain. He added a promising buttplug and a jar of lubricant and closed the lid.

By the time he turned around, Sebastian found Zaria watching him like a bird hypnotized by a snake.

Oh, yeah. This was going to be fun.

And when he was finished, he'd put his plans into action.

Chapter Eight

SEBASTIAN gave her his best menacing male smile and sauntered over to slide a knee onto the bed. Tossing down the dildo
and the jar of lube, he leaned over and opened one of the clamps
right in front of her eyes. Slowly he let it squeeze closed. "You
know where I'm going to put this, don't you?"

She blinked, and her eyes dilated with helpless arousal.

"Don't you?" he barked.

Zaria jumped and nodded.

"You ever wear one of these?"

She shook her head, her nostrils flaring as she breathed in hard
over her gag.

He gave her an artistic snarl. "And yet, I'll bet you just love putting them on your poor Thralls." Actually, he'd wager she didn't. But
he captured one full, pretty breast, thumbed its blushing nipple, and
glared into her eyes anyway. "Were you planning to use one on me?"

Her gaze flickered. To his astonishment, she lifted her chin and gave her head a short, defiant nod.

Sebastian barely managed to contain his shout of laughter. The little minx! He knew good and damned well she'd intended no such thing, but she wanted to play the role of deserving victim. He managed another growl despite his amusement. "Yeah, I'll just bet you were. Well, the clamp's on the other nip now, isn't it? Or," he added, hovering the little device over her eager peak, "it's about to be."

He let the tiny jaws close slowly, listening to her gasp of surprised arousal at its gentle bite. Sebastian smirked. "Bet that stings." Not much, though.

Slowly he pulled the clamp upward until it lost its hold, then attached it again and twisted his wrist. Zaria whimpered deliciously, and her eyes drifted closed. "Mmmm. I've been dreaming about tormenting your big, pretty tits all day. I knew it was going to be hot." Picking up the other clamp, he rumbled, "Let's do both of 'em."

+ + +

ZARIA moaned as the second clamp closed over her nipple with a hot, erotic bite. Slowly, tauntingly, Sebastian began to flick and play with the two little toys, sometimes twisting first one and then the other, sometimes pulling them both off so he could suckle her, only to reattach them a moment later. She found herself writhing at the blend of pleasure and pain, rolling her hips in short pleading thrusts, desperate for him to mount her, pound into her with that big, curving cock. She could smell her own arousal.

Suddenly he levered off her and moved down her body. She lifted her head, dazed, only to see him settle between her legs, the width of his shoulders forcing her thighs apart. "Now," Sebastian rumbled, "let's make sure you're good and wet."

Zaria caught her breath as he spread her folds with two fingers and bent his head. His first sampling lick brought her arching off the bed. "Ummm," he rumbled. "Creamy." Another lick. She whimpered. "If I didn't know better, I'd say getting your tits tortured made you hot."

If it hadn't, it would have as he went to work, licking and suckling her lips and clit as he used the clamps to tease her hard peaks. The ferocious pleasure-pain soon had her twisting on the edge of a pulsing orgasm.

Until he lifted his head and met her eyes with a savage glare. "You'd better not come, you little witch."

With that, he started dancing his agile tongue over her clit until her entire nervous system thrummed. She yowled, the sound muffled.

"Don't come," he growled again, and twisted the clamps. From behind her gag, she begged him to take her.

"You heard me, Zaria," he rumbled again, giving her clit another lick and the clips another twist. "By God, you'd better not let yourself climax until I say you can." Then he closed his mouth around her hard, aching clit and suckled.

The orgasm rolled up in clenching pulses that built and built and built until she screamed into the gag, unable to hold back her cries of maddened pleasure.

✦ ✦ ✦

THE aftershocks were still rippling through her twitching muscles when she lay dazed and limp in the aftermath.

Sebastian reared over her. Before she knew what he was doing, he snatched her off the bed and dragged her head down over his lap, sending the clamps flying. "I told you not to come!" he growled.

The first impact of his big palm on her naked ass sent her jolting in shock. Her yowl this time was more astonished outrage than pain.

Another slap landed, loud and stinging.

That was when she realized where she was—draped over Sebastian's powerful thighs, bound and naked, getting a hard spanking.

Just like in all her darkest fantasies.

The next slap was even harder, jarring her nether lips against her swollen clit. The last of her instinctive anger died without a whimper, drowned in lust.

He went to work on her ass in earnest, and she found herself bucking and kicking. With every bounce, her nipples rasped over his hairy thighs as her clit ached and throbbed.

She'd thought she couldn't get hotter. She'd been wrong.

+ + +

WATCHING Zaria's pretty cheeks turn a blushing pink under his hand, Sebastian grinned in pure male pleasure. Carefully he changed the aim of his next smack, angling it to reverberate right into her clit.

"Let's get one thing straight," he growled, still paddling her ass, "from now on, you're my Thralline, and I'm the Dom. Got that?"

She groaned something that sounded suspiciously like agreement, her voice throaty and erotic even muffled by the gag.

He gave her another swat. God, he loved the way she

squirmed, unconsciously humping his thigh, obviously burning to be taken. As he burned to take her.

But he intended to get both of them even hotter before it was all over, so he picked up the jar of lubricant he'd dropped on the bed and unscrewed the lid.

She stirred uneasily at the sound and lifted her head as he dipped two fingers into the cool, oily cream. Then he spread her pretty little cheeks, and she jolted with a protesting squeak that made his dick twitch in sadistic anticipation.

She started squirming in earnest as he slid one well-oiled fore-finger into her deliciously snug backside. Between her shocked "Mmmmph!" and the sensation of her tiny anus clamping around his exploring digit, his balls tightened in lust.

"Oh, come on, Zaria," he purred. "I know you've seen Doms use tight little Thralline ass. Especially after a good, hard spanking . . ."

Her next helpless "Mmph!" held a distinct note of surrender.

He allowed himself the wicked pleasure of spinning out his exploration of her anus. She was going to be a delicious fuck when the time came.

Then, reluctantly, he withdrew his finger. "Luckily for you, though, I think you need to be stretched a little first." He grinned evilly. "I'd hate to rip anything with my big, hard cock."

She whimpered. He felt the cock in question get even bigger as he reached for the little buttplug.

Sebastian took his time working it into her snug ass. A series of rings flared out from its bulbous nose, each bigger than the last, specifically designed to torment the victim's anus.

When he'd sunk it in all the way to the first ring, he breathed, "Now, brace yourself sweetheart. This is going to hurt."

Twisting his wrist, he screwed the ring past Zaria's tight muscles. Her moan sounded more like pleasure than pain as it popped inside.

"You do realize, of course," he said, "that I'm a lot bigger than this little plug?"

Then he forced the next ring in.

✦ ✦ ✦

ZARIA whimpered and squeezed her eyes shut at the fiery heat of the plug entering her, centimeter by wicked centimeter.

She'd watched guardsmen sodomize Thrallines before, of course. She'd found the sight darkly erotic, but it had never crossed her mind that anyone would actually do such a thing to her.

She was astonished at how hot it was, being forced to submit to a man this way.

It made her feel how utterly she was at Sebastian's mercy. Even the spanking hadn't made her feel so dominated. If he wanted to give her a brutal assfucking, there was absolutely nothing she could do about it, bound and gagged like this.

She was his.

Zaria moaned, helpless—and desperately, blindly aroused.

She could feel the cream rising between her pussy lips even as Sebastian forced the buttplug all the way home. "There," he told her. "We'll let that stretch you a while. In the meantime, I think I'll stuff that wet little pussy."

He stood, lifting her effortlessly in his arms before tossing her lightly back on the bed. She whimpered as the impact drove the buttplug even deeper into her ass.

Then he leaned over and jerked off her gag. "Got anything to say?" he barked.

She looked up at him, dazed and hot with need. "Fuck me!"

It wasn't a plea. It was a demand.

He grinned, grabbed her under her backside with one hand, and jerked her hips off the mattress. She cried out helplessly as the buttplug moved inside her. With the other hand, he seated his cock between her thighs, found her opening, and drove home.

Zaria convulsed at the sensation of his big cock filling her so completely, raking past the plug in her other channel. "Ten Gods, Sebastian," she gasped in shock, and wrapped her legs around his waist.

"Like having both holes stuffed, Zaria?" Grinning in triumph, he pulled her close and began to fuck her in long, slamming lunges.

The sensation of that big cock cramming its way into her was even hotter and more overwhelming than it had been when she'd taken him. For one thing, she'd always ridden her partners in the female superior position, but now he was thoroughly in control.

And he seemed determined to prove it, looming over her and bracing his weight on muscled forearms as he pumped relentlessly deep. Each stroke jolted the plug, which scraped her rectal tissues deliciously.

He lowered his head, and she felt his beard brush her ear. "Yeah, that's it, take every last centimeter. God, you're tight."

And he was hard. She moaned helplessly as he pumped, driving her closer and closer to another shattering climax with every stroke.

Some prim part of her objected. It was wrong to submit to him. She was a Domina. She was shaming herself and her mother and her House.

And she didn't give a damn.

Opening her eyes, Zaria looked up at him, wanting to see his expression as he came inside her. Yet the look in his eyes wasn't, somehow, quite what she'd expected. The dark pleasure was there, yes, and the hot satisfaction of claiming her. She'd even anticipated his raw male possessiveness.

But what she hadn't expected was the tenderness mixed in with all that savage heat.

Then he threw back his head with a shout. "God, Zaria!"

He slammed to the balls, coming. Filled to bursting with the two shafts he'd driven into her, Zaria screamed in pure, helpless delight and followed him over.

Chapter Nine

ZARIA lay limp and dazed in Sebastian's arms, her body still quivering. His head rested in the curve of her neck as he panted with exertion, and she was surrounded by the sweet-smelling, golden curtain of his hair.

She blinked, finally becoming aware that her arms were aching, bound as they were beneath her. Her abused ass stung even harder.

Sebastian sighed and drew her close, then began pressing soft kisses to the underside of her jaw and up over the line of her chin. Hardly the gesture of a ruthless dominant in pursuit of some inexplicable revenge.

The fog of arousal began to clear, added by the ache in her wrists and backside. She moaned in pleasure as his gentle lips found her mouth and drew her into a sweet, slow kiss.

It seemed he'd been playing some kind of game with her after all. *A wonderful, wonderful game,* Zaria thought, kissing him back, loving the sweetness in the aftermath of all that delicious violence.

Then she sighed. It had also, of course, been completely unacceptable. Not only had he taken her, he'd spanked her and plugged her ass. Not the kind of thing she could permit. "We can never do that again," she said softly.

He went still. "What?"

"I can't . . . you can't . . ." Zaria stopped, suddenly unsure how to put it. "Dominating me like that—it was wrong."

He lifted his head, and his green eyes met hers. She could actually see the afterglow in them cooling into something chilling and assessing. "Are you saying you didn't like it?"

"I think you know better than that." She shifted uncomfortably. "Untie my wrists. They're beginning to ache. And remove this plug!"

"Not yet. Why don't you want me to dom you again when we both enjoyed it?"

Zaria huffed out a breath, suddenly impatient with him. "You're a Thrall, Sebastian. I'm a Domina. It's not natural."

"And yet, if you were the Thralline and I was the Domince, it would be perfectly acceptable."

She frowned at him. "You're being deliberately obtuse."

"No, you are. What we just did was a particularly delicious and arousing game. There wasn't a damn thing unnatural about it, any more than it's unnatural for two children to play starships and pirates."

Zaria lifted a brow. "Neither of us is a child, Sebastian."

"I'm not, but I'm beginning to wonder about you." He pushed off her and rose, towering over her beside the bed. "You do a damn good imitation."

Temper began to spark and snap in her. "You forget yourself, Thrall!"

"No. You do. So it's perverted and wrong for you to enjoy submitting to me? What, then, would you call kidnapping a man and sexually tormenting him to force him into submission?"

For a moment she stared at him in shock, unable to believe he'd dare talk about her mother's treatment of Arnoux Ferrau. "Do you realize I could have you flogged for that?"

A faint, cold smile touched his mouth as he scanned her bound nudity. "Not at the moment."

She rolled off the bed, tugging furiously at her bonds. "Who in the Ten Hells do you think you are?"

He straightened to his considerable height. "Commander Sebastian Cole, executive officer of the interstellar mercenary warship *Starrunner*. And I'm here to rescue Arnoux Ferrau."

The bottom seemed to drop out of her stomach. "You're an Outworlder?" she asked numbly.

Then she pushed the idea away. He couldn't be, because if he was, he'd leave. Zaria squared her shoulders and gave him her best cold look. "No. Stop playing games, Sebastian. This is no time for your jokes."

"I'm not joking." And for once, there was no humor in his eyes at all. "Dominor Xarles Ferrau hired me to get his son away from your mother."

She stared at him for a long, sick moment, trying to grasp the depth of his betrayal. "You're not a Thrall?"

"No. That was only my cover so I could get into the palace."

"You lied to me!"

He shrugged. "A man's life was at stake."

The anger drained away at those words, and Zaria slumped.

He was right, curse him to the Ten Hells. "But why tell me? Why not just . . . do whatever you came here to do?"

His green gaze grew searching. "I wanted to give you the opportunity to help avert the war your mother is courting." He stepped closer, and she looked up at him, feeling the ache grow in her chest. He wasn't hers, and now he never would be. "Help me free Arnoux, Zaria."

"I can't," she said numbly.

"You can. Particularly given that helping him escape might be the one thing that will keep his father from declaring war." Sebastian's sensual mouth drew into a cold line. "Or would you rather watch men and women die for your mother's ego?"

She shook her head in despair. "What you're talking about is treason, Sebastian! She's not just my mother, she's my Dominess!"

Silence spun between them, swirling with tension and suppressed anger. His eyes seemed to freeze into green ice. "Fine." He went to the chest where she kept her armor and dug through it. When he returned to Zaria again, he held a new set of leathers. "Come here."

She took a wary step back. "What? Why?"

Sebastian looked at her, his face utterly without emotion. "If you won't help me voluntarily," he said coolly, "you'll make an excellent hostage."

Stunned and heartsick at his betrayal, Zaria didn't resist as he dressed her in her armor, his movements as impersonal as if she were a doll, even when he pulled the plug from her ass. He did not, however, offer to untie her wrists. She was surprised at how much his distance hurt.

Yet somehow she knew he wouldn't physically injure her.

And despite everything, she was very much concerned

about what the palace guard might do to him. He was one man alone. One man against the three hundred who protected the Dominess.

Those weren't good odds, even for an Outworlder.

As Zaria watched Sebastian dress in the loincloth that was all a palace Thrall wore, images kept flashing through her mind: of sword wounds marring that magnificent chest, of his glorious hair matted in blood, of his green eyes blank in death.

She swallowed bile.

No, Zaria told herself, fighting panic, *He's got some kind of Outworlder weapon hidden somewhere, something that will allow him to free the Domince and escape. They would hardly have sent him in alone otherwise.*

Yet there was nothing on his body that looked like it could hide a weapon. Not even so much as an earring. "Are you . . . are you armed?" she blurted.

He lifted a brow at her and took a sword down from her weapons' rack. "I am now."

"That's not enough, Sebastian. All the guards have swords."

His smile stretched coldly in the frame of his goatee. "I also have you, darling. Let's go." He reached for her.

"You can't parade me through the castle bound like this," Zaria protested. "You'll never even make it to the Dominess's pleasure quarters."

Sebastian hesitated a moment, frowning as he considered the point. Finally he stepped behind her. Cold steel brushed her wrists as he sliced her bonds with one easy pass of his blade. Before the relieved sigh was out of her mouth, however, he rested the sword lightly against her throat. "Bound or not, I suggest you remember you're a hostage."

Zaria swallowed. "Even with me as a prisoner, they're not going to let you take the Domince."

"Oh, I think they will."

"But—"

"But nothing. I've got it all planned, my sweet. First, it's the middle of the night." Looping his free arm around her waist, he drew her tight against his hard, powerful body. "Second, I've got the guard's patrol routes scanned and timed. Right now we have the perfect window of opportunity." He angled the blade up, forcing her to lift her chin. "And finally," he whispered in her ear, his voice silken and suggestive, "I have you." His tone hardened. "Come along, my sweet. I'm sure the Domince is more than ready to go home."

Sebastian lowered the sword and caught her shoulder, pushing her lightly toward the door. Despairing, she went where he directed.

Why did she feel so bereft? He had been with her barely two days. True, she'd been wildly attracted to him, but then, her mother surrounded herself with beautiful males, so it was more than that.

He was intelligent, though this scheme to march through the palace and liberate Arnoux smacked of recklessness. And she enjoyed his irreverent wit, even as it sometimes scandalized her.

But more than that, Zaria had felt a sense of kinship, despite the supposed difference in their respective status. He, too, did not seem to fit the role he'd been assigned: She'd never met a less submissive Thrall in her life. It had made her feel less alone, less . . . wrong to feel this hunger to submit to him.

But he hadn't been a Thrall at all, so she was once again alone in her deviance.

Yet . . . Zaria frowned, remembering what he'd said to her just before he'd revealed himself. *What we just did was a particularly delicious and arousing game. There wasn't a damn thing unnatural about it, any more than it's unnatural for two children to play starships and pirates.*

Could he be right? After all, she felt no particular need to submit in the rest of her life. She commanded Dom and Thrall alike in the course of her duties and thought nothing of it.

But if it was all nothing more than a game, what did that say about the rest of her culture, with its castes of Dom and Thrall, its Dominesses and Dominors?

And how immoral *was* it to kidnap a man in order to sexually torture him into becoming a Thrall?

Suddenly Sebastian stopped, grabbing her shoulder to bring her to a halt. Jolted from her preoccupation, Zaria glanced around at him. "What—?"

"Shhh." He was looking toward the head of the corridor, a hard, intense expression on his face.

Then she heard it—a rapid swish and crack, punctuated with soft male grunts of pain. A sound she knew too well: a cat-o'nine tails being used to beat a man.

And that meant . . . *That bitch.*

Fury roared over Zaria, and she started forward, forgetting all about her status as a hostage. Sebastian dragged her back. "Let me go!" she snapped.

He didn't even glance at her as he frowned. "If that's Ferrau being beaten, my scans say he's in a bad way."

"Of course he's in a bad way," Zaria growled. "My idiot mother let my sadistic bitch of a sister have him! Let me go!"

+ + +

ASTONISHED, Sebastian looked down at Zaria's small, furious face, then reluctantly released his grip on her arm. So much for that submissive streak. She promptly whirled and snatched the sword from his hand. Bemused, he let her take it.

"Come on, we've got to move fast," she snapped, "or he's dead!"

"Lead the way."

She sprinted off down the corridor with him striding at her heels. They rounded the corner to see two stone-faced guards standing before the Dominess's pleasure quarters. Zaria didn't even break step as she headed for the double doors.

The two men automatically drew their blades and moved to block her. Sebastian swore softly as his heart jammed into his throat.

He knew he shouldn't have armed the little lunatic.

Chapter Ten

"OUT of my way!" Zaria snarled, lifting her weapon.

Both guards looked uncomfortable, probably not sure how to handle their sweet little Domina in what appeared to be a homicidal rage.

One of them stuttered, "But . . . but, Domina, the Domina Marcelle left orders she is not to be disturbed."

"I'm sure she did, the sadistic bitch. Stand clear!"

"Domina . . ."

It was time for a little strategic intervention. Putting on his best expression of diffident concern, Sebastian shouldered between them and Zaria. "Now, mistress," he began, "these men are only doing their . . ." Spinning, he slammed his fist into the first guard's jaw. The man went down like a sack of meal, knocked cold by nanotech-enhanced strength.

Before the second could bring his weapon into play, Sebastian grabbed his sword hand and twisted. Something snapped wetly, and the guard howled in astonished agony. The cry cut off as another hard punch put him down on top of his partner.

He turned to see Zaria staring at him with startled respect. "Well," she said finally, "I don't suppose you did need a weapon."

Before he could reply, a male voice screamed beyond the double doors, the sound raw with suffering.

✛ ✛ ✛

ZARIA spun and jerked at the double doors, but they didn't budge. "She's got them bolted," she said, wincing as another savage swish and crack sliced the air.

"Let me worry about that." Sebastian lifted one muscled leg. She opened her mouth to warn him about the door's steel-reinforced core and frame; there was no way he could kick it open.

Then his bare foot hit the portal with a thunderous boom. Wood splintered, steel hinges and bolts shrieked, and the door toppled in with a crash. She heard Marcelle's started yelp.

Reminded of her fury, Zaria ducked around Sebastian and plunged inside to find Marcelle gaping at her, a bloody whip hanging forgotten in one hand.

Arnoux was chained to one of the room's marble pillars. Her stomach twisted at the condition of his back. If anything, he was in even worse shape than the Thrall she'd rescued a couple of days before. They had to get him to the Outworlders or he wouldn't live out the night.

"What are you doing here, Zaria?" Marcelle demanded, lifting the whip threateningly. If she'd noticed her sister was armed, it didn't seem to worry her.

Zaria fell into guard, sword held at a threatening angle. "Give me the key to those shackles, Marcelle."

The Domina gaped at her demand. "I will not!" she spat. "I told Mother I would break Arnoux to the collar, and I won't stop until I have."

"Think, you vicious little fool," Zaria snapped, out of patience with her family's blind indifference to reality. "If you kill him, his father will raze this palace to the ground and murder every last one of us!"

Marcelle's eyes flickered, but she quickly recovered enough to sneer. "When I've broken him to the collar, he'll say he enjoyed it."

"No!" Arnoux's voice was weak with pain and blood loss, but there was hate in the look he cast them over one bloody shoulder. "I will never yield to you, bitch. Never. Never. *Never!*" The last word was a hoarse bellow.

"All right, I've had enough of this." Sebastian stalked over to the other man, wrapped a big hand in one of the shackles, and jerked. Its chain snapped with a musical clink. Arnoux's eyes widened.

"What?" The word was a shriek as Marcelle whirled toward the two men. "You dare!" She lifted the cat to strike.

Zaria lunged to grab the lash, jerking the whip from her sister's hand. "You will *not* touch him!"

Marcelle spun, her face twisted with the wild rage Zaria had always found so terrifying. "Oh, you're going to pay for that!"

"I don't think so." She brought up her sword, the point inches from her sister's chest.

That got the little bitch's attention. "What do you think you're doing?" The Domina backpedaled, her gaze flicking down to the menacing blade.

Before Zaria could reply, Marcelle whirled and lunged, sweeping up her own scabbarded sword, left lying in a chair. Jerking the weapon out of the scabbard, she threw the sheath aside and fell into guard. "I repeat," she hissed, "you're going to pay."

A prick of fear pierced Zaria's righteous rage. Her sister was taller and heavier than she was, with a longer reach and a stronger build.

Her gaze flicked to Sebastian. He'd freed Arnoux of his chains, and now he supported the smaller man with an arm around his chest to spare his bloody back. He looked from Zaria to Marcelle, and his mouth tightened as he started to lower the Domince to the floor. He intended to intervene.

"No!" Zaria ordered fiercely. "Get the Domince out of here!"

Then she lunged for Marcelle.

✦ ✦ ✦

BEFORE Sebastian could step in to put Bitch Sister down for the count, a male voice bellowed from down the hall. "Ten Hells, what's this? Guards! The Domina has been attacked!" Running footsteps sounded, pounding in their direction.

"Shit!" The men he'd knocked cold had been discovered. Urgently he looked at Ferrau's haggard face as he let the man's feet take his weight. "Can you stand?"

The man's dazed, swollen eyes met his. "I can . . . run to . . . get out of here!"

Sebastian doubted it. Judging by the Domince's pallor, he wasn't even sure how much longer Ferrau could remain on his feet.

But before he could say anything more, two guards plunged through the door. Releasing Ferrau, Sebastian whirled to intercept them. In one nanotech-enhanced move, he slammed his fist into the first's jaw and grabbed the sword out of his hand as he toppled.

Metal flashed toward his head. He brought his own blade up and around barely in time to block the vicious sword stroke. Batting his opponent's weapon aside with sheer muscle, he drove an elbow into the guard's head.

Unfortunately, three more guards thundered in, with more on the way as shouts of warning went up.

It was a damned good thing the doorway formed a natural bottleneck. Sebastian went to work defending it with a combination of nanotech-enhanced sword work and gutter fighting. Blades thrust at him, only to be knocked away as he ran their owners through. But for every guard he put down, another appeared.

And none of this was getting the Domince out of the palace.

At the same time he was intensely aware of Zaria's furious battle with her sister. His sensors told him that though she was fighting hard, she was tiring as Marcelle's greater strength and longer reach began to tell. It was past time to call for reinforcements.

If only they'd arrive in time . . .

+ + +

"FOOL!" Marcelle hissed as they circled one another, looking for an opening. "You've finally given me the excuse I've needed to kill you! Not even Mother will question it, when she sees you fell in an act of treason!"

"The treason," Zaria gasped, "is plunging . . . our people into war!"

"A war we'll win!" Marcelle brought her sword down in a two-handed blow intended to cleave her head in two.

Desperately Zaria brought up her weapon. She felt the jarring impact all the way to her shoulders, and her sweating hands slipped on the sword hilt. Somehow she held on to it and forced the blade away.

Unfortunately, she knew too well her strength was failing. Sooner or later Marcelle would overpower her and take her down. And then the bitch would cut her to pieces like the sadist she was.

Over her sister's shoulder, Zaria spotted a flash of motion: Sebastian, his big body dripping with sweat and blood, golden hair flying as he fought savagely to keep the guards from the room. Another glance found Arnoux, lying in a heap on the floor. His eyes met hers before they slid closed. Silently she prayed to all Ten Gods to spare him.

"Surrender, Zaria. I'll make it quick!" Marcelle panted. Her mouth curled into an ugly smirk. "Besides, you know you want to. You've always had a taste for submission!"

Staring into that smug gaze, Zaria realized her sister had no doubt at all she'd win. She really did think it was Zaria's nature to surrender.

At that realization, welcome fury surged into her blood, hot and strengthening. "Not to you, bitch!" She brought her sword up and around in a savage swing.

Her sister blocked it, but she felt the satisfying ring of the blow all the way to her bones. For an instant she saw surprise in Marcelle's eyes.

And then Zaria went after her with everything she had. She pounded her sword against Marcelle's in a frenzy of rage as years of remembered torment boiled up from her soul. All the times her sister had belittled, shamed, insulted, and beaten her. The times her mother had turned a blind eye. The day the Dominess and Marcelle had driven her brother Brys away.

Most of all, she remembered all the good men Marcelle had flogged half to death out of her lust for the suffering of others.

Dimly she realized her sister was in full retreat, barely parrying the blows Zaria rained on her in her fury.

Then Marcelle took one more step—and her foot slipped in a pool of blood on the floor where she'd beaten Ferrau so mercilessly. With a cry of shocked fear, she fell to one knee.

Zaria pounced, sweeping her sword down and around to hook her sister's blade with her own. She jerked upward. The weapon flew from Marcelle's hand and hit the opposite wall with a clatter that rang loud even over the howls of the men fighting in the doorway.

A savage grin stretched Zaria's mouth as she brought her blade around again to hover over her sister's bare head. "Now . . ." she breathed as hot victory stormed through her blood.

Marcelle stared up at her with terror in her eyes. "No! Sister, you can't!"

"Oh, don't you dare beg, when we both know you'd have killed me without a second thought!" She set her feet apart in preparation for the blow.

"Zaria, don't! Mercy!" Marcelle threw her hands up, cringing back. "I beg quarter!"

For one searing moment their eyes met. Temptation and blood lust sang in Zaria's heart. It would be so easy. . . .

Zaria reversed her swing to slam the hilt into her sister's head with both hands. Marcelle slumped into unconsciousness.

Panting as sweat streamed down face, Zaria eyed her slumped form with satisfaction. "On second thought I've decided I want you to live. A long, long time." She wiped the sweat from her face and spat at her sister's feet. "And every day that goes by, I hope you remember what it was like to beg me for your life."

Then she turned to stride toward the doorway. "Enough! Stand down!"

Startled faces turned toward her. The fighting paused. Taking advantage of the opening, Zaria shouldered in front of Sebastian, raising her blade with a roar. "I gave you an order! Stand down!"

Searle, at the head of the pack, lowered his blade. Blood dripped from a cut down one cheek. "It's the Domina!"

A confused mutter rose as the guards quickly dropped their weapons and stepped back, frowning at the cuts that scored her body in a half-dozen places. "Domina, are you hurt?" Searle asked, concerned.

"I'm fine." They had to move fast before the Dominess arrived to countermand her orders. Over her shoulder Zaria snapped, "Sebastian, get Ferrau."

He nodded, went to the Domince, and hauled him across his shoulder. Ferrau's head hung limp.

"Ten Gods," Zaria muttered, wincing at the sight of his savaged back, "let him live!"

Chapter Eleven

Behind her, she heard one of the guardsmen say, "Look! She actually beat Marcelle!"

"Good," another guard replied, his tone grimly pleased.

Zaria smiled at the lack of respect for her sister as she turned to them and gave them a bold gesture of dismissal. "Back to your quarters."

"But, Domina," Searle protested, "you can't just take Domince Arnoux! Her Dominance—"

"Will appreciate our taking him for treatment before he dies of his injuries," Zaria said firmly. She narrowed her eyes. "Are you going to stand in my way?"

Searle looked at her a long moment. "No, Domina." He stepped back, clearing the way for her. She strode out into the corridor, Sebastian at her heels.

"Is Arnoux all right?" Zaria asked him softly.

Sebastian looked grim. "No, but I think he'll make it if we can get him some decent medical attention."

"Then that's what we'll do." She turned back toward her men. "Searle, prepare a wagon—"

"That won't be necessary," Sebastian interrupted. "My crewmates are on the way. They'll transport him."

Zaria lifted her brows. "How did you manage to alert them?"

He shrugged. "I have my ways."

"Zaria!"

Oh, Ten Hells.

The Dominess stood in the corridor, staring in shock at the guardsmen as they started gathering up their injured comrades. Ila's gaze flicked to Sebastian and the limp, bloody body slung across his shoulder. "What in the name of the Ten Gods is going on here?" she demanded.

"At the moment I'm rescuing your prisoner," Zaria told her coolly.

"What?" Ila gaped. "That's Arnoux?" Fear widened her eyes as it dawned on her what the Domince's condition might mean. Then she drew herself to her full height. "Return him to my quarters."

Weary anger rose in Zaria again. "Mother, look at him!" She gestured at Arnoux's flayed back. "Marcelle cut him to ribbons. What were you thinking, giving him to her?"

Ila's face went slightly green as she looked—really looked—at her captive. "Marcelle did that?"

"Yes, and it's not the first time." Zaria shook her head. "You've got to face the truth, Mother. The Dominor was right. Something's twisted inside Marcelle. If you're half the Dominess you should be, you'll name my brother as your new heir. Brys would make a far better ruler than any of us." *Including you.* But she didn't say that last. Instead, she turned and followed Sebastian as he strode off with his burden.

"Brys?" her mother called. "But what about you?"

"I have no interest in the throne," Zaria said, without looking around. "I'm going to save you from this war, and then I'm done with you."

"Permanently?" Ila's voice went shrill in alarm. "But . . ."

"Dominess," someone called. "Domina Marcelle has been hurt!"

"What? Marcelle!"

Zaria didn't even turn as her mother hurried off to tend her sister.

+ + +

BEFORE they rounded another corner, they were met by a grim-faced contingent from the *Starrunner* in full boarding armor, Nathan in the lead. Zaria stumbled to a shocked halt.

"It's all right," Sebastian told her as he moved to meet his crewmates. *"Where's the trauma team?"*

"Here!" The medical unit was already pushing its way through the crowd, towing a float stretcher behind them. Sebastian loaded Ferrau into the tube and watched as it closed around him, lights flashing as it began treatment.

Nathan walked over to join him. Sebastian saluted him with a grin, and the captain returned it crisply.

"Sorry it took us so long," Nathan said, shaking his head. "Ran into a contingent of mounted troops coming back from some kind of patrol. Took longer to dispatch them than I expected." He looked Sebastian over, then eyed Zaria as she hovered behind him. "In any case, you seem to have done pretty well. You managed to fight off that entire horde practically naked?"

"I had help." Sebastian turned and took Zaria's hand. She looked up at him, her gaze searching and uncertain. "This is Domina Zaria Orva. She saved a lot of lives today."

The smile that lit her face made something warm and sweet expand in Sebastian's chest.

✝ ✝ ✝

ZARIA insisted on accompanying the medical team to the clinic to make sure Arnoux pulled through his injuries.

In the facility's waiting area, she and Sebastian sat together on one of the strange, Outworld couches that molded itself under them in a particularly disconcerting way. Zaria tried to ignore it as she clung to his hand. He seemed the only stable thing in her world.

"What are you going to do now?" Sebastian asked at last. "And what exactly did you mean when you told your mother you were done with her?"

Zaria shrugged, feeling more exhausted than she'd ever been in her life. It wasn't fair. She'd finally beaten her sister. So why did she feel so . . . defeated? "I have no idea what I'm going to do," she admitted finally. "I just know I'm not going back to the palace."

He hesitated. "You might want to give it time. Reconsider. Being Dominess sounds like a pretty good job."

"Yes, but unfortunately it comes with the necessity of dealing with my family. And frankly, I've got no more interest in that." She shrugged. "Besides, I don't really have the temperament. My brother will make a far better Dominor."

"I don't think I've met him," Sebastian said.

"You didn't. Brys is an army captain, and he's rarely home." She grimaced. "I suspect he had some kind of run-in with Marcelle, but I don't know the details. I think when it came right down to it, though, Mother took Marcelle's side. And that was it as far as he was concerned."

Sebastian frowned. "Given that, do you really think your mother will disinherit Marcelle and give the throne to him?"

"Oddly enough, yes." She lifted a hand to rub at the knot of muscle between her shoulders. "The Dominess may be blind when it comes to Marcelle, but she's keenly aware of her duty to the dominality. When she saw what Marcelle had done to Arnoux, I think she finally realized just how . . . broken she is." Zaria shook her head. "Marcelle is just not suited to be Dominess. That temper of hers would drive her to plunge the dominality into war until someone finally invaded and killed her."

"I suspect you're right." Sebastian nodded slowly. Then he gave her one of his wonderfully wicked smiles. "By the way, I saw some of your fight. I was impressed. Marcelle's a hell of a lot bigger than you, but you beat her anyway. That took both guts and skill."

Zaria laughed. "Yes, well, she managed to make me mad, and the whole thing got surprisingly easy. Evidently she's not the only one in the family with a temper."

He snorted. "Your temper's not that bad."

"Oh, yes, it is."

He lifted a blond brow. "She's alive, isn't she?"

She sighed. "Good point." Silence fell between them. He held his arm out for her, and she settled into the curve of it to rest her head against his chest. A lock of his long hair lay under her cheek. It felt like raw silk.

Zaria listened to his heartbeat for a while before she said, "She threw the same thing in my face she always did. About my being a deviant. She said she knew I wanted to surrender because I have a taste for submission." She laughed shortly. "That was when I went for her throat."

Sebastian chuckled warmly. "Good for you."

"What you said about my submitting to you being a game, not who I really am . . ." She looked up at him. "You were right. It really *doesn't* make me weak."

"Yeah, you definitely proved that in spades with the way you dealt with Mommy and the Bitch."

Zaria nodded thoughtfully. "On the other hand, Marcelle is weak. When she realized I had the advantage, she caved right in. I never knew that before."

Sebastian shrugged. "But it's not all that surprising, Zaria. People like Marcelle dominate others because secretly, they *know* they're weak. Only by breaking someone else can they convince themselves they're strong." He slanted her a wicked little smile. "Now, people like me, on the other hand"—he reached over and hauled her into his lap as she shrieked out a giggle of surprise— "are just kinky as hell."

She lost the laughter when he claimed her mouth in a dark, devouring kiss. When he finally lifted his head again, he said, "Come to the *Starrunner* with me."

Zaria blinked at him in surprise. "You mean—visit your ship?"

"No." He met her eyes in a long, steady gaze. "I mean move in with me."

She gaped at him in shock for a long moment before she was able to manage a reply. "But you just met me, Sebastian! You don't know anything about me."

"I know I've never met another woman like you," he said, his voice low and fierce. "And I know I don't want to ever let you go."

Zaria didn't even have to think twice as a fierce, hot joy swept over her. "Yes," she breathed. "Yes, I'll go with you!"

And then he was kissing her again. She had no idea what she'd just agreed to, or what it meant, or where they were going with their relationship.

As long as they were going together, nothing else mattered.

The Dominor Xarles Ferrau of Rabican arrived twenty minutes later. By the time Sebastian and Zaria had finished relating their rescue of Arnoux, Ferrau was feeling so generous he offered to give Zaria anything she wanted as a reward for helping save his son.

Zaria promptly extracted a promise he wouldn't go to war against Orva. He reluctantly gave his word, which was a good thing, because by then Outworlder medicine had seen to the regeneration of Arnoux's back, and the young man was conscious.

Once the Domince finished relating his experiences at Ila's hands, Ferrau was ready to go to war again.

With a sigh of resignation Zaria went back to work.

✦ ✦ ✦

WHILE his lover conducted her passionate argument with the Dominor, Sebastian kept a watchful eye on the proceedings, half afraid Xarles would turn on her as the nearest representative of her family. To his relief, though, he quickly realized he'd underestimated her charm.

He was watching her work the Dominor and trying to keep the grin off his face when he heard a familiar voice over his com. *"Sweet gods, look at him. I told you he's smitten."*

Sebastian looked up just as Nathan and Trin strolled into the room. He tried out a mock-offended glare on his captain, though he strongly suspected he hadn't pulled it off. *"Smitten? Me?"*

"You," Trinity agreed. *"I could almost hear the strains of an angelic chorus as you gazed at her."*

Nathan snorted. *"The word 'angelic' has no business being applied to Sebastian Cole."* The Captain tilted his head and studied him thoughtfully. *"He does look a little sappy though."*

"Sappy?" Subastian glowered. *"I've never looked sappy in my life."* He paused and cleared his throat. *"I would, however, like to make a formal request."*

"Yeah?" Nathan folded his brawny arms with a this-should-be-good lift of his eyebrows. *"What kind of formal request?"*

"Zaria's told me she's leaving the palace permanently. I'd like your permission to bring her aboard the Starrunner. *I'll pay for her passage, of course."*

Trin and Nathan exchanged a look. *"Told you,"* she said.

The captain nodded. *"Smitten."* He looked at Sebastian. "She's welcome."

Grinning, Sebastian returned his attention to the conversation between Zaria and Ferrau. "Declaring war would actually be a less effective way to deal with my mother than a trade embargo," she told the Dominor. "Ila would be stubbornly brave in the face of a physical threat, but hit her in her purse, and she'll yield to your demands."

Ferrau nodded thoughtfully. "And you believe she'll name this brother of yours as her heir?"

Zaria shrugged. "She's halfway there now. The look on her face when she saw Arnoux's back . . . she was genuinely appalled. She's been lying to herself for a long time about how bad Marcelle is, but she won't be able to ignore what she saw. Anyone whose temper would drive her to such viciousness has no business being Dominess, and my mother knows it."

"But you believe I will be able to deal with your brother?"

She nodded. "Brys has always had a profound sense of justice. When he learns what . . ."

"Damn," Sebastian commed, *"she's good. Isn't she good?"* He looked at his captain, a proud grin stretching over his face.

Nathan gave his wife a knowing smile. *"I give it a month."*

Which was the same thing Sebastian himself had said about Nathan and Trin when the captain had asked her to become his lover last year. Sebastian had predicted his friend would propose within the month, and he'd been right.

Now Sebastian looked at the woman he himself was falling for. Her beautiful face glowed with passion as she argued her case to the Dominor. He felt his smile fade. "That depends on Zaria, doesn't it?"

Chapter Twelve

ZARIA started having second thoughts about moving in with Sebastian as she boarded the *Starrunner* with him and the combat contingent who'd mobilized to rescue them.

Though Captain Nathan August and his wife, Trinity, seemed to go out of their way to welcome her, the ship struck her as alien and intimidating with its warren of corridors and bewildering array of Outworlder technology. After all the rich fabrics and gleaming gold of her mother's palace, the *Starrunner* seemed a chill, too-professional place. Its curving bulkheads looked alien and artificial, despite the bright colored walls Sebastian said signified the different decks. Men and women hurried around, talking highly technical jargon at each other. Most disturbingly, computers sometimes joined in on the conversation, sounding far more human than machines had any business being.

By the time Sebastian ushered her into his quarters, she was having serious doubts. The cabin's walls curved, like those of every other room on the ship. Three-dimensional images hung on the bulkhead or stood displayed on furniture, depicting alien worlds she'd never even heard of.

Sinking down on the bed that looked wide enough for Sebastian and at least three partners, she gazed around in bewilderment. A gleaming weapon she vaguely recognized as some sort of gun hung on one wall, while one entire corner of the room was occupied by a massive console showing all kinds of bewildering displays.

And the strangest part of it all was Sebastian, who had covered his magnificent body with some kind of matte-black uniform that looked nothing like her own leathers. Zaria felt primitive and ignorant next to his sleek blond beauty. "I don't think this is going to work," she managed at last.

He looked up from the console as his clever fingers stroked over the controls. A frown tightened his mouth. "What do you mean?"

"This. Me. This ship." She gestured at the console. "I don't even know what that is."

A sliding panel opened in its top, and two glasses lifted into view. "It's a drink dispenser, among other things." He picked the goblets up and carried them over to her, handing her one. "I'll show you how to use it. And once we get you a com implant, you'll find it much easier to make sense of what's going on."

"A what?" Zaria eyed the glass cautiously, evaluating its dark, foaming contents.

"A communications implant. It's what we use to speak to each other and the equipment, particularly when we don't care to be overheard."

"Where do they . . . put this implant?" She sipped cautiously. The cool, yeasty liquid foamed on her tongue, and she nodded in approval. "This is good. What is it?"

"A Star Mead. And the implant goes in your jaw, right under one ear. It'll build nanotech neural connections with your brain's cerebral cortex, and . . ."

Zaria shook her head. "And that's what I mean. I didn't understand any of that at all."

He looked down at her, his green eyes intense. For a moment she saw desperation in their depths.

Then he plucked the glass out of her hand and put it down on the bedside table with his. Sinking down on the bed beside her, he slid open a drawer and reached into it. "So you don't understand the technology," he said, turning back toward her. "How about this?"

He held a length of gold cable in his hand. Before she knew what hit her, he'd jerked her facedown across his lap, grabbed her left wrist, and wrapped the cable around it.

"What are you—stop that!" she yelped, squirming as he bound the other wrist, too. "Sebastian!"

"You may not understand the technology"—he stood and pulled her effortlessly to her feet, then hooked one big hand in her leathers. A hard, strong tug, and the laces snapped, leaving her breasts bare. He gave her a wicked smile—"but I'll bet you know exactly what this means."

✦ ✦ ✦

"SEBASTIAN, this is not going to solve the problem," Zaria protested, but her voice sounded breathless, and Sebastian's sensors told him she was alrady beginning to respond to him.

"Maybe not, but it'll make me feel a hell of a lot better." He bent down and attacked her leather groin band, ripping the tough hide apart in a deliberate display of strength that made her dark eyes widen. Throwing the shreds aside, he whirled her around and knelt to finish off her leggings.

Finally he had her completely bare, from elegant shoulders to dainty feet—and especially that beautiful, peach-shaped ass. He stroked his fingers over the rise of one cheek and found the skin as irresistibly smooth as he remembered.

"Sebastian . . ." She moaned. Oh, yeah. She was as aroused as he was.

Remembering the tight, clamping grip of her virgin anus, he felt his cock twitch in lust. God, he was going to enjoy this.

But he had to make sure she enjoyed it even more—enough to forget her entirely reasonable doubts and stay with him.

Testing, he slid a forefinger down the delicate cleft of her backside and grinned as she squirmed. "You know, I think I want to bend you over this time." Discovering the tiny rosette pucker of her backside, he slid his finger deep. Her little muscles clamped hard around him, and she yelped in protest mixed with arousal. "As I recall, my cock has an appointment with this tight little ass." Unable to resist, he lowered his head and gave one perfect cheek a nip.

She jumped. "Sebastian!"

He grinned, continuing his exploration of her tight channel. "Yes, Thralline?" With the other hand, he delved between her soft nether lips to find her deliciously wet.

On, yeah, it was working. But how could he make her even hotter?

Thoughtfully he stroked the index fingers of both hands in and out of each snug opening, enjoying the way she tightened around him and groaned in pleasure.

His thoughts flashed to Zaria's barracks inspection, when they'd seen the two guardsmen with the girl tied to the chair. One of them had fucked her mouth while the other took her from behind. Zaria had found the sight wildly arousing. But had it been the idea of being taken by two men at once that so turned her on? He pondered the question, circling his thumb over her clit as he watched her writhe, the strong muscles of her backside working as he fingerfucked her.

Come to think of it, she probably *had* been taken by two Thralls at once—an image he refused to consider in any more detail because it pissed him off. But . . .

Suddenly an idea occurred to him, and he grinned wickedly. "You know, all of the sudden I'm in the mood for a blow job. Ever sucked cock, Zaria?"

Even without the slight shake of her head, he would have known the answer just from the way her slick inner muscles tightened.

It was all Sebastian could do not to moan to himself at the idea of being the first to slide his dick between Zaria's lush lips. Followed by a slow conquest of her virgin ass. "Well, now," he purred. "That sounds like the perfect appetizer."

He could, of course, simply make her kneel, but he instantly decided that wasn't good enough. He wanted her to feel completely helpless, utterly at his mercy.

Then he thought of the Thralline tied to the chair.

Perfect.

✦ ✦ ✦

ZARIA yelped in surprise as he swooped down on her and snatched her into his arms. Before she knew what he was up to, he'd deposited her a chair so that she knelt on its seat, facing its back. "What are you doing?" she squeaked.

"Getting my little Thralline in position to entertain my cock," he told her, his goatee tilting up with his lecherous grin.

Actually whistling, he untied her wrists, then lashed one of them to the arm of the chair. She twisted around to watch anxiously as he retrieved several more cables from his toy drawer, along with what she strongly suspected was a jar of lubricant.

Then he went back to work on her bonds, tying her ankles and free wrist to the arms of the chair. Finally he propped her chin on its padded back so her mouth was precisely at the height of his bobbing erection. By the time he was done, Zaria was all but panting in arousal as she imagined what it would be like to feel Sebastian's long, curving cock sliding into her mouth.

But if she thought he'd simply plunge between her lips, she'd underestimated him—and forgotten his feral fascination with her backside.

Once he had her bound in a helpless crouch, he picked up the jar he'd left on the desk and moved around behind her. The lid rattled as he unscrewed it. Zaria licked her dry lips nervously.

"I figure," he said in an arousing rasp, "that by the time I finish with your mouth, I'm going to be in the mood for a little virgin ass. So to save time, I think I'll get you all greased up and ready for cock."

Zaria stiffened at the touch of a fingertip on her sensitive asshole. He increased the pressure slowly, forcing the well-greased digit deep in her channel. She quivered. "Sebastian . . ."

"Yeah?" He withdrew from her backside and entered again,

this time with two fingers, stroking slow and deep. At the same time he used his thumb to tease her clit, sending hot little jolts of pleasure up her spine to compete with the sensation of his anal probing.

Zaria swallowed, feeling the delicate tissues stretch, the sensation both erotic and delicately painful. "Your cock is so big . . ."

He laughed, the sound deep and male and dark with anticipation. "And getting bigger." He twisted his wrist, deliberately goring her tight opening as he raked his thumb over her clit again.

She shivered. "It's going to hurt."

"Oh, yeah. Especially when I start doing you deep and hard." He leaned over her to whisper in her ear. "But maybe if you do a really good job sucking me off, I'll be in the mood for a little mercy."

Oh, she doubted it. She really did.

Finally he stepped around in front of her. As she watched breathlessly, he opened the fasteners of his dark blue uniform, revealing the magnificent body she loved.

"Ten Gods, you're beautiful," she managed as he stripped before her hungry eyes. Here, surrounded by this cold, technological world of his, he looked even more barbaric and primal—and intensely male.

Sebastian laughed. "Not as beautiful as you." Threading one big hand in her hair, he tugged her head up gently, until she was face-to-head with his massive erection. "I particularly admire that luscious mouth. Open wide, Zaria." His voice dropped to a sensual rumble. "Your master wants in."

Shivering in delicious arousal, she obeyed.

But he didn't thrust between her lips as she expected. "Lick it. Stick out that tongue and taste me."

Swallowing, she gave the flushed head a slow pass of her tongue. The texture was like nubby satin, and it tasted salty. Deciding she liked the sensation, she licked him again, then again, until he groaned and thrust into her mouth. Instantly she closed her lips around the thick shaft and began to suck.

"Nice," he purred. "Now swirl your tongue around it and suck harder."

Quivering, Zaria did as he demanded. He began rolling his hips slowly, forcing his cock in and out over her laboring tongue.

She was acutely aware of her own helplessness, bound to the chair, cable lashed tight around her wrists and knees. In this position Sebastian could punish or fuck her at his whim. Her excitement rose as she sucked harder, servicing him with his mouth as eagerly as any Thralline she'd ever seen.

For a moment she felt a hint of shame at her own arousal. Then she forced the embarrassment away. Whether she chose to submit to him here and now or not, she'd proven herself worthy of her name. She'd fought Marcelle and won.

She earned whatever pleasure she took, just as Sebastian had.

"More," he growled, playing the dominant to the hilt as he stroked, feeding his massive cock even deeper.

With a moan, she angled her head and took him, swallowing him down right to the balls. Wanting it all.

The feel of Zaria's hot, eager mouth sucking his cock with single-minded attention sent heat spinning into Sebastian's balls. The need to spill himself inside her pounded in his blood. And his sensors told him she was just as aroused as he was.

But blowing his come down her throat wasn't good enough. He had to claim her fast and deep and hard. First her cunt, then that deliciously tight ass. Ream her until she knew she could never belong to anyone but him. Could never belong anywhere but with him.

So she'd never leave him.

"Enough!" He dragged himself free of her talented lips with a growl of mingled frustration and pleasure.

"Noo," Zaria sighed, lifting her gaze to his. Her eyes were dazed with arousal, her mouth pouting. "Please, Sebastian, take me!"

"Oh, I will!" He grabbed the back of the chair. "In every single orifice." Spinning it around so her lifted ass faced him, Sebastian slid a knee into the seat of the chair between her wide-spread legs. Aiming his aching erection for her slick cunt, he drove it deep in one hard thrust.

Zaria's gasp of pleasure, combined with the mind-detonating sensation of entering her, almost ripped him to orgasm on the spot. Somehow he managed to hold on to his self-control as he worked himself deeper.

"Ten Gods, Sebastian," she groaned. "You feel so good!"

"Yeah," he panted, and pulled out, sliding slickly through her deliciously tight core. "So do you. Hot and slick and submissive . . . Ah! . . . when it suits you." She yowled in pleasure as he slammed himself all the way to the balls. "Ready for this. Perfect for this. Perfect for me!"

"Oooh, gods! Sebastian!"

So he fucked her like that, driving her closer to climax with every long, demanding thrust. And kept right on fucking her, though he had to order his computer implant to keep him from blowing his load every time he slid deep. He had no intention of coming until he'd claimed her. Completely.

"I'm coming!" she gasped breathlessly.

"No, not yet." Gritting his teeth, he jerked his shaft out of her deliciously creamy grip, ignoring her wail of protest.

"Don't stop!"

"Sorry, darlin', but you don't get to come yet. Not until you've had your ass stuffed."

She jerked in instinctive protest, but he was already spreading her delicious, peach-shaped butt to reveal her last virgin orifice. He studied the tight little opening, imagining how it would feel to claim her so completely. Beyond any possibility of denial.

He licked his lips. "Here it comes, Zaria." Taking his dick in one hand, Sebastian pressed the big head against her anus. For a moment he allowed himself to savor the contrast between his own aching width and her tiny, well-greased pucker.

She whimpered in instinctive anxiety.

God, this was going to be so good.

Then he leaned into her, pressing his cock against her anus until it began slowly, reluctantly to yield. She was just as impossibly tight as he'd expected, and he grinned in sheer, nasty pleasure as he forced his way up her ass a centimeter at a time.

"Mmm," Sebastian purred in her ear. "You're tiiiight."

Zaria gasped helplessly as his broad rod slid another blazing fraction deeper. For all her wicked fantasies, she'd never imagined anything like this—being bound and helpless over the back of a chair while her former Thrall skewered her backside. Her rectum burned in protest as it stretched impossibly wide around Sebastian's shaft. "It hurts!" she gasped.

"Oh, I know." He leaned into her, forcing her to take more and still more of the endless rod. "And you love it."

She groaned. He was right. She did. She loved being wrapped in cable and spread wide while he impaled her ass. She'd been taken by the ruthless dominant of her dreams, a man intent on using her body without mercy, on wringing savage pleasure from her with every brutal thrust.

"There," he murmured in her ear at last. "All the way in, right to the balls in my pretty Thralline's tight little butt." He leaned closer to her ear. "Ready to be fucked?"

"I don't think . . ." she gasped, "you care if I am or not."

Sebastian laughed. "Well, I *am* the Dom," he said, and began pulling out.

The retreat of that massive cock brought a wicked pleasure that made her whimper in surprise. At that delighted sound, he began fucking her more quickly.

In. And out. In. And out. Pain and ecstasy surged through her in glittering waves that rolled her inexorably toward climax. Zaria writhed, yanking mindlessly at the cable that bound her as Sebastian rode deep and hard in her butt.

"Oh, yeah," he growled. "Come while I screw your tight little ass, Zaria. I want to feel you milk my dick."

His next merciless inward thrust shot her straight into a shuddering climax. "Sebastiiiaaan!!!" she screamed.

✣ ✣ ✣

ZARIA was coming, coming even as he reamed her. Groaning with pleasure as her inner muscles clamped down on him, Sebastian grabbed her hips in both shaking hands. Pumping savagely as she writhed on his impaling cock, he gasped, "Just so"—thrust— "you know"—thrust—"I'm not letting"—THRUST!—"you go!"

"Sebassstiiaaaaaan!" she screamed again, her inner muscles clamping down on him even tighter as her climax strengthened under the lash of his driving dick. Just as he'd known it would, that sweet, inner milking kicked Sebastian over into his own fiery orgasm. His bellow of raw pleasure blended with her shriek of surrender.

✦✦✦

IT was much later before he found the strength to untie her and carry her to bed. Curling around her, he wrapped her in his arms, surrounded her in his warmth.

Zaria, still quivering from the blinding force of their pleasure, was about to drift off to sleep when he spoke. "Marry me."

The words were a rough command, but the faint tremor of need in his voice gave him away.

Zaria, curled in his arms, lifted her head to meet his eyes. "I have no desire to do anything else."

"Good," he said. "I'd never have lasted another month anyway."

As he dragged her down into a hot, soul-searing kiss, it occurred to her she didn't know what he was talking about.

Then again, she knew there'd be a great deal else she'd have to learn about this new world of his. Yet suddenly, it no longer seemed quite so intimidating.

With Sebastian by her side, she could handle anything.

Claiming Cassidy

✦

Chapter One

A klaxon was screaming, a buzzing howl of warning that made the hair rise on the back of Cassidy Vika's neck. The cockpit was hazed with smoke, and every breath stank of ozone. Sweat rolled, stinging, into Cassidy's eyes, but she couldn't wipe it away with her faceplate closed. And she had no intention of opening it with God knew what burning in the cockpit.

Besides, such distractions were minor. She couldn't afford to divert her attention from the Dharani fighter, or she was dead.

He'd zeroed in on her the moment she took off from the *Starrunner*, his fighter a slim silver stiletto darting against the stars, lit up with the hot blue glow of his jump generators. She'd fired off a shot that almost clipped one of his engines, but he'd juked and the blast went wild.

Then the dogfight was on. Other fighters streamed from the two warships, engaging in dozens of savage battles. Though she saw some of her comrades exploding in fireballs while others blew up their enemies, Cassidy kept her attention focused on the Dharani she fought. Only an idiot would have done anything else. The Tribesmen had a reputation as the deadliest killers in human space.

Cassidy gathered they'd spent a little too long trapped on the wrong side of the Tormod Front, cut off from the rest of humankind. Now that they'd been reunited with humanity, they were intent on building their collective wealth by any means necessary. Including hiring out to the Kalistans in their campaign to conquer New Galveston.

This particular Dharani was certainly a determined bastard. He and Cassidy had chased each other from the *Starrunner* to the Dharani Tribeship and back, looping around New Galveston twice. Fighting every millimeter of the way. Yet no matter how they'd maneuvered, neither had managed to get the other in his sights long enough to get off a good shot.

At least until the Dharani grazed one of her nacelles with a beamer blast, sending all that menacing smoke boiling through her cockpit.

Cassidy had zoomed off then, trying to get room enough to turn the tables, but he'd stuck to her butt like a burrworm. He smelled blood, and if she didn't do something, he was going to get it.

Cassidy glared at the three-dimensional cockpit readouts floating in front of her face. There was far too much red in the systems pane. She needed to either ditch or kill the Dharani before the engines went critical on her.

Her attention was caught by another readout pane, this one showing three globes floating off to starboard—New Galveston's sister planet, Dallas, and its two moons. The former was habitable; there were even a few colony towns there.

An idea made her eyes narrow. With any luck . . .

Cassidy punched it. Gs slammed her back in her seat, pressing hard on her chest as the fighter screamed toward the planet. Dallas swelled in her viewscreen, blue and green, swirling with cotton-white clouds as it grew larger.

The ship's computer suddenly screamed in her com. *"Warning! Enemy weapons lock! Warning!"*

Shitpissfuck. She jerked the fighter into a roll. A mental command to the computer, and the ship's rear guns fired off a beamer blast and a burst of sensor chaff designed to confuse the Dharani's weapons.

Didn't work.

Light flared off to starboard. Something banged hard into the fighter. Her roll became an out-of-control tumble. The computer's klaxon howled, "Starboard engine hit! Critical damage!"

Dammit, not the good engine! The other was at half-function as it was.

Grimly Cassidy scanned the sensor readouts. Most of the damage seemed electrical rather than structural. The Tribesman hadn't actually managed to hole her fighter's skin, so it was just possible she could land. *If* she could make it through the atmosphere, and *if* the Dharani didn't get her first.

All in all, she wouldn't bet a bucket of warm spit on her chances.

+ + +

MAJOR Rune Alrigo felt a savage grin spread across his face as his computer told him he'd damaged the enemy's starboard engine. It appeared the pilot was going to try to land his crippled craft on the planet ahead.

Rune, of course, had no intention of allowing any such thing.

He allowed himself a flicker of regret. The other was a skilled and brilliant warrior who had fought well. Which only made it more imperative that the enemy pilot die. He couldn't be allowed to survive to fight again, or worse, breed more warriors to oppose another generation of Dharani. Despite his admiration, Rune could not afford mercy.

Rune sent a mental order to his combat computer, which in turn shot a command through the fighter's interface. Behind his head, the engines howled in response, vibrating through the cockpit like the screams of the damned. Acceleration smashed him back in his seat as the fighter tore after his enemy. Trid displays shimmered around him, revealing system functioning for his own craft as well as sensor data on the enemy. He monitored them automatically as he piloted his fighter, the vessel responding to the silent orders he sent through his comp.

The cockpit canopy began to heat as the fighter hit the atmosphere. A soft whistle sounded as the air thickened, the sound swiftly escalating into a howl. In minutes the gentle cherry glow of friction built to a hellish blaze. Finally the light abruptly cut off as the canopy went opaque, but the howl of the wind continued to build.

A glance at his sensor readouts told him the enemy fighter was still shooting along ahead of him, pitching and rolling wildly as its pilot fought for control. Rune admired the man's skill even as he tried to get a weapons' lock.

It was only a matter of time. Even if the mercenary survived the landing, he'd be an easy target on the ground.

The planet zoomed closer. Blobs of green and sand brown resolved themselves into land masses, then into forests, then finally into trees. A patch of blue glittered in the sunlight, became a lake. The enemy fighter headed for that blue shimmer, apparently intending to land in the clearing on its leeward side. Rune followed, reverse engines thundering as he slowed his craft for the killing pass. Deceleration sent his body surging against the harness.

The enemy's port nacelle dipped as he approached the ground, and for a moment Rune thought he wouldn't have to kill the man after all.

No such luck.

Somehow the pilot brought it back under control, the craft rocking furiously as he played force against force in a desperate bid for life. At last all three wheels touched, and the fighter slid to a neat stop.

"Very nice," Rune murmured regretfully. "You really are good." To his computer he added, "Fire . . ."

Before he could get the rest of the command out of his mouth, something boomed. His fighter rocked wildly. *"Warning!"* the comp howled. *"Tachyon torpedo hit to the fuselage. Control systems failing!"*

Blazing angels, the bastard had hit *him*! Swearing, Rune fought to regain control of the fighter as it shot helplessly past his enemy. The nose dipped, and the ground spiraled toward him. He commed order after order to the ship, forcing the craft to stabilize right side up just long enough to . . .

Boom!

Light exploded in his skull. Metal shrieked. Rune tasted blood as he bit his tongue, and his torso slammed with bruising force against the straps. The crash seemed to go on and on, an endless kaleidoscope of pain and brutal sensation as the craft pinwheeled around him. He knew he was dead.

And then . . .

The fighter rolled over once more and stopped, rocking a moment before it went still. Metal creaked and groaned. Cautiously Rune opened his eyes. He was hanging upside down in his harness. Only a dim bloodred emergency light illuminated the cramped interior of the cockpit.

He could sense the power dying. Only seconds left. *"Computer,"* Rune commed, *"activate Tach Pulse."*

"Activating Tach Pulse."

Static roared white-hot in his head, blinding him as his sensors picked up the savage tachyon pulse that blasted from the ship's systems.

Then everything went black. Even the emergency light was gone.

Grimly Rune hauled off his helmet; the Pulse had killed his suit's internal oxygen system. If the planet hadn't had breathable air, he wouldn't have dared use the weapon, last ditch or not.

Reaching over his head to the cockpit release, he grabbed it and jerked down with all his considerable strength. The canopy plummeted to the ground below. Freeing his shoulder harness, Rune dropped a few centimeters before the webbing caught him, then quickly twisted his way free and fell.

He landed in a crouch, looking around for the enemy pilot. The bastard's fighter sat demurely a couple of dozen meters away, despite its scorched nacelle. To his irritation, it had emerged from this engagement better off than his own craft.

At least until he'd fired the Tach Pulse. At close range, the blast of tachyon radiation was powerful enough to punch right through the shielding that would normally protect electronics. Now every power supply for every piece of equipment on both fighters was dead, including those of any beamer pistols or energy weapons.

All of which ensured the bastard wouldn't be shooting him.

Rune's nanotech computer and muscle enhancements alone survived, since they were biological rather than electronic. So had the enemy pilot's, of course, but the odds were that Rune now had the advantage. Dharani nanotech was generally superior. In any hand-to-hand battle, he had the edge.

Drawing the knife from his boot, Rune started off to find the enemy.

✦ ✦ ✦

BLOODY hell, the bastard had Pulsed her! Cassidy jerked her helmet off and started flicking the manual switches, but everything remained stubbornly dead.

Maybe—*maybe*—she could set up the solar collectors to recharge the main batteries, then use the batts to recharge her suit, communication system, and weapons. But that would take hours.

What if the *Starrunner* left the system before the process was completed? How the fuck was she supposed to get rescued if she couldn't send a com message? Her internal implant couldn't punch a signal much farther than orbit. And the nearest town was on the other side of a mountain range that would block her transmission.

What's more, her foe was in the same boat. The Dharani really were nuts.

Growling to herself, she grabbed the canopy release and popped it, then levered herself out of the cockpit. With a surge and flex, she vaulted over the side and dropped to the ground.

Straightening, Cassidy took a look around. She could have landed in worse places. Just as sensors had indicated, Dallas was more than habitable. The lake was a clean, clear blue under the crystalline sky, and the leafy lavender-tinted vegetation underfoot reminded her of Terran crabgrass. The air felt just right—warm without being hot, scented with a medley of alien perfumes from God knew what plants.

All of which was why they were fighting this war to begin with. It was very rare to find two naturally habitable planets in the same star system. Usually only one was located at the right spot for a temperature range humans could stand. Dallas, however, orbited at a screwy angle to the rest of the system. The local star must have captured it at some point in the distant past. It wasn't a stable arrangement; computer simulations said eventually Dallas and New Galveston would collide—in a few million years. Until then, the colonists intended to take full advantage of the situation.

Unfortunately, they weren't the only ones. The inhabitants the next system over had a yen for a little empire building, and Galveston and its settlement here had looked like easy pickings. So the Kalistans had mounted an invasion force, hiring three Dharani Tribeships to give it some muscle. The Galvestonians didn't have a navy big enough to defend themselves against that kind of attack, so they'd called in several mercenary companies, including the *Starrunner*.

Enemy approaching, her computer whispered in her mind.

Cassidy whipped around. A tall male figure stalked toward her around the curve of the lake. Dammit, she'd hoped the bastard had been hurt in the crash. No such luck.

Jesus, he was big. She took a wary step back. Easily the size of

Captain August, maybe a little bigger, tall and broad-shouldered in his skin-tight black body armor. There was some serious muscle under that suit, too, backing up whatever implants he had. From the look of all that beef, he was probably even stronger than she was. Dammit.

Adding to the stark, menacing look created by the suit, he wore his hair in a stiff black brush that emphasized the stark lines of his angular face. As he moved closer, she saw that his eyes were very pale against his tanned skin, a smoky silver. Their expression was cold, flat. As deadly as the big knife he carried in one hand.

His features were strong and intensely male, with broad, high cheekbones, a hawkish nose, and wide, full mouth. She'd have considered him handsome if he hadn't been planning to kill her.

Cassidy crouched and drew her own knife from her boot. If he wanted a fight, she'd give him one.

Chapter Two

THE enemy pilot was female.

Rune stopped in surprise, his Tribeship instinct to revere women warring with his training against giving an enemy quarter.

She was tall, long-boned, and lean-muscled, her white-blond hair braided in an intricate arrangement designed to accommodate a helmet. She met his gaze without flinching, her expression professional and wary, her grip on her combat knife steady. Very different from the pampered, voluptuous *Mahiris* who ruled the women's deck, dispensing pain and pleasure at whim.

Even so, her lean body had some very lush, pretty curves not even combat armor could hide. Her eyes were an exotic green in her heart-shaped face, and her mouth looked soft, kissable, despite its grim line.

Desire closed a hot, tight fist around Rune's balls. It had been too long since his last visit to the women's deck. It was too bad he couldn't have encountered his pretty foe under better circumstances.

Unless . . . A daring idea made his eyes widen. He stopped as his heart began to pound.

Though a male warrior with her intelligence and skill could not be allowed to live, a woman with those traits would make an invaluable addition to his tribe. And Rune had no doubt this one would breed magnificent warriors.

What's more, she would be his. His as no other woman ever could be.

The problem, of course, was that any female fighter worthy of being Claimed would slit a warrior's throat for the attempt. Which was as it should be. A woman who would yield easily was not worth having.

Slowly Rune began moving toward her again, evaluating the grim determination in her eyes. No, she wouldn't go down easily.

She would have to be captured and disarmed, then courted and seduced. Trying to force her would be profoundly stupid. She'd either fight him to the death, or pretend to yield and kill him when his guard was down. That would be what he would do himself, faced with an overwhelming foe.

And Rune fully intended to overwhelm her. In every sense of the word.

He began his campaign when he reached a respectful distance, his slight bow wary as he watched her pretty face. "I am Major Rune Alrigo of the Dharani Tribeship *Conquest*. I offer challenge to a Claiming Duel."

Rune could tell by her lack of reaction that she had no idea what he meant. She probably assumed he simply intended to kill her. She gave him a short, sharp nod in return. "Lieutenant Cassidy Vika of the mercenary warship *Starrunner*. What the hell was the business with the Tach Pulse? I don't know about you, but I'd actually like to get rescued."

"As would I," he told her coolly. "After our business is completed. My people do not duel with beamer pistols."

Her pretty mouth tightened. He wondered how it would feel against his. "Look, asshole, this is not a duel—it's war. There's no time for whatever elaborate ceremonies you lunatics have constructed to entertain yourselves when you're bored. This is for real."

"Oh, most definitely." He would have to teach her about the nature of honor. Not surprising; the Dharani conception of honor was a difficult one for those not of the Tribes.

Her expression went even colder. "Fine. Let's dance." Holding her blade in a competent knife fighter's guard, she advanced, light and graceful on the balls of her feet. Rune fell into a crouch, his attention focused on her eyes. If she felt fear, it didn't show. Good.

Cassidy stopped a little more than a pace away, her hands moving in hypnotic patterns designed to confuse. Rune waited, knowing she'd find his stillness more unnerving.

Without warning, he lunged with a hard slash designed to test her strength and reflexes. Even as he attacked, Rune prepared to pull the blow; he had no desire to kill her.

She did not disappoint him, slipping aside like a ghost. Her return slash scored his tough armor, but didn't penetrate it. "Very good," he told her, pleased with her speed.

"Condescending prick," she growled, and came after him in a flurry of steel that forced him to retreat, blocking knife thrust after knife thrust with flicks of his own blade. Her nanotech implants made her strength something to respect, though he still had a considerable advantage in muscle.

Assured she could handle herself, Rune launched another series of attacks, moving faster this time, pushing harder. He wanted
to wear her down so he could get in close enough to begin her seduction.

Close enough for the secret weapon in his erotic arsenal to
take effect. *If* she was susceptible. It would certainly simplify matters if she were.

✦ ✦ ✦

CASSIDY had the ugly feeling she was in serious trouble. For one
thing, the top of her head barely came to the Tribesman's shoulder, and she figured he outweighed her by a good sixty kilos. She
still could have taken him if he'd been merely human—her implants would have seen to that. Unfortunately, this Rune Alrigo
had implants of his own. To make matters worse, her sensors told
her somebody had done some intensive genetic modifications on
the bastard, probably before he was even born. His bones and
muscle were denser, tougher, than that of a normal human, even
one that had been enhanced.

If Cassidy wanted to get out of this alive, she was going to
have to out-think him.

It helped that Alrigo was playing with her. Given his strength
and implants, he should be hitting her a lot harder, a lot faster. At
least once she'd caught him pulling a knife stroke that would have
sliced right through her armor.

What the devil was he up to? Why take the risk of playing this
game if he didn't plan to kill her? Alrigo had to realize that despite
his physical advantages, she could still outmaneuver him. Hell,
sheer bad luck had killed many a strong fighter; all he had to do
was trip. So why take the chance?

Unless he planned to rape her.

The thought sent a stab of cold fear through Cassidy, but she suppressed it ruthlessly. She'd always known being a mercenary could go very bad in a hurry. Getting blown to quarks in a space battle was actually one of her preferred ways to die, compared to some she could name.

And if she didn't get her mind back on the fight, she was going to buy it with a knife in the guts.

Hell, it didn't matter why he was playing with her. The point was to win.

Cassidy surged at him, slashing and stabbing in a flurry of attacks. He ducked or parried every one of them, but he had to work at it.

Better. Much better.

Breathing hard now, she circled him, looking for an opening in his rock-steady guard. Sweat rolled under her combat armor to pool at the base of her spine, sticky and itching. The suit normally had a heating and cooling system that would keep her comfortable in much worse conditions than this, but that damn Tach Pulse had disabled it. Cassidy wished she could strip off and let the breeze blow across her overheated skin.

Probably not a good idea, given the way Alrigo was watching her. His gaze was a little unnerving. Unusual eyes—smoky blue irises threaded with silver, predatory and intent. His nostrils flared, reminding her of a wolf catching a scent. A bead of sweat rolled down one high cheekbone and right past the corner of his sensual mouth.

Sensual mouth? Where the hell had that come from? She must be more exhausted than she thought.

She had to wrap this up.

Cassidy attacked in a brutal thrust to the belly, and the Tribesman parried with a flick of his blade. She kept going, slamming into him, grabbing for his knife wrist with her left hand as she tried to drive her own weapon into the underside of that square jaw. Alrigo clamped a hand over her wrist so hard, she felt the bones grind. She fought him anyway, trying to force the knife point that last few centimeters.

Suddenly he quit holding back. Dragging her weapon hand down and to the side, he twisted and yanked. The knife went flying. She shouted in rage as he rammed her, forcing her over backward.

They hit the ground hard, the breath whooshing from Cassidy's chest as Alrigo's full weight slammed down on top of her. She bucked, managed to throw him off, then flipped around and started to scramble after her fallen knife.

He pounced on her like a mountain lion on a rabbit. He weighed a ton. Cassidy's arms and legs went out from under her so fast she tasted dirt. But the knife glittered in the ground vegetation barely a meter away, so she threw herself toward it anyway, lifting both of them off the ground with her enhanced strength.

Until Alrigo got an arm around her throat and braced a leg against her progress. Suddenly they weren't going anywhere. "I think not," he breathed in her ear, and forced her down again. One of his legs hooked under and around one of hers as he applied ruthless pressure against her windpipe. The other arm wrapped under her own to clamp a hand around the back of her neck. She managed to jerk her head to the side so she could suck in a breath. Throwing her weight against him, she rolled them both over.

A mistake. He wrapped his free leg around hers, and she was immobilized, stretched across his massive body in a bow.

Luckily she still had one arm free. Cassidy grabbed the forearm across her throat and dug for a nerve, trying to force him to let go, but the tough armor of his suit protected him. She couldn't get a grip.

Where the fuck was Alrigo's knife? Both his hands were occupied with holding her. He had her immobilized; this was a perfect opportunity to slide a blade between her ribs, but he'd evidently dropped it. Why?

He wasn't even pressing on her throat hard enough to choke her. In fact, he was making no effort to finish her at all, though she could think of a dozen ways to do it.

Furiously Cassidy twisted and fought, digging with her free hand, trying to force him to let go. No matter how she bucked and writhed, she couldn't seem to break his hold. "What the hell are you doing?" she panted at last, furious and frustrated. "If you're going to kill me, quit fucking around!"

"I have no intention of killing you," he rumbled against her ear. The sensation tickled.

"Yeah? Then why the hell did you challenge me?"

"You'll figure it out." At least he was breathing hard, the son of a bitch.

She growled and went back to battering at any part of him she could reach, but her free arm felt as if it were turning to lead.

He was so damn big. It was as though God had carved him from solid granite, all ridges and hollows and swells of hard muscle against her back.

Didn't he ever get tired?

It was too bad they'd had to meet like this. She'd bet he'd be delicious in the sack. He was built just the way she liked them: big and brawny. Her nipples hardened as she imagined him surging against her in passion.

As the sudden wave of lust rolled over her, Cassidy blinked. Good God, she was actually getting turned on. The guy had tried to kill her a dozen times today, and damn near succeeded. Now he had her pinned like an eelsnake coiled around a rat, and damned if there wasn't a ball of heat gathering in her belly.

Thing was, she liked the way he smelled. God knew why; they both reeked of sweat and smoke and the oily tang of body armor. Cassidy should have been grimacing, yet she found herself inhaling instead. Hungrily, as if Alrigo was a rare delicacy and she wanted to take a big bite. She fought the desire to turn in his arms and find out if he tasted as good as he smelled.

What was more, every breath she took only made her hotter. She wanted to . . .

Something was wrong.

Unease snaked through Cassidy's building arousal. She'd fought a lot of men hand-to-hand, but she'd never wanted to fuck any of them. Yet this one had her ready to rip off his clothes just from his scent alone.

His scent. Her eyes widened.

Analyze his scent, Cassidy ordered her comp. *See if there's something in it that shouldn't be.*

Seconds later the answer came back, and she swore viciously. "You're trying to *drug* me, you son of a bitch!"

Chapter Three

"IT'S not a drug," Rune told her. "It's nothing more than pheromones. And it's not something I do voluntarily. My body produces them when I am . . . aroused." Which he most definitely was, with her lush little body grinding against his groin even through two layers of armor.

"You planned this!" The fury in her voice made him wince.

"Not exactly. There was no guarantee your body would respond to mine," he said, controlling her ferocious struggles with an effort. "Though I'll admit I'm pleased it did."

"Why?" Cassidy jerked against his hold and sneered. "Are you that desperate for a woman?"

Oh, yes—on any number of levels. Not that he had any intention of admitting it. One did not advertise vulnerability, particularly to a woman. She'd use it.

Rune put a confident purr in his voice. "What do you think?"

She was silent for several long, simmering moments. "If you're going to rape me, get it over with and leave me the fuck alone."

The insult stung. True, some Tribesmen didn't care about a Breeder's consent, but he was not one of them. "I'm not a rapist."

"You drugged me. Even if I give in, it's rape."

"You're not drugged. You're fully capable of fighting the attraction. If you choose."

"Well, I choose. Let me go."

"To cut my throat? I think not."

"You seem more than capable of defending yourself." Cassidy gave another furious jerk against his hold, arching against him with a surging flex. Rune closed his eyes as his body leaped in reaction. She smelled of feminine sweat and the tang of sex, and she'd washed her hair in something floral. The contrast between those womanly scents and the masculine smell of her armor was unbearably erotic.

"I challenged you to a Claiming Duel," he said hoarsely. "And I won. I'm not releasing you."

+ + +

CASSIDY went still in the Tribesman's grip, her mind working feverishly—no small accomplishment, considering the arousal steaming through her.

That's right—Alrigo had said something about a Claiming Duel when he challenged her. At the time she'd been so focused on the coming fight that the words hadn't really penetrated. It couldn't possibly be what it sounded like. "You don't really think you can keep me?"

"Actually, I do." He sounded utterly calm, utterly sure of himself.

Cassidy wanted to punch him. "If you think I'll be a docile slave, you bastard, you're in for a—"

"Slave?" Offended astonishment rang in his voice. "My people do not keep slaves. I mean to wed you."

"*Wed?*" Several seconds clicked by before she could speak without sputtering. "You really are out of your mind! Why in the hell would you want to marry me? More to the point, why do you think I'd marry *you*?" She twisted in his arms, punching at any part of him she could reach.

Alrigo only coiled more tightly around her. He felt like living steel, seductive and warm. And his scent—God, his scent! Like distilled sex. To her irritation, Cassidy's body responded, nipples peaking beneath her armor.

"As to the first question, you are intelligent and quite strong for a woman," he told her, his voice deep, rich, and so calmly assured she wanted to scream. "Your reflexes are very fast, your aim is good . . ."

"Not good enough!" She bucked against him.

He tightened his grip until bone ground. She went still with a gasp of pain. ". . . You have a strong grasp of strategy and tactics, and you are courageous. All of which are qualities I wish for in my warrior sons."

Cassidy went limp in shock. "Your sons?"

"Yes. If a warrior encounters a female with the qualities you have, it's his duty to attempt to obtain her for his tribe." He said the words simply, as if the logic was obvious instead of insane. "Our population is small, and we need the genetic diversity of new blood stock."

"Let me get this straight." She twisted her head around to glare at him from the corner of one eye. "You actually expect me to accompany you back to your ship and become a baby machine for the Dharani."

"Not for the Dharani as a whole," he said. "For me. I found you, I defeated you. It's my right to claim you."

"And it's my right to slit your throat from ear to ear as you sleep!" Cassidy gritted. "Let's get a few things straight—I'm not marrying you, and I'm not having sex with you, and I am sure as hell not having your children!" Teeth gritted, she strained against him so hard her back bent like a bow. All she got for her trouble was the sensation of his groin grinding into her backside. He might as well have been cast from neutronium.

"I will convince you otherwise." There was that infuriating assurance again. She wanted to scream. Which of course, would do her absolutely no good.

And neither would fighting him like this. Getting pissed off only played into his hands.

The thought sent cold common sense pouring through Cassidy's fury. She had to calm down and start thinking, instead of letting him pin her down where his pheromones could do their work.

And they were doing a damn good job. Angry as she was, need hummed underneath her rage like a high-voltage line, just waiting to fry her.

Think, Cassidy.

Force obviously would not work. Alrigo was too damn strong. She had to turn the tables on him somehow.

First step to doing that, of course, was to get him the hell off her. The good news was that he couldn't hold her like this forever. If nothing else, he'd have to let go to try to get his ship's communications systems working again so he could call his Tribeship.

Which meant he was going to have to secure her somehow. He probably had a set of mag restraints on his fighter; everybody did.

She couldn't afford to let him tie her up. The situation would be completely out of her hands then. There'd be no way she could keep him from taking her back to his Tribeship, where he could rape her at his leisure.

Which meant she had to get Alrigo busy doing something else *now*.

The choice was obvious, if galling, particularly given her rash declaration of a few minutes earlier. She was going to have to have sex with him.

Her hormones gave a muted little cheer. Cassidy snarled at them. *This is just business. The idea is to distract the son of a bitch, sucker him into dropping his guard so I can bash his skull in and get loose.*

Unfortunately, Alrigo would probably realize she was planning something if she simply offered to bang him. She had to make him believe she was being overcome by those damn pheromones of his. Then once his dick started doing his thinking for him, his ass was hers.

✦ ✦ ✦

CASSIDY collapsed against Rune, panting, so furious he could smell her rage. According to his sensors, she'd exhausted herself.

Not surprising, since he, too, was feeling the effects of their brawl. She'd fought him with a stubborn fury that made no allowances for his superior strength. Fought him so long, he'd thought she'd never give up.

Rune wasn't at all sure she'd given up now. More than likely, she was scheming to overcome him by trickery.

He had no intention of being overcome. He did, however, have every intention of seducing her into yielding to their mutual desire.

Fury wasn't the only emotion his keen sense of smell detected in her scent.

Rune lowered his head until he could whisper into one delicate ear. "It will not be so unpleasant being my wife, Cassidy." He breathed out slowly, letting the warmth gust against the curve of her jaw. "I am very, very good."

Cassidy went still. He heard her swallow and smiled. "What you are," she said in a low, tight voice, "is very, very egotistical."

"Perhaps." Rune eyed the delicate flesh of her lobe. It looked soft and pale against the gold of her hair. "But then, perhaps not." He nuzzled the delicate nubbin, licked it tenderly. Her flesh tasted deliciously feminine, reminding him of the three endless months since he'd last had a woman.

If he could make her his, he would no longer be dependent on the whim of the Mahiris. He could make love to her whenever he wanted, however he wanted.

"Cut it out, Alrigo." But her voice wasn't quite steady. Good. He'd make it more unsteady yet.

Delicately Rune licked her ear, then took the lobe between his teeth. And, with exquisite care, took a careful bite. Suckled slowly as she stiffened against him. "But your flesh is so sweet," he purred.

"Let me go."

"No. I wonder how your mouth would taste."

"You wouldn't like it. It's full of sharp teeth." The words were gritted, but the scent of female heat was rising.

"And I'll wager you bite, don't you?" He twisted his head so he could reach her throat, then pressed his mouth against a straining tendon running from her jaw. Her skin felt like satinweb against his lips. "But then, so do I." He raked his teeth across it until her breath caught. "Ahhhhh. Very nice. But . . . it strikes me that you're overdressed. All this armor leaves so little bare flesh for my teeth. . . ."

Taking a chance, he released his hold on her throat and trailed his fingers across the front of her armored suit. Even as he did it, he waited for her to launch another furious attack with her free hand.

But she didn't. Instead she simply lay across him, breathing hard from exertion—and, he suspected, more than a little arousal.

Rune allowed himself a slight smile. Either his pheromones were getting to her, or she'd decided to try to lull him into complacency. Most likely both; there was definitely arousal in her scent, but she was too ruthlessly disciplined to let it matter. So she was playing him—but he was playing her, too.

They'd discover who played with more skill.

He found the seal of her armor. Located the first clip. Pulled it. It opened with a sigh. "Mmmmm," he breathed. "That's better, isn't it? It's probably hot in that suit."

Rune opened another clip. The edges of the suit sprang open, revealing the upper curves of her breasts. He gazed down the arrow of cleavage, shamelessly admiring them. "Pretty. So full and pale."

His gloved hand found another clip. Snap. The arrow lengthened. Her white flesh seemed to swell under his gaze as if silently begging for his touch.

"Is that any"—he smiled—"cooler?"

"Go to hell."

"Not right now. I have another destination in mind." His hand continued down the line of clips. Snap. Snap. Snap. The arrow widened, revealing her smooth belly right down to a glimpse of blonde curls right at the top of her groin. She squirmed, as if unable to help herself.

It was not a gesture of rejection.

Smoothly, as if he had every right, Rune reached a hand down her open neckline and claimed one of those lovely breasts. It felt deliciously yielding, and he longed to take off his gloves so he could enjoy the sensation.

When she spoke again, her voice was tight with control. "You're quite the bastard, aren't you?"

"Sometimes." He found her hard jutting nipple. Delicately plucked. Listened as she caught her breath. "And then, again, sometimes I'm not."

Chapter Four

ALRIGO caressed her slowly, his fingers gentle and skilled on her nipples as he plucked them into a hot ache. Despite her determination to remain unaffected, Cassidy's breathing grew rough with hunger.

He paused in his erotic assault only to lift his hand to his mouth and catch the fingertip of a glove between his teeth so he could work it off. "I find I need to touch you," he told her, tossing the gauntlet aside. "Skin to skin."

Something about the way he said "skin" made her heart leap in a hard thump. It began to pound in earnest when his long fingers took her again.

Alrigo was right. It was so much hotter when bare flesh touched.

His fingertips were just slightly rough with calluses, and his hand felt deliciously warm as it cupped her. "Sweet," he breathed. "And soft. So soft . . ."

With a muscular flex, he rolled them over. Her first impulse was to struggle, but then he turned her in his arms so they were face-to-face. His eyes were a pale, smoky silver. The deep tan of his face made them even more striking, particularly framed by those dark, long lashes of his.

Suddenly Cassidy realized he'd gathered both her wrists in one of his hands. Now he pinned them to the ground over her head. He was nuts if he thought he could hold her that way. His strength advantage, while considerable, wasn't enough to let him get away with it.

But her intent was to seduce him into lowering his guard, so she didn't fight. Instead, she gave in to the temptation to gaze up into that stern face while he studied hers.

He was a handsome bastard, she'd give him that. The knife-blade cheekbones and square chin contrasted with the sulky sensuality of his mouth. She was seriously tempted to bite that lush lower lip, just to see how it would taste.

He lowered his head. Cassidy caught her breath. Considered turning her face away. Didn't. And not just for strategy's sake.

One thing was immediately clear: Alrigo knew how to kiss. He started out warm and slow, a light brush of the lips that made her want more. Only when she started kissing him back did he deepen it, sipping at her lips, first the upper, then the lower, gently licking and nibbling.

Despite her firm intentions to kick his ass at the earliest opportunity, Cassidy found herself yielding, enjoying the hot sweep of his tongue. She returned the favor, determined to work her own erotic magic.

So they dueled with kisses and tender bites, growing bolder with each taste of hot skin.

Alrigo settled against her, his weight so welcome between her thighs, she grew impatient with their armor. She wanted to feel him naked against her, wanted to see what he looked like under all that hard plate. The edges of own her suit pressed against her nipples, teasing them until need roiled in her blood.

As if sensing her growing desperation, he left her mouth to string kisses along the line of her jaw, right to her throbbing pulse. For a moment he pressed the edges of his teeth to her jugular, not quite biting. The gesture of dominance and claiming made something ancient in her want to spread itself and yield.

Then he was working his way down again, right to the opening in her suit. With his free hand, he lifted one breast until its nipple popped free of her armor's parted neckline. He took the tight little point, sucking it gently into his mouth, raking it with his teeth until she squirmed at his skill. His male rumble of approval made her sex clench in hunger.

At last Alrigo released her wrists and sat up so he could grab the shoulders of her suit. "I want to see you," he said, his voice low and rough, his eyes hot. "All of you."

When he began stripping the suit down, she helped him, wriggling her way out of it. He paused to wrestle with her stubborn boots, and she sat watching him, her heart thumping hard, her bared breasts tight in the cool, springlike air.

As he tossed the first boot aside, Cassidy growled, "Strip."

About to pull off her other boot, he stopped to look at her, dark brows lifted.

"I want to touch you," she said. "Got a problem with that?"

His lips quirked. "No."

She watched him as she took care of the rest of her clothing. The boot joined its mate, followed by her gloves, then the rest of her suit.

Rising to his feet, he reached for the seal of his own armor, his gaze challenging. Naked now, she licked her lips, palms braced in the soft, blue tinted vegetation as he revealed an arrow of brown, brawny chest.

Alrigo stripped as quickly as she had. When he was finished, he stood over her a moment, letting her look her fill at him even as he stared hungrily down at her.

Well, if I've got to seduce an enemy pilot, I sure as hell could have done worse, Cassidy thought, taking in his sheer muscled size. The suit had actually minimized and compressed his brawn. He was all sculpted honey skin, covered with a fine ruff of dark hair. What she'd taken for a tan must be his natural skin color; the shade was too even to be anything else.

His cock was a thick, ruddy stalk thrusting from the cloud of soft hair at his groin. A single pearl of pre-cum glinted on its meaty, heart-shaped glans. His balls hung heavy between his braced thighs.

Cassidy didn't think she'd ever seen a more thoroughly *male* man, from his short-cropped hair to his big feet. Adding to the effect of delicious barbarism were odd designs on the skin around his nipples, belly button, and cock—not tattoos, exactly. Raised patterns, like intricate scars. Tribal markings of some kind.

"Where'd you get the marks?" Cassidy asked. Her voice was so low and rough with arousal, it startled her. She cleared her throat.

"The women of my ship," he said, his voice equally rough. He sank to his knees beside her. "When I became a man."

She looked at his urgent erection surrounded by its starburst of scarring. "Did it hurt?"

He smiled tightly. "Oh, yes. It was supposed to."

Cassidy frowned, her mind conjuring an image of Alrigo stoically enduring while women sliced into his most delicate flesh. She found the idea a lot less satisfying than she'd have expected, considering his offenses against her.

Without conscious intent, she reached out, brushing her fingers against the taught muscle of his abdomen, feeling the slick, raised designs. He drew in a hard breath. She looked up to see heat blaze high in his eyes.

One big hand cupped the back of her head, and he kissed her again, his mouth intoxicating as he licked and sucked at her lips. He hooked an arm behind her waist and leaned her back as he started kissing his way down her bare throat. When Alrigo paused to nibble her collarbone, she caught his head. His short hair felt like a silken pelt against her fingers.

He found her breast, lifted it gently, teased the nipple with a thumb. "Lovely," he rasped. "Such a pretty pink." Then his mouth closed over the peak, suckled with a slow, seductive power that made her eyes close in bliss.

Alrigo lowered her to the soft, short alien leaves and went to work in earnest with delicate nibbles and a slow, swirling tongue. As he settled between her thighs, she gave into impulse and stroked the bunching muscles of his shoulder, the skin like velvet over granite.

Watch it, Cassidy, she told herself. *You're supposed to seduce him into dropping his guard, not let him seduce you into dropping yours.*

But, God, his mouth felt good as he gently tugged and suckled. It felt even better when he reached between her thighs. Tender fingertips traced her vaginal lips, stroking the soft hair before slipping between.

She was so slickly wet, even she was surprised. Alrigo groaned in lust. "No," he rasped, his gaze flashing up to meet hers with sudden fierceness, "you can't claim this is rape."

Cassidy stiffened—trust a man to find a way to spoil the mood—but then he brushed a skillful thumb across her clit as he raked her nipple with his teeth, and her eyes rolled back in her head.

Damn, he was *way* too good at that.

By the time he abandoned her breasts to work his way down her abdomen with tiny nipping bites, she was all but writhing. Anticipation curled in shimmering waves of heat in her belly.

Then Alrigo stopped to explore her bellybutton, and she thought she was going to explode. Despite her best intentions, she found herself spreading her legs and rolling her hips.

His pale gaze met hers across her panting breasts. "Like that?"

"You're a teasing son of a bitch, you know that?" she gasped.

Rune smiled slowly. "Why, yes." He gave her navel another taunting swirl of his tongue.

Slowly, deliberately, Cassidy drew one long leg up his side in a long caress. She hooked a foot against his ass and dug in as she rolled her hips up. To her satisfaction, his eyes widened and a flush of lust rolled up his cheekbones.

She gave him a mocking smile. "I can play too, stud."

He grinned, humor lighting his face, making him look almost boyish. "So you can."

Then he rose off her, slid down between her thighs, and caught her behind the knees. She sucked in a breath as he spread her wide and buried his face against her sex.

He licked her once, slow and deep, as if she were some exotic sweet he wanted to capture on his tongue. Cassidy gasped, arching her spine at the burning intensity of the pleasure. He growled something guttural and settled in, almost attacking her flesh with a flurry of tongue flicks and slow laps and small, careful bites centered over and around her clit.

The ruthless pleasure rose, spiraling in a molten corkscrew up her spine until the muscles in her thighs quivered and jumped with the ferocity of her building orgasm.

Close. So close. But not quite.

It was all she could do not to beg him. She had to clench her teeth against the need.

He lifted his dark head to study her face. His mouth was wet. "You see?" he purred. "This is what I can do to you. Anytime."

It took effort, but she managed a sneer. "You talk big, but I still haven't come."

His teeth flashed. "You will."

He rose onto hands and knees and crawled up her body like a big predator. Despite herself, she caught her breath as she watched him take his cock in hand and aim it for her wet, aching sex.

Don't let me get pregnant, comp, she managed, despite the hot arousal steaming through her.

Understood, the comp replied. It would mobilize her body's defenses against his sperm just as it would against any microbial invaders he happened to be harboring.

Cassidy didn't want any souvenirs of this little encounter. She suspected she'd have enough trouble forgetting it as it was.

Alrigo entered her slowly, taking his time as he worked his thickness into her tight sex. It had been too long for her, and Cassidy hissed through her teeth at the raw, dark delight. He felt huge, overwhelming, though God knew she was no virgin.

His pale silver eyes locked on hers, fierce and triumphant as he slid deeper and deeper. "Nice," he breathed. "Very nice." In to the balls at last, he started pulling out. "And tight. And wet."

Panting, she managed to bare her teeth at him. "Give it your best shot, stud."

He bared his back. "Oh, I will. Let's go."

And then he started to thrust.

Chapter Five

A hot flush rode Cassidy's high cheekbones, and her pupils were dilated so wide they almost swallowed the gem green of her eyes. She gripped Rune's cock like a slick, breathtaking fist, so tight that every stroke sent blazing ecstacy rolling up his spine. He could feel the tiny contractions of her sex milking him, demonstrating just how close she was to coming herself.

Yet so much defiance blazed in that emerald gaze, he knew that though he might have won over her body, the battle for her heart hadn't even been joined.

Luckily, he enjoyed a challenge.

Rune braced his palms beside her shoulders and rolled his hips, using every bit of skill he'd learned on the women's deck, keeping his thrusts slow and deep.

It wasn't easy. She felt so slick and delicious that all he wanted to do was ride her hard, grind deep and ruthlessly until he came.

And judging from the challenge in her eyes, she expected him to do just that.

But Rune had learned discipline from harsh teachers, so he clamped down hard on his control. He'd damn well bring her before he went over.

As if reading his mind, Cassidy wrapped her endless legs around his waist and began to hunch her hips in short, teasing strokes that tested his control. "How long do you think you can hold it, stud?"

He gritted his teeth. "Longer than you."

"I don't think so." But to his satisfaction, she was panting.

Tits of the Goddess, he liked her. Liked her defiance, her determination to win, her intelligence.

And of course, he loved her lush little body, from those snapping green eyes to those full breasts to the tight, creamy cunt and long, long legs. She was everything he'd ever wanted. And he was damn well going to claim her.

So Rune reared off her, scooped her long legs up, draped her calves over his shoulders, and slid back into her again. Just to make sure she got the full effect, he thrummed his thumb over her hard little clit.

She might be stubborn, but so was he.

✛ ✛ ✛

CASSIDY caught her breath as delight drove up her spine like a spike.

God, he was good.

She could see how close he was. She knew she could have forced him over, but in this position, Alrigo was firmly in control.

And he felt like a beamer cannon in her cunt—thick, hard,

merciless. Every single stroke maddened her, an effect heightened by his thumb circling her clit. She fought to hold her climax off, determined not to give in until he came.

Then he rose up on his knees, leaned hard against her, and ground. "Come," he rumbled, with a single devastating stroke across her tight pearl timed at just the right moment.

Her climax came boiling out of nowhere, savage and irresistible. With a cry of mingled ecstacy and frustration, she came, her back arching with the frenzy of her orgasm.

"Yes," he growled. "Yes!"

Alrigo threw his head back and slammed his hips against hers, circling hard, pounding deep. Spurring her climax to jolting new heights as he roared and came, the tendons standing rigid on his throat, every muscle in stark relief.

The sweet, dark pleasure was merciless, a luscious firestorm. By the time it retreated, Cassidy felt drained and boneless, sprawled beneath his hot weight in the leaves.

With a groan he dropped her legs and collapsed over her, fists braced on the ground. Panting hard, he grinned into her eyes. "I'll have you yet."

Cassidy snarled at him even with her nervous system still jolting from the ferocity of her climax. "Fuck off."

He laughed, a long, rolling boom of delight and anticipation. "I didn't think it would be easy."

✦✦✦

DRESSED in his armor again, Rune sat in the cockpit of Cassidy's fighter and studied the equipment he'd jury-rigged. A dim red light gleamed on the otherwise dark console.

It meant he'd succeeded in deploying the solar collectors on the wings, despite the damage that had forced him to go out and pop them up by hand. Evidently something mechanical had broken somewhere, either during the fight or the landing. In any case, the collectors were recharging the fighter's battery array now. Barring too much cloud cover, systems should be up and running again in forty-eight hours. Then he'd be able to recharge his beamer pistol and use the fighter's com system to call the *Conquest*.

Assuming they hadn't sent someone to look for him by then. When Rune didn't report back, his Wing Brothers would start the search even if nobody else did.

Unless the *Starrunner* and her sister ships won. His stomach sank at the thought. There were more than ten thousand men, women, and children on the *Conquest,* including the Wing Brothers he'd known since his boyhood on the *Invader*. If his ship was destroyed, he might as well be dead.

There was, of course, another possibility—that the *Conquest* had survived, but a search party from Cassidy's ship would arrive first. If that happened, Rune was finished anyway. His people would expect him to kill as many of the enemy as possible—including Cassidy.

Grimacing, he dragged a hand through his short hair. The idea of hurting her wound a knot of pain in his chest. Despite the demands of duty, he simply didn't think he could look into those brilliant green eyes and end her.

Suicide would be much easier—and that was just what he'd do, rather than let himself be taken prisoner. A captured warrior was considered shamed beyond redemption.

Bowing his head, Rune sent a quick prayer to the Warrior Goddess. He only hoped she granted him the luck he asked for. He'd need it. There were far too many things that could go wrong.

Too many of them were already doing just that. His own fighter had been so badly damaged, he couldn't even deploy the solar collectors. He'd been lucky he could figure out how to get Cassidy's operational.

"Shitpissfuck!"

Despite the situation, Cassidy's muffled curse lightened his grim mood. Grinning, Rune called, "Are you all right out there, Cassidy?"

"Fuck off!"

He laughed, his spirits lifting. He'd used mag restraints to secure Cassidy's wrists to one of the fighter's wing nacelles. She'd been fighting to free herself since he'd climbed into her cockpit; he'd used his sensors to monitor her increasingly frustrated struggles. Strong as she was, she still couldn't break the cables.

"You know, I am really looking forward to kicking your ass!" she shouted.

"And I'm looking forward to fucking yours."

Something thumped hard against the wing—likely her foot. Her string of inventive curses had his brows rising and his lips twitching. She really was everything he'd ever wanted.

He just hoped he wasn't forced to kill her.

+ + +

CASSIDY hung upside down, both booted feet braced on the underside of the fighter's starboard wing. Once again, she threw herself against the mag restraints. The muscles in her neck, back, and shoulders howled as she fought to break the magnetic seal that bound her to the wing. Sweat rolled up her forehead, and tendrils of blond hair wafted around her sticky face. Between the fight and the sweaty roll on the ground, her braids were history. And if it hadn't been for her suit gloves, her wrists would have been in no better shape. The cable would have chewed right through her skin.

This just wasn't working. The mag seal was too strong.

With a grunt of frustration Cassidy let up the pressure and allowed her feet to fall back to the ground. Her shoulders ached so savagely, she wondered if she'd torn something.

Panting, wrists bound over her head, she rested a moment and considered her options. Rune was still busy in her cockpit, trying to get the main batteries charging. He'd stopped cursing a half hour ago, which probably meant he'd succeeded.

Figured. Even her equipment couldn't resist him.

Cassidy's stomach chose that moment for a growl. At least between the two fighters, they had enough rations for a few days. Rune had said his stores were intact, and hers had taken no damage. She licked her dry lips and considered abandoning her pride long enough to ask him for something to drink.

And when the hell had she started thinking of him by his first name? Yet another bad sign he was getting under her skin.

She sighed and rolled her aching shoulders. She'd put her armor back on, and now drying sweat was making all kinds of uncomfortable places itch. At least the breeze was relatively cool as it blew into her face, carrying the scent of alien vegetation and . . . something rank.

Cassidy stiffened, straightening in her bonds as she stared across the lake toward a stand of ferny alien trees.

Something was moving in, out there in the brush.

Her sensors showed several massive life forms advancing toward her in a way that suggested more than casual curiosity.

What the hell are those things? Cassidy asked her computer through her mental link with it.

The colonists call them caravores, the comp responded. *Five of them, ranging in weight between five hundred and a thousand kilos. Data suggests a hunting pack consisting of four females and a lone male.*

Damn, the things were huge. *A hunting pack?*

Caravores are predators.

That figured. She raised her voice in a bellow. "Hey, Rune—get out here! We've got company!"

Enemies were one thing. Getting eaten was something else again.

He stuck his head out of the canopy he'd replaced, stared toward the woods, and cursed. Vaulting out of the cockpit, he dropped to the ground beside her as the restraints around her wrists fell away, probably at a command from his computer. He looked in the direction of the advancing predators, no doubt doing a sensor scan. Judging from the way his mouth tightened, he didn't like the results any better than she did. "I have no desire to take five of those things on with nothing more than a knife. Better get in the fighter. It's the only shelter we've got."

She jumped for the wing and chinned herself up. "Yeah, well, if you hadn't triggered that Tach Pulse, we'd have beamers!"

"I didn't know anything about those . . . things. What are they?"

She scrambled for the cockpit as he hoisted himself after her. "Caravores. Apparently they're something like a cross between a tiger and a bear. Meaner than hell."

He strode ahead of her and dropped into the cockpit first, then lifted a hand to help her in. "Sit in my lap. We're going to have to get friendly until they go away."

Cassidy hesitated a moment, but it wasn't as if she had a hell of a lot of alternatives. With a sigh she climbed in and settled on top of him while he dragged the canopy closed and activated the mag seal. At least that still worked.

For a moment neither spoke, too busy looking out the canopy as the caravores slipped from the trees and headed toward the fighter.

"Good God," Cassidy murmured. "Look at the size of those things!" Though easily as big as an old Earth grizzly bear, they moved with a liquid grace that was more feline than anything else. Their bodies were long and sleek, with pointed wolflike muzzles, and their fur ranged from a bloodred striped with slash markings to a black so deep it was almost blue.

One of them stopped to roar, the sound clearly audible even through the canopy. Its gaping jaws revealed a mouth full of teeth that looked like daggers.

Rune and Cassidy exchanged appalled looks. "Oh, God," she breathed. "If they break open the canopy, we're dead."

Chapter Six

"THIS fighter was built to withstand interstellar dogfights," Rune pointed out. "I doubt a bunch of animals are going to be able to crack it open."

"I'd agree with you if you hadn't shot me down," Cassidy told him tartly. "Considering the crash, I'm not sure it's still up to specs."

He winced. "Good point."

Something roared. Something else answered. The fighter rocked on its wheels.

"Leave the wing alone, you bastard," Cassidy growled as her sensors reported that one of the caravores had stood on its haunches to give her craft a testing shake.

"The brakes on?" Rune asked, tightening his grip around her waist.

She licked her dry lips. "Yeah. I don't think we're going to go anywhere—shit!" Her heart lunged into her throat as they rocked violently.

One of the caravores has jumped on the port wing, her comp told her.

The craft shook as the huge animal walked up the wing toward the cockpit. Eyes wide, Cassidy met Rune's grim gaze. He lifted his right leg beneath her and reached down to pull his combat dagger from the top of his boot.

"I don't suppose you've got another one of those tucked away somewhere?" she asked. Her own blade was still lost in the vegetation where she'd dropped it during their fight. She'd rather have a beamer, but just now she'd take anything she could get.

Without a word he lifted his left knee. She reached down into the top of his boot and found the hilt of the second knife. It felt cool and heavy in her hand.

+ + +

"THIS blows the airlock," she told him as her sensors reported the beast had stopped to sniff a weld. "It's one thing to fight humans—hell, even aliens—but something that *eats* people . . ."

Rune flashed her a look cold with determination. "They're not going to touch you, Cassidy. I've claimed you, and I defend my own."

She had never felt a need to be defended by anyone or anything. Yet looking into his savage expression, Cassidy realized the statement wasn't hyperbole. He'd defend her to the death.

She frowned, caught between gratitude and discomfort. "Rune, with your strength you could probably take one of those things—but *five*?"

His mouth tightened, and a muscle flexed in his jaw. He knew as well as she did how impossible it would be. "I'll think of something." Then he sighed and gave his knife a restless toss, looking up at the canopy. "If necessary. With any luck, it won't be. We should . . ."

A head twice the size of hers appeared overhead and looked down at them through the transparent laminate with feral hunger. Despite herself, Cassidy flinched. "Holy God!"

A massive paw planted right in the center of the thick canopy. Daggerlike claws screeched as the caravores tried to dig through it. As one, Rune and Cassidy winced at the grating sound.

The fighter rocked again.

Another caravore has leaped onto the ship, her computer reported.

Blessed anger replaced her fear. "This is ridiculous!" Cassidy glared upward at the beast. "If I had my beamer, I'd burn those furry sons of bitches into barbeque."

"Yes, well, unfortunately neither of us has a beamer."

She aimed a hot glare at him over her shoulder. "Thanks to you and your fuckin' Tach Pulse! What were you thinking, using something like that on a planet with man-eating predators?"

"I wasn't aware this planet *had* man-eating predators!" Rune snapped back. "Our database on this colony consisted of little more than the fact that it was habitable."

Which only made sense, she supposed. Rune was working for the invaders, while Cassidy had been hired by the New Galvestonians who'd colonized Dallas. Naturally, their information would be more complete. "It was still a dumb thing to do," she grumbled.

"If I hadn't fired that Pulse, you'd have shot me. Or vice versa." The caravores gave the canopy a smacking blow with one huge paw. Rune's arm tightened protectively around her. "In any case, we wouldn't be having this conversation."

"Personally, I think I'd rather be shot than eaten!"

A grim smile tilted his mouth. "I didn't realize those were the choices."

Something groaned as the fighter shifted hard to one side. One of the caravores was pushing up on the starboard wing. Cassidy clutched at Rune's arm and cursed ripely. The caravore over their heads began raking at the canopy like a dog trying to dig up a bone.

"You'd look really good as a rug," Cassidy told one. "I'd skin you slowly and display you in my cabin."

Rune chuckled suddenly, his breath warm against the side of her face. "It is galling to sit here like this, helpless." The fighter shook. "But there is no honor in being eaten, either. As much as I'd like to take a knife to those things, we are safer in here."

The caravores climbed on top of the canopy, reared, and slammed their forelegs into the glass. Cassidy swallowed a yelp.

"I don't suppose you have any chemical grenades?" Rune asked.

She licked her lips. "No. Well, I did, but they all had powered detonators."

The caravores flopped down and started trying to gnaw at the glass. The fighter rocked again as one of the other animals advanced up the wing to the canopy. This one was stark black, its eyes a hungry yellow. It, too, started raking and biting at the shield.

Cassidy eyed them. One suddenly threw back its head and roared, taking a swipe at the other with its claws. "I feel like a package of rations in here, Rune." She blew out a breath. "Time for a change of subject. So—just why the hell do you want to marry me? Don't you have any women on that ship of yours?"

He lifted a brow. "You want to talk about that now?"

She looked up at the caravores and grimaced. "Beats wondering about how much pressure that canopy can take."

"Good point." Rune settled her more comfortably against him. Cassidy braced her back against his chest. Surprisingly, his solid warmth was comforting. Enemy or not, he made a damn good ally just now. "To answer your question, men outnumber women on a Dharani Tribeship five to one."

She turned to look around at him in astonishment, so astonished she didn't glance up when one of the caravores jumped on the canopy again. "You're kidding me! *Why?*"

Rune shrugged, watching the animals prowling overhead. "We spent two hundred years trapped on the wrong side of the Tormod Front, cut off from the rest of human space by those damned aliens. The ships in our convoy were huge—intended to transport an entire population, along with everything we'd need to set up a self-sustaining colony."

"How many ships?"

"Ten of them, each with a population of five thousand. Most average twice that now." He grimaced. "Population pressure is a continuous problem."

"So what did you do when the Tormod started moving against the humans?"

Rune sighed. "We happened to be crossing a quadrant that was already heavily populated by other alien races. We tried appealing to them for help, but they refused. Mass starvation had already begun to set in when we discovered two of those worlds were fighting a war."

"So you became mercenaries."

"It was that or die."

One side of the fighter suddenly lifted a meter in the air, then dropped with a crunch. Cassidy swallowed a yelp as the two caravores above them tumbled off the canopy. "Well, that's some improvement, anyway." The ship shook. "More or less." She returned her attention to his story. "I still don't understand how you got from there to a predominantly male population."

"My leg is going to sleep." Rune shifted under her, drawing a thigh up. She obligingly shifted on his lap, seeking another position. "That's better. Come here." He drew her against him once more. "We were fighting aliens who were much stronger than humans, and our tech wasn't advanced enough to make up the difference. Many of us were killed. We turned to genetic engineering and the new nanotechnology we got from the aliens, hoping to improve our chances. Because our survival depended on creating the most effective warriors we could, we began producing more males."

"Not sure I'd agree with the underlying assumption."

He shrugged. "Men are bigger and generally stronger. Makes them easier to enhance. Besides, that wasn't the only reason. Our ships were big, but not that big, so . . ."

". . . Controlling the number of females made it easier to control your population."

"Right."

"Except after two hundred years of that, you've ended up with a lot of hyperaggressive men, and not nearly enough women to bleed off the sexual pressure." The fighter shimmied on its wheels. She threw a glance upward, but at least the caravores weren't digging at the canopy again.

He lifted one broad shoulder. "We manage. Successful warriors receive passes to the Women's Deck and—"

"Passes to the Women's Deck?" She gaped at him. "Like for sex?"

"Yes."

"Jesus. No wonder you tried to kidnap the first woman you met."

"Not the first," Rune corrected. "The first who was worthy."

She folded her arms and braced a shoulder against his chest, the better to meet his gaze. "Worthy. Right."

Evidently not recognizing the danger in her tone, he nodded. "Yes, based on your intelligence, your skill in battle, your courage. These are characteristics I wish for my sons."

"Who would also be my sons. And so far, the environment you're describing is not one I'd want for any child of mine."

Rune glowered as if stung. "You should. We're a strong people. Honor is all to us—unlike most in human space, who do whatever is convenient, no matter whom they must betray."

"I'm curious, Rune. How exactly is methodically scarring a young man's groin and nipples an 'honorable' activity?"

He stiffened, offended. "It's a very solemn religious ceremony, Cassidy. And it gives new warriors an opportunity to demonstrate their determination and worthiness to the tribe."

"Yeah? Just how old are these 'new warriors'?"

"Sixteen."

She gave him a long look. "So they sexually torture sixteen-year-old boys?"

"Among my people, a sixteen-year-old is no boy. I flew my first combat mission at sixteen."

"What'd your mother think about that—the combat mission and that 'ceremony'?"

His silence went on a little too long. Cassidy swore. "She was the one with the knife, wasn't she?"

Rune met her gaze, his level and defiant. "Should she have let another woman do such a delicate task? It was her duty."

She snorted. "Hell of a mother. Literally."

"Ulmana loved me, Cassidy. Until I was six years old, we were inseparable."

"Yeah?" She studied the hard, handsome lines of his face. "What happened when you turned six?"

He lifted a shoulder. "I went to live with my father and the warriors of my tribe. I learned combat skills, the importance of duty and hard work." Correctly interpreting the pity in her eyes, Rune glowered. "How many of your children are neglected and unwanted? We value our young."

"Oh, yeah. They make such good cannon fodder."

Rune glowered at her. "That was uncalled for."

"But true." She frowned, a detail of his story niggling at her. "Wait a minute—if you've got a population of ten thousand with one in five of them being women, that's only a couple of thousand females. How do you avoid committing incest? Sounds like a very shallow gene pool."

"No, because every ten years, the ten ships gather and trade off their teenagers."

"Ahhh. So you weren't raised on the *Conquest*." She considered the implications, envisioning thousands of teens suddenly cut off from their families. "Must have been lonely for you, losing everybody you knew."

"Not everybody. My Wing Brothers went to the same ship."

Cassidy lifted a brow. "Wing Brother?"

Rune nodded. "My best friends. We grew up together. Even

today we fly in the same combat wing. We . . ." He broke off, his eyes widening in horror. "Goddess curse it!" He lunged forward and hit a button, then swore again.

"What tripped your—shit!" The battery system light had gone out. Cassidy looked up at him in horror as the realization hit. "The solar collectors were on the wings!"

"With the caravores." He reached up for the canopy release. She started to protest, then realized the beasts had finally given up and wandered off. Rune pushed the canopy aside, lifted her off his lap, and vaulted out.

Grimly she followed him.

Chapter Seven

RUNE looked down at the smashed globe protruding from the wing and swore viciously. All four solar collectors had been wrecked—one snapped completely off its base, the other three crushed.

"Why the hell didn't you retract them back into the wing?" Cassidy demanded, her fists braced on her hips.

He raked a hand through his hair in frustration. "Because they were jammed—the manual controls weren't working. I had to come out here and deploy them by hand. And then there wasn't time to push them back in when the caravores came." Rune turned away from the device in disgust and stalked back up the wing. "I assumed they'd be sturdy enough to withstand the beasts."

She followed him, her boot heels clicking on the wing. "Yeah, well, you assumed wrong. Now what are we going to do?"

He shrugged. "Wait for a search party from my ship."

"*If* they send one, and *if* they can find us."

"I assure you, my Wing Brothers will make it their business to find us."

Cassidy bared her teeth at him. "Assuming my people don't get to us first. Or that those damn caravores don't come back and fuckin' *eat* us."

"If you have an alterative, I would be delighted to hear it."

"There's a settlement about a week's walk from here," she said. "There's a mountain range between us and it, but I don't think we'd have trouble climbing it. They'd have communication equipment, maybe a transport."

He turned to look at her. "Cassidy, I'm an enemy combatant. They will not willingly help me."

"We can't stay out here indefinitely, Rune."

She had a point. "I could take what I need—a beamer, a com system capable of reaching the *Conquest*." He surveyed the wrecked fighter. "Better than sitting out here waiting for a surprise visit from the enemy. However . . ." Rune turned to look down into Cassidy's clever face. "Once we climb that mountain range of yours, we will be in com range of the settlement. I can't allow you to call them."

Something flickered in those green eyes, and he knew that was just what she planned to do. His lovely enemy did not lie well. "Rune . . ."

"I will not be taken prisoner, Cassidy. If you bring the local authorities down on us, my duty as a Dharani warrior will require me to kill you, then as many of them as I can, and then myself."

Green eyes widened. He'd actually managed to shock her. "You'd do that?"

"Yes. My honor would not permit anything else."

"But it's not necessary." Cassidy shook her head. "Rune, even if you were captured, you'd be sent back to the *Conquest* after the war's over."

"I wouldn't even be allowed to set foot on that ship. I'd be expected to suicide in the airlock rather than bring my stained honor aboard. And I'd do it without hesitation. I have no desire to live with that shame of being captured."

"That's ridiculous!"

He sighed, realizing it would be difficult to make her understand. "Cassidy, honor is all a Dharani warrior has. Without it, we're nothing."

"Look, no matter how good a warrior is, sometimes he just has bad luck. That has nothing to do with honor or ability, and anybody with any knowledge of combat knows that."

"You don't understand. You're not Dharani."

"Thank God!"

They were wasting time. "Pack up your rations. We're going to need something to eat on the walk."

With a huff of frustration, Cassidy slid down into the cockpit, jerked open a panel in a console, and dragged out her emergency pack. She unsealed it, revealing spare beamer batteries—dead thanks to the Pulse—ration bars, and a couple of tight bundles his comp identified as a sleep sack and a tent. Cassidy dug around until she located a canteen, then pulled it out and tilted it to her mouth for a drink.

Rune licked his dry lips, suddenly realizing how thirsty he was. He'd have to get his own supplies out of his wrecked fighter. With any luck they had survived the crash better than the craft had.

To his surprise, Cassidy reached up and handed him the canteen before scrambling out of the cockpit. Giving her a long look, he took a sip and handed it back to her. "Thank you."

"Figured you were thirsty," she said gruffly, tucking it away before slinging the pack across her shoulder.

Together they hopped off the wing; Cassidy followed him as he strode back toward his own fighter. He could almost feel her tension.

Despite her generosity with the canteen, she still had the knife he'd given her when the caravores had attacked the ship. And judging by the agitation his sensors detected, she was trying to decide whether to use it.

"I'm tempted to tie you up," he told her as they walked. "But the chances are good we'd encounter some more of the local predators on the trip, and I'd rather you could defend yourself. On the other hand, I really don't want that blade in my back, either. If you give me your word you won't attack me, I'll leave your hands free."

Cassidy studied him, her gaze speculative. She didn't seem surprised he'd read her intent. "You're assuming you can tie me up again."

"I can."

She made a sound halfway between a snort and a laugh. "Every time you say something like that, I itch to prove you wrong."

Rune sighed and stopped, dropping into a combat crouch.

For a long, vibrating moment they stared at each other. Finally she broke the stalemate with a roll of her eyes. "Hell with it. It's been a long, exhausting day, and I'm not in the mood for another fight."

"Give me your word you won't attack me."

Now faint amusement broke through her tired frustration. "You'd take the word of mercenary?"

"Most mercenaries, no."

She stopped and looked at him thoughtfully. "But I'm an exception?"

Rune shrugged. "I fought you. I know how you think. And yes, you are an honorable opponent."

Cassidy huffed out a laugh and shook her head. "Just when I want to punch in your teeth, you say something like that." She sighed. "Look, I can't promise I won't fight you, but I won't ambush you, either."

Rune contemplated the compromise, then nodded slowly. "Keep the knife."

✢ ✢ ✢

THEY walked through the alien forest in silence. His emergency pack slung over one shoulder, Rune moved with all his senses alert as his computer did a constant scan for predators. He had no intention of being taken off guard again.

At the moment it looked as if they were safe. There was nothing larger than small rodents and birds for kilometers.

Which meant he could safely attend to Cassidy.

Though she walked freely at his side, she had withdrawn from him. *What do you expect, fool?* Rune's mouth tightened into a grim line. *You just threatened to kill her if she calls the authorities.*

Still, he didn't regret telling her the truth. First, it might make her hesitate to com the colonists.

More than that, he'd rather be honest with her. She needed to know what her situation was. Deception had never suited him anyway, regardless of the cause.

On the other hand, he had to do something to tear down the emotional barriers she was busily constructing between them.

And sex was the best weapon he had.

He knew she liked his body. He'd glimpsed admiration in her gaze even before he'd challenged her back in the clearing. So as they walked, padding through the thick ferny undergrowth, Rune opened the seal of his armor and shrugged out of the sleeves.

"What are you doing?" she demanded, turning to watch as he peeled the top half of the suit down to let it hang around his waist.

"It's too hot to wear all this armor without a functioning coolant system." Rune let his head fall back, sighing in elaborate pleasure at the cool breeze that kissed his bare, sweating chest.

Cassidy gave him a tart glare. "You'll wish you kept it on if more caravores show up."

"My sensors will detect them in plenty of time, now that I know they're a threat." He glanced at her slyly. "You might want to loosen your suit, too. You wouldn't want to get heatstroke."

"I'll risk it," she said tightly.

Controlling a grin, Rune reached for his canteen, popped the top, and lifted it to his mouth. The distilling unit in the little device pulled water molecules out of the air, so it wouldn't run dry.

He pretended not to notice the way Cassidy watched him, eyes darkening as he tilted his head back to drink. *Just wait, sweet,* he thought, silently toasting her. *This is only the opening salvo.*

The heat was only part of the reason he'd taken the suit top off. Without the thick armor to absorb them, the pheromones in his sweat would soon start to work on her libido again. And judging by past experience, it wouldn't take Cassidy long to feel the burn.

"Beautiful day," Rune commented, clipping the canteen to his belt again.

"It's too damn hot," she grumbled. One gloved hand went to the top clip of her suit and opened it. She hesitated a moment, then opened two more, revealing a narrow V of pale flesh. Her cheeks were flushed and sweating.

He glanced over at her and frowned. He really did need to get her out of that armor, and for more than carnal reasons. She was dangerously close to overheating.

"Drink more," Rune ordered.

Cassidy lifted a brow at him. "Who died and made you my captain?"

"I'm not your captain—I'm your captor. And I don't want to have to stop and nurse you back to health when you keel over from heat stroke. Drink more water, curse you, or I'm going to strip you out of that armor myself."

Giving him a long, steady look, she unclipped her canteen and took a drink. "Feel better now?"

"Much. Open a few more of those clips."

"You're pushing it, Alrigo." But she opened the suit all the way down to her flat little belly.

He still didn't like her color, though. *Computer, are there any bodies of water nearby?*

Senors indicate a pond 1.2 kilometers southwest.

That'll do. He changed direction.

"Where are we headed?" Cassidy lengthened her stride to keep up with him.

"There's a pond up ahead. We both need to cool off. Besides, it's time to make camp."

✦ ✦ ✦

THE pond was perfect.

Rune surveyed it with satisfaction. It was no bigger than the warrior's bath on the *Conquest*—barely a hundred feet across, backed on one side by a cliff. A waterfall tumbled down the rock wall, hissing and thudding on the surrounding stone. Apparently the pond had an underground outflow somewhere, since there was no river to carry the water away.

"It looks . . . cool," Cassidy said, longing in her voice.

Rune looked over his shoulder at her and smiled darkly. "Yes, it does."

Without another word, he started stripping, toeing off his boots and pushing the suit the rest of the way down his legs.

"Uhhhhh . . ." Cassidy said, sounding strangled.

"Nothing you haven't seen before." Balancing on one leg, he pulled the other from the suit. Finally free, he picked the armor up, folded it neatly, and started for the pond.

As he waded into the water, Rune was intensely conscious of Cassidy's fascinated gaze. His comp scanning for hidden dangers, he headed toward the waterfall at the other end.

"I know what you're doing, and it's not going to work." She glowered at him, attempting defiance. "I'm not having sex with you."

He looked back at her just before he stepped under the cool tumble of the waterfall. "Aren't you?"

Chapter Eight

THE falls pounded Rune's broad shoulders as he threw back his head under the stream. The muscles in his tight, delicious ass shifted under the brown satin of his skin. His sigh of pleasure made her nipples peak.

"Not this time," Cassidy gritted, as much to herself as him. "I'm *not* letting you seduce me. Or have you forgotten you threatened to kill me an hour ago?"

He turned to face her, spreading his brawny arms wide. The spray hit his muscled body and bounced. "I merely wanted you to know the risks. I could have hidden the truth from you, but that's not my way."

"I noticed—jerk," Cassidy grumbled. That was Rune. Honesty and honor, the cost be damned. She lifted her voice to be heard over the falls. "But I'm still not having sex with you."

He only laughed and turned his back again. For a moment he

stood looking up at the falls, letting the spray splash on the hard, strong planes of his handsome face.

"It feels good." Rune turned to face her with a groan of pleasure. "Very good. You should join me."

Cassidy caught her breath at the sight of him. The water bounced and danced on his broad shoulders, rolling down his sculpted torso and the tight ridges of his abdomen. His cock stood high and hard, bouncing slightly under the gentle pounding. His wet skin gleamed in the sunlight, the effect throwing the intricate scarring around his cock into high relief.

She cleared her throat. "You do realize you're washing off all those sweaty pheromones of yours?"

His pale gaze met hers as his teeth flashed in a wicked smile. "I don't need pheromones to get to you, Cassidy." Slowly he brushed one big hand down his chest and wrapped it around his meaty cock. "Do I?"

Cassidy glowered and propped both fists on her hips, trying to ignore the hungry knot of need gathering in her belly. "You are *such* an arrogant asshole."

He lowered his lids and cupped his heavy balls in his free hand. "I have a lot to be arrogant about."

God, he did. He really did.

With a huff Cassidy turned her back on him. Dammit, she was not letting him do this to her.

Not again.

No matter how gorgeous and sexy he was, no matter how delicious that big dick was, he was Dharani, and he'd taken her captive.

She'd thought she could use his potent sexuality against him, but he'd turned out to be a lot better at that than she was. It was time to cut her losses and keep her distance. There was absolutely nothing to be gained from playing his game.

Well, except for the howling orgasm.

Cut it out, Cassidy.

Rune groaned in pleasure again, the sound mixing with the musical patter of the water. He raised his voice to be heard over the falls. "Goddess, this feels good. Aren't you hot?"

In more than one sense of the word. She growled in frustration, feeling sweat rolling in itching trails between her shoulder blades and down the crack of her backside. "You're a sadistic bastard, you know that?"

"And *you* are a masochist," he shot back. "Otherwise you'd be in here with me, instead of courting heatstroke inside all that armor."

"Dammit!" With a growl she grabbed the edges of her suit and started stripping it off. Pride notwithstanding, she wasn't an idiot. He was right—if she didn't get cool soon, she was going to be in serious trouble.

She thought she heard him laugh.

The minute she was naked, Cassidy turned around and waded in before plunging her entire body underwater. When she surfaced again, he was waiting. She wasn't surprised.

Rune stood with those brawny thighs braced wide apart, one hand still caressing his impressive cock. Instantly a searing memory flashed through her consciousness—the way he'd felt as he'd worked his way into her by slow, delicious increments.

He was looking at her breasts. The tip of his tongue touched his lower lip, and he slowly slid his hand from the base of his cock to just behind the plum-sized glans. "Feels good, doesn't it?" he asked. "All that water touching you, sliding across your skin. So cool, so soft. Making your nipples so hard." His lids dipped. The long, dark fingers of his left hand rolled his heavy balls. He let his head fall back. "I remember the way they taste. Musk and heat and sex." His right hand pumped again, slowly. The head of his erection glistened as it bobbed. The spray struck his face, rolled down his chin and the powerful column of his throat. Slid into the thatch of wet, slick hair on his chest, then down his belly with its intricate patterns of barbarism and suffering. "I want you in my mouth again."

God, Cassidy ached to taste *him* too. She wanted to close her lips around that tempting glans and drive him as insane as he was driving her.

And why not? Why not let him feel her power for once? It would be so sweet to make him beg. . . .

Dumb, a soft mental voice protested. *Very dumb. Touch him and he's got you.*

Oh, yeah, a softer, darker voice purred. *And it'll be delicious.*

Until he tries to kill you. Or worse yet, until he drags you off to be his whore.

He'll try to do all that anyway, whether you touch him or not, the dark voice pointed out. *At least this way you'll have a taste of him. At least this way you'll have a chance to make* him *beg.* And she wanted him to beg her. At least once.

He kept getting the best of her.

It was her turn.

Cassidy moved toward Rune, her gaze fixed on that slowly pumping hand. Eyes closed, he gasped in pleasure as the water struck his face. Dropping his head, he grimaced, droplets beading on the blade of his nose. She felt her sex clench and heat even more at the sight of his extravagantly feral pleasure.

"Let me." She dropped to her knees in front of him. Gasped as the cool water closed over her hot breasts.

His eyes flared wide as he looked down at her, very silver, oddly startled. "What are you doing?"

"What do you think?" She leaned forward and caught his wrist. Pulled his hand away from his cock and replaced it with her own. Aimed the fat, luscious head toward her mouth.

"That's not something my people . . ." Then he sucked in a breath and stiffened as she closed her lips around him. Sucking hard, she took him deep, one hand cupping the taut muscles of his ass as the other held his thick cock.

"Goddess!" Rune drew back, trying to pull his cock free of her lips. She refused to let him go, instead sucking so hard her cheeks went hollow.

"Cassidy, don't . . ." He sounded shocked. "You should not . . ."

Damn, she realized in delight, *he's never had a blow job before!*

How was it possible that Rune, hyper-masculine Dharani warrior, had never had a woman suck him off?

Oh, Cassidy thought in delight, *I've got him now!*

Wickedly she swirled her tongue over and around the satin head. Sucking hard, she drew back to the tip of his shaft, raked it gently with her teeth, then slid him back into her mouth.

She'd never tried to deep throat a man—her gag reflex made it too uncomfortable—but Rune's stunned groan goaded her. Greedily she fed more and more of him into her mouth, tilting her head and shoulders to find the right angle.

He moaned, the sound helpless and erotic coming from such a powerful man. His long fingers curled around the back of her head with a strength that felt involuntary. He began to roll his hips in tiny thrusts.

She nibbled. Suckled. Licked. Found his heavy balls and stroked them between her fingers.

"Stop," Rune gasped. "I will come if you . . ."

Cassidy grinned around his cock and sucked harder. He tasted like distilled masculinity, hot and potent and fierce.

She loved it. Loved the way he writhed as she suckled him. She could feel his balls tightening in her hand.

Power surged through her, intoxicating, deliciously arousing. He was at her mercy now, and she loved it.

"I said *stop*!" Strong hands closed around her upper arms, dragged her up and off the luscious shaft.

Before she knew what hit her, she was in his arms. He turned with her, pushed her against the wet cliff wall. Rough, cold stone pressed into her back. Blazing silver eyes met hers through the falling spray as he caught her behind the legs, jerked them upward. Spread her.

Cassidy yowled as Rune found the opening of her slick cunt and speared it in a rush of stone-hard erection. Bracing her against the cliff, he began to thrust, grinding hard. "I . . . told you— that's . . . not something . . . our women . . . *do*!"

She gave him a savage grin. "But you liked it!"

Rune's glittering gaze met hers as the water thundered around them. "Yes. Goddess, yes!"

He kissed her, his lips hungry, demanding. Licking and nipping at her mouth just as she'd worked his cock. Giving her no quarter.

Not that she wanted any.

Rune began to thrust, slowly at first, then harder, faster, in long, creamy strokes that jarred her against the stone and made her shudder at his thick power.

Cassidy tore her mouth from his and cried out, digging her nails into the bunching muscle of his back. God, it felt so good!

Bracing her bare heels against his thighs, she ground back at him, taking him, feeling her climax build like a burning storm.

He growled something at her in Dharani, the words liquid and alien as he surged into her grip. Grabbing the back of her head, he pulled her into another devouring kiss.

Moaning, on fire, she rolled her hips as he pounded her without mercy, his strokes long and savage and impossibly delicious.

Until at last he hurled her into a screaming orgasm, heat and pleasure surging through her body until her every nerve and muscle jerked and danced. Even as she writhed in his arms, he bellowed, a raw male cry of pleasure. She felt him pump deep within her slick depths.

"Rune!" She clawed at his shoulders, maddened.

"Cassidy . . ." He gasped, shuddering against her. "Goddess, Cassidy . . ."

Long, fiery moments went by before his arms lost their impressive strength, and he let her slide down his body. He took a staggering step back.

Cassidy braced her trembling legs apart and managed a grin of triumph. "Got you."

She half expected him to get angry at the taunt. Instead he threw back his head and laughed. "Oh, yes. You certainly did." Then that cool silver gaze met hers again, and heat flashed through it. "This time."

Cassidy shivered, knowing he was going to seek a deliciously erotic revenge.

She also knew she'd probably enjoy every minute of it.

Chapter Nine

"OKAY, I'm dying to ask—how is it you've never had a blow job?"

Rune shrugged. They had staggered out of the pool to collapse together on the sun-warmed ground. Now his chest hair tickled Cassidy's cheek as she lay draped over him in sleepy lassitude. "As I said, it's not something our women do. It's . . . servile."

She lifted her head and stared at him. "Do I look servile to you, stud? Besides, you don't seem to have a problem doing it."

He grinned. "On the contrary, I don't give blow jobs, either."

"Smartass. You know what I mean."

He threaded his hand through her hair and contemplated the remains of her braids. Casually he went to work unwrapping them. "A Dharani warrior is expected to know how to pleasure and arouse a woman. It's a necessary skill, if one expects to be invited to a *Mahiri's* bed."

Cassidy fisted one hand on his chest, then propped her chin on top of it. "I had the impression you just flashed your pussy pass and the ladies just . . . accommodated you. And what's a *Mahiri*?"

Rune frowned, a line forming between his dark brows. "It doesn't translate well. High woman? Mistress?" Releasing her hair, he reared up and braced his elbows behind him, the better to meet her eyes. "But what was that you called it? *Pussy pass?*"

She shrugged, realizing there was genuine offense in his eyes. "Well, you said something about getting a pass to the women's deck, and I thought—"

"It's not a brothel, Cassidy. A warrior is invited to the women's deck to recount his exploits, to display his skills—not *those* skills," he added, reading her grin. "Singing, poetry, dancing, perhaps hand-to-hand combat with another fighter. If he manages to impress, one of the *Mahiri* may invite him to her bed. And he'd best know what to do when he gets there, or he won't be invited back."

"Dancing?" Biting down on her lip, Cassidy managed to suppress her snort of laughter at the sly image that appeared in her mind. Fierce Dharani warriors staging *Swan Lake* for a bunch of pampered women, all in hopes of getting laid . . . "I gather you fight."

"No, any tribesman is expected to be able to fight. I sing. It gains their attention." Reading her skepticism, he said, "I'm considered to have a very good voice."

"Yeah? Sing something."

She expected him to demur—most men of her acquaintance would have. But Rune being Rune, he wasn't going to back down from a challenge of any kind. He sat up as Cassidy moved back to give him room, folding her legs under her as she settled in to listen.

For a moment he looked across the pond, a distant look on his face. A slight smile curved his seductive mouth.

Then he began to sing.

His voice was a lush baritone, deep and seductive. Even though she didn't understand Dharani, the liquid, slightly guttural words made the song sound like distilled sex. The effect was only enhanced when he turned to give her that hot, heavy-lidded silver gaze.

Yet there was more than sex in his eyes—there was a tenderness and admiration that seemed completely genuine. Looking into his handsome face, Cassidy felt something draw into a tight, warm ball in her chest.

When his song finally drew to its gently pleading end, she had to clear her throat before she could manage anything suitably teasing. "It's really not fair. Women would sleep with you just for that voice. Add the rest of the package, and we don't have a prayer."

One corner of Rune's mouth curled up in blatant male satisfaction. "Good."

"You've got no shame at all, do you?"

"Not really, no."

She shook her head and tried throw off his spell with a change of subject. "So what do your women do when they're not having sex or being entertained? *Do* they do anything when they're not having sex or being entertained?"

"Of course." He looked a bit indignant at the suggestion. "They raise the children, of course, but they also serve on the ship's council, deciding maters of justice, administration, and policy. And they perform the genetic engineering to create our warriors, deciding who will be permitted to father children. That is one reason they have such power."

Cassidy asked the question softly, seriously. "But do they pilot fighters?"

Rune went still, as if realizing where she was going with that. "Our women don't serve in combat. They're too precious to risk."

Bracing an elbow on her knee, she met his gaze steadily. "Rune, all I ever wanted to do was fly. I can't let you take that away from me."

He flinched just slightly. "Cassidy . . ."

"My parents weren't mercenaries," she said softly. If she could only make him understand that he couldn't turn her into some kind of hothouse plant, she wouldn't have to kill him. And the more time she spent with him, the more she hated that idea. "They were hydroponics farmers. But from the time I was a small child, I was fascinated by flight—by the freedom of it, by the romance of the air."

Naked, he rose to his feet and moved away from her, but she stood and followed him.

"I joined my colony's space defense force. I loved being in the cockpit, watching the ground fall away and curve below me. I loved the punch of acceleration, the roar of the engines."

Rune crouched to examine one of the bamboolike stands of trees that surrounded the pond. The set of his shoulders shouted that he didn't want to hear what she had to say, but Cassidy had no intention of letting him off that easy.

"Then Acron's Space Force went through a budget crunch, and a bunch of us were released from service. I found myself without a job—or a fighter to fly."

That got his attention. He looked at her, frowning. "What did you do?"

"What could I do?" As she watched, he drew his knife and

began to hack at the base of the small tree. "I couldn't give up fly-ing, but I had no interest in becoming a passenger pilot. I wanted to fly fighters."

"So you became a mercenary." He broke the trunk free and began to cut off the small branches.

"Yes, though it wasn't that easy. I had to get nanotech im-plants before I could find a ship willing to take me on. I had to use all my payoff from the service to pay for the procedure, and I was flat broke for months."

Rune frowned, obviously troubled at the idea of Cassidy in such straits. Encouraged, she continued, "Eventually I was able to sign on with a mercenary vessel. I served on three other ships be-fore I met Captain August and joined the crew of the *Starrunner*."

Still frowning, he turned to carry his knife and pole back toward his pack. Cassidy strode after him. "You don't seriously think I'm going to let you take away my wings?"

He tossed down the pole and got to work unloading his pack. The frown he aimed at her was forbidding. "Cassidy, I challenged you to a Claiming Duel, and you lost. You belong to me."

Frustrated, she glared at him. "Stud, I don't belong to anybody but myself."

"Does your honor mean that little to you?"

"Dammit, Rune, I didn't know what a 'Claiming Duel' was! You didn't tell me. I thought it was to the death. You can't hold me to—"

"I can. I do." He turned and took one long step until his boots tapped her toes. "You are mine."

"Fuck off."

"I won your life. I could have taken it, but I spared you. Every breath you take, you owe to me."

Cassidy bunched her fists and gritted, "You are *not* doing this to me! *I will not allow it.*"

"You can't stop me."

"Watch me, stud. And watch your back." She whirled to stalk off, but a big hand landed on her shoulder.

Rune spun her around and snatched her into his arms. His mouth crashed down on hers, muffling her outraged snarl. She planted her hands against his chest and shoved, knocking him back a pace. For a moment they stood staring at each other, breathing hard in fury and frustration.

Then he surged toward her.

The fight that followed was short and nasty, but it ended with Cassidy on her face in the leaves as Rune bound her wrists behind her back. To her grim satisfaction, blood streamed from his upper lip. She'd gotten in one good punch.

But she'd still lost.

✝ ✝ ✝

PATIENTLY Rune wrapped coil after coil of cord around the hilt of his knife, working to tie it to the pole he'd found to create a serviceable spear. The balance would likely be poor, but at least it would give him some reach if the caravores attacked again.

Though at the moment he supposed he should be more concerned about what Cassidy would do to him when she got free. And it wasn't as if he could keep her tied up forever.

He glanced over at her as she lay on her side against the wall of the tent he'd erected. Her green eyes burned with sullen rage. Her arms moved restlessly as she pulled at her bonds. Despite his superior strength, it had been all he could do to get the restraints on her.

He'd say one thing for Cassidy: She didn't give up.

Suppressing a sigh, Rune studied the new spear, then put it aside and picked up the other knife and pole. As he went to work making the second weapon, he brooded.

He'd thought he was making good progress in stirring her affections. Her body definitely responded to his, and he'd sensed a warming in her attitude.

Now he knew he had a very long way to go.

But he'd get there, Rune thought, wrapping the cord around the knife hilt.

He didn't give up, either.

Eventually he'd make her care about him. She'd find his love and the love of their children would compensate her for what she'd lost.

His hands slowed in their work, and his frown deepened as he remembered the light in her eyes when she'd spoken of flying. There was no question she loved being in the cockpit.

Did he have the right to take that away from her?

Dharani philosophy insisted he did. He'd won their battle, and he kept proving he could seduce her no matter how she tried to fight him. She belonged to him by right, and she should feel honor bound to yield.

Yet . . . he also knew that if he'd been in her place, he wouldn't have stopped fighting, either. That was one of the things he found so appealing about her: He understood her. Admired her fire and her courage, her intelligence and sense of duty. Her beauty added to her attraction, but wasn't the deciding factor. After all, there were many beautiful women on the Tribeship. None of them spoke to his spirit the way Cassidy did.

He was falling in love with her.

It felt as if the bottom had dropped out of Rune's stomach. It couldn't be. They barely knew one another. Only a few hours before, he'd been doing his best to kill her.

And yet . . . he felt as if he'd met the other half of his soul, like a hero in some Dharani ballad. He knew her, recognized her, on a level that went beyond thought or reason. She wasn't just a warrior with desirable virtues he wanted as the mother of his sons—she was Cassidy Vika, pilot and mercenary, as fiery and brilliant as she was beautiful.

And he needed her. He'd been lonely far too long. Even among his Wing Brothers, he'd had the sense of being isolated. Though they'd grown up with him, Kaveh, Ymir, and Tyrkir did not really understand him. They lived only for flying, sex, and honor. If any of them needed anything more, he'd never seen any evidence of it. Goddess knew when he'd tried to talk of something beyond dueling and women, he'd gotten nothing more than blank looks.

But did winning a fight—or even falling in love with Cassidy—give Rune the right to take her wings away?

Chapter Ten

CASSIDY dreamed of engines. For several long, sweet moments, she was back in the cockpit.

Then the familiar rumble pulled her out of sleep.

When she opened her eyes, she found Rune sitting up, his attention focused on the tent flap. The low-pitched rumble grew into a howl, as if a craft hovered right overhead. Probably a transport of some kind; the pitch was wrong for a fighter.

"Who the hell is that?" She tried to sit up, only to discover her wrists were still bound behind her back.

"My people."

Cassidy's stomach dropped like a stone. *No!* As she silently cursed in dread, he rolled to his feet and left the tent. Despite her bound wrists, she scrambled to her feet and followed him.

She wanted to throw up.

They were here. He was going to take her to that ship of his, and she'd be trapped on the *Conquest* for good. Never to fly again. Nothing but a toy for him and a baby machine for a culture she already knew she'd hate.

Fury steamed in to drown her despair. *How dare he do this to her!*

As she shrugged her way out of the tent, Cassidy saw a transport shuttle just sitting down. Its stubby wings rocked before it settled into a patch of moonlit vegetation.

"Mushy landing," she muttered, not at all impressed. The pilot either didn't have Rune's skills, or he was drunk. And what kind of idiot flew drunk, when his implant could sober him up in seconds?

Drunk or not, though, the pilot had come ready for damn near anything. The transport was a boxy, heavily armed affair, bristling with beamer cannons that looked as if they'd seen recent use, judging from the sear patterns around them.

Yet instead of running to meet his rescuers, Rune held back as the airlock cycled open and three men leaped out to swagger toward them, calling greetings in Dharani.

Computer, translate, Cassidy ordered. She damned well wanted to know what they were talking about.

. . . Come to rescue our lost Wing Brother, and how do we find him? one of them was saying, her comp translating his words in a mental whisper. *Safe, warm, and all cuddled up with a woman.*

Another, a big blond, gave Cassidy a dark look as the three stopped to eye her and Rune. "An enemy female, at that, by the looks of that uniform."

Rune stiffened, but his tone was calm and level as he answered. "I challenged her to a Claiming Duel and won."

The third one barked out a laugh and elbowed his friends. "Rune caught himself a Breeder!"

Laughing, all three men pushed in close, jostling Rune as they tried to get a look at her.

"Hey! Back off, you lot," Rune protested, stiff-arming the blond back. "She's mine."

"Actually," Cassidy said coolly, "I'm mine." Raising her chin at them, she glared in warning.

The three hooted and elbowed each other. Judging from the fumes, they'd done some celebrating before they'd come looking for their Wing Brother.

Funny job to attempt drunk, Cassidy thought waspishly.

"Sounds like Rune hasn't taught her her place yet," the blond told the others, giving her a narrow-eyed sneer.

Drunk or not, she had to admit they were a handsome trio, just as tall and broad-shouldered as Rune himself. Beefy, muscular warriors in full armor, each was as strikingly handsome as her captor.

Yet there was a faint unsteadiness in each move and a trace of something ugly in their eyes.

Definitely drunk.

A moment later her comp confirmed that suspicion, and she silently cursed. Just great. Worse yet, all three wore holstered beamers. Beamers that worked. And here she was, tied up and unarmed.

Surreptitiously she twisted her hands around and began plucking at the cold cable around her wrists, knowing even as she made the attempt that it was useless. There was no way to untie or break mag restraints, even with her strength. The cable was keyed to respond only to Rune's touch or the orders of his computer.

Definitely a problem, because something told her she didn't want to be bound and helpless with these three around.

When the big blond reached for her a second time, Rune stepped in his path with an easy smile. "I'm grateful for the rescue, but I'm surprised to see you so soon. Did we win?"

The blond snorted. "Not likely. The idiot Kalistans sued for peace."

Rune frowned, obviously as surprised as Cassidy. The war had certainly been in full swing when they'd taken off yesterday. "Why?"

The tall, dark-haired warrior spread his hands in a gesture of disgust. "The Galvestonians may not have much of a navy, but thanks to those trillite mines, they've got more money than the Goddess. And they used it to hire a second mercenary fleet."

"Six hours ago that fleet popped into Kalistan space and locked weapons on the capital city," the redhead finished. "The dirtsucking Kalistans caved right in."

Rune swore. "The Galvestonians used their mercenaries here as a diversionary force."

"Exactly. And with the Kalistan navy tied up in this system running the invasion, they're not in a defensible position." The blond shrugged. "So they declared a truce and started negotiations. I suspect the war will be over in a week, if that."

Cassidy hid a satisfied smile. At least the bastard Kalistans had lost, even if she'd ended up on the wrong end of her battle with Rune.

"So we took the opportunity to search for you and do a little raiding," the redhead put in. "And here you are—with the perfect way to kill time." He gave Cassidy a genial leer.

She definitely didn't like the way this was going. Time to nip this in the bud and pray her captor would back her up. "Rune, if you seriously think I'm going to do all four of you, you're out of your mind." Her tone did not leave him room for argument.

"Of course not. I . . . ." Rune turned to look over his shoulder at her. The blond picked that moment to snake out a hand and snatch her from behind him.

Suddenly Cassidy was plastered against the big bastard, one of his hands clamped onto her butt, the other gripping her head. Before she could even spit a protest, his mouth crashed down over hers, wet and blatantly contemptuous.

She promptly caught his thrusting tongue between her teeth and bit down.

With an muffled shout of outrage, the blond shoved her back and lifted a big fist. Rune grabbed his wrist before he could hit her. "What in the Goddess's name do you think you're doing?"

"She bit me!" the blond growled.

"What do you expect?" Rune threw his hand off. His obvious fury made Cassidy feel a little better. At least he didn't plan to feed her to his drunken friends. "You touched her without her permission. You know better than—"

"Permission?" Contempt rendered the blond's handsome face tight and ugly. "I need no permission from the likes of a Breeder!"

"But you need mine, and I have not given it."

Cassidy frowned, not liking the sound of that at all. These guys could just grab her whenever they wanted? Rune hadn't said anything about that.

The dark-haired one stepped between Rune and the blond, his tone elaborately reasonable. "As I recall, we four took a vow—the first to capture a Breeder would share her with the others. You swore to it, too, Rune."

"That's right!" the redhead caroled. He was obviously the drunkest of the three. "And I haven't had a woman in months!" He reached for Cassidy, but she stepped nimbly out of the way.

Eyeing the three, she glared. "Rune, you are *not* going to pass me around like a party favor."

"You heard her, she's not willing," Rune said, shoving the redhead back a pace when he tried to lunge past again.

"So?" The blond glowered. "She's a Breeder—she allowed herself to be taken captive instead of choosing an honorable death. She doesn't have the right to refuse."

"Besides, we get in that tent with her and let her breathe pheromones from all four of us, and she'll be plenty eager for it." The redhead gave her a drunken leer. "In ten minutes she'll be begging. We just need to hold her down for a bit, and—"

"Are you rapists, then?" Rune's tone was so cold, even Cassidy flinched.

"You can't rape a Breeder," the dark one protested. "That's what they're *for*."

Suddenly the blond stepped right up against Rune, so close their weapons' belts touched. "I have fought by your side since we left the Women's Deck as boys. How many times have I saved your life?"

Rune lifted his chin. "As many times as I've saved yours."

"We all have," the dark man added.

The redhead lifted his voice in a drunken shout. "Wing Brothers for life!"

"Yes. Wing Brothers." His expression chill, the blond looked directly into Rune's eyes. "Now. I want to sample your Breeder, Wing Brother. *Get out of the way.*"

Cassidy sucked in a breath and waited to find out if she was about to be raped.

One way or another, she wasn't going to go down easy.

+ + +

RUNE looked into Kaveh's cold gray stare and felt his life spiraling out of control. Sweat rolled down his back under his armor, itching savagely. He ignored it.

These men were his brothers. He'd grown up with them, fought for them, bled for them, got drunk and schemed and seduced *Mahiris* with them. When they'd been traded to the *Conquest* as boys, Kaveh, Ymir, and Tyrkir had been the only friends he'd had.

Now they wanted Cassidy.

But he'd seen them with Breeders before. They'd try to use her like a piece of meat, and he was damned if he'd allow it.

Yet it was also brutally obvious Kaveh had no intention of letting him refuse.

Agonized, he looked over his shoulder at her. She was staring at Kaveh, her expression grim and set, every muscle in her lean body obviously ready for battle. It wasn't in her to let them take her. And if she fought them, they'd hurt her.

At that thought, a cold, angry determination filled him. Nothing and no one was going to abuse Cassidy Vika as long as Rune was alive to stop it. If he had to take them all on, so be it.

But maybe it was still possible to talk some sense into Kaveh. Though the group often followed Rune's lead, it was Kaveh they looked to when he opposed them. If Rune could only convince him to back off, the others would follow. If not, the situation would implode.

"You said she has no honor. That's not true. She fought with courage, intelligence, and skill. She will be the mother of my sons. I will not allow her to be hurt."

"And I am your Wing Brother." Kaveh curled his lip. "Does some defeated cunt mean more to you than your brothers?"

He was losing control of this, and Cassidy was still bound and helpless. *Comp, release her mag bonds.* "I vowed to protect her, Kaveh."

"We're not going to hurt her," Ymir said, throwing his red hair back from his face with a toss of his head. "Just fuck her a little." He smirked and turned a predatory leer on the open front of her armor. "All right, a lot."

Rune's anger turned to rage. "I said no. I gave her my vow!"

"You took a vow to us, too," Tyrkir pointed out. "And we've shared women before. It's not like you to be so possessive."

Kaveh laughed, the sound an ugly bark. He wheeled toward the others. "He's smitten! Our Wing Brother is smitten with a Breeder! He thinks himself in love!"

Tyrkir gave him a long look as he silently cursed. "Is this true?"

"Look at his face," Kaveh spat. "You know it is."

"Hey, now—it's one thing to become infatuated with a *Mahiri,* but a Breeder?" Ymir said, drunken concern in his blue eyes. "That's not good. People will say you've gone weak."

Rune turned to give his friend a long narrow look. An accusation of weakness would be fatal. "Any man who says such a thing of me will soon be stuffing his guts back in his belly."

"Then you'll find yourself fighting every warrior on the *Conquest,* because it's true." Sick jealousy burned in Kaveh's green eyes. "I can smell it on you like a stench. You've fallen in love with her. It's been less than a day, and already she's got you wrapped up tight."

Rune hit him.

The jolt of fist on face was visceral and satisfying. It sent Kaveh flying. He hit the ground rolling and flipped himself back to his feet.

His beamer was in his hand, aimed right at Cassidy. "I can't believe you'd choose a cunt Breeder over your brothers."

Kaveh fired.

Chapter Eleven

CASSIDY was already diving for cover. She felt the blazing tingle of the blast's nimbus wash across her calf, heard the *chokzaaaap* of its passage. Close. Too close. He'd nail her with the next shot.

An arm clamped hard around her waist, lifting off her feet, throwing her forward. Another sizzling jolt, this one so close she cried out in pain at the heat across her face.

Rune bellowed hoarsely in her ear, his grip tightening as he reeled on, dragging her with him.

Shit. He'd shielded her with his body—and he'd been hit. If he hadn't taken it himself, the bolt would have struck her right in the head.

Another step and she landed on her feet as Rune went down on one knee. Cassidy kept going, segueing into an attack on the nearest warrior even as she prayed Rune's armor had taken the brunt of the blast. If it had, it was just possible he'd survive.

The redhead's startled gaze met hers in the instant before her fist slammed into his face. She snatched the beamer out of his holster as he fell.

Stupid bastard. He should have had his comp sober him up when he'd seen it was going bad.

"Rune!" It was the blond. Cassidy pivoted and fired at him, but he was already on the run.

Rune was up again, thank God, bulling right into the dark-haired one. There was a flurry of punches Cassidy didn't see clearly; the redhead had tried to get up. She kicked him in the head and he went back down.

"Come on!" Rune shouted, his voice hoarse with pain. "Run for the transport!"

Cassidy obeyed, sprinting in a zigzag pattern, Rune at her heels. She heard him fire, the buzzing chok of the beamer loud in her ears.

"Traitor!" the blond screamed, agony in his voice. "Step foot on the *Conquest* and I'll see you dead!"

The airlock ahead opened, probably at some command from Rune. Cassidy leaped inside, then whirled just in time to catch Rune as he half-fell through the door. "Lift off!" he gasped.

"In a minute!" She slid an arm around his waist and half-carried him to the cockpit, her nanotech implants scarcely laboring under his weight. "How badly are you hurt?"

"Bad enough," he gritted. His face was paper-white beneath its golden tone. She lowered him into the copilot's seat.

"Go!" he gritted as she hit the pilot's seat. "Take off!"

Cassidy grabbed the control yoke between her thighs, but it wouldn't budge. "The ship's comp doesn't recognize me! You'll have to unlock it."

Sweating, he closed his eyes. "Try now."

The yoke suddenly moved. The trid controls flashed on around her. Heart pounding, she brought the engines to roaring life. A flick of the controls and the vessel leaped straight up.

"The *Conquest* is in orbit," Rune gasped as acceleration mashed them both back in their seats. "Kaveh has notified them we've taken the transport. They're going to try to shoot us down."

"Kaveh's the blond, right?" She poured on more speed. "Charming bastard. Were you two lovers, or what? That wasn't just brotherly indignation."

He rested his head back against the seat, eyes closed, his lashes a dark fan against his cheeks. His lips looked faintly blue. "The warriors often turn to each other between visits to the women's deck. But I never felt as he did." Rune's pale lips curled into a slight smile. "I prefer the company of women."

She flicked him a look as the sky went black around them. She really didn't like his color. *How badly is he hurt, comp?*

He took a beamer blast to the side. His armor protected him from the full brunt, but since the suit wasn't powered, he sustained internal injuries. The comp rattled off details she would rather not hear.

Basically, he'd cooked half his guts saving her life. If she didn't get him into the *Starrunner*'s sickbay in the next twenty minutes, he was a dead man. As it was, only his comp was keeping him from sliding fatally into shock.

With one hand, she stroked her fingers through the trid com unit controls, changing the frequency to that used by the *Starrunner*. "Lieutenant Cassidy Vika, aboard captured Dharani transport, to *Starrunner*."

"Vika?" It was Captain August's familiar deep rumble. "What the hell are you doing with a Dharani transport?"

"Long story." The planet's horizon was starting to curve. "And I'm about to come under fire. Somebody get sickbay ready. I've got a seriously injured passenger with a beamer burn in the side."

"We've got a lock on your position. We'll rendezvous."

A glittering white star shot over the planetary curve toward them. Cassidy's hands tightened on the yoke.

"It's the *Conquest,*" Rune husked.

"Yeah, I figured that one out." She sent the transport yawing hard to one side, narrowly avoiding a torpedo. The craft's klaxons began to yowl, the sound an unfamiliar wavering wail. Cassidy ignored it, intent on evasive maneuvers as the *Conquest* did its best to blow them out of space. Its fire was so withering, she had no attention to spare on returning the favor. She was far too busy sending the transport in rolls and yaws designed to evade the next blast.

Sweat beaded her forehead, and she prayed the transport wouldn't take a hit. With their pressurized armor still unpowered, losing atmosphere would kill them both.

Out of the corner of her eye, she saw Rune reach for the fire controls. Without a word he sent a tachyon torpedo on its way. The transport vibrated as it fired.

Catching her startled glance—he'd fired on his own ship?—he bared his teeth in a smile that was more grimace than anything else. "Aiming wide. Just trying to divert their attention from shooting us."

But as he started to launch another torpedo, a second star appeared over the planet's horizon, also headed for them. Cassidy caught her breath. Another Dharani?

A beamer blast shot from the second vessel. The *Conquest* veered off, barely avoiding it.

Cassidy gave Rune a feral grin. "Captain August to the rescue."

✦ ✦ ✦

A squadron of small bright stars poured from the *Starrunner*— August had launched a fighter wing to cover their landing. As they streamed after the Conquest like a swarm of angry bees, Cassidy brought the transport to an uneventful landing in one of the ship's docking bays.

Waiting for the atmosphere to pump in, she turned her attention to Rune. He lay lax in his seat, unconscious.

"Damn you, Rune," she whispered. "You just had to go and be a hero."

He didn't stir.

✦ ✦ ✦

SHE popped the transport's airlock the moment the all-clear signal sounded.

A medcrew hurried aboard, towing a float stretcher. Cassidy watched anxiously as they loaded Rune into the transparent capsule. It flooded with stasis foam, freezing his body functions for the trip to sickbay. Her heart in her throat, Cassidy followed the stretcher out of the transport and into the docking bay.

✦ ✦ ✦

CASSIDY stared at Rune's still, pale face through the transparent wall of the regeneration tank. He was naked, comatose, and completely submerged in the clear nanogel that was currently at work repairing his damaged organs.

"Thought you'd want to know," August said, stepping into the treatment room, "everybody's back home and safe. The *Conquest* finally broke it off and headed for open space."

She sighed. "That's a relief."

The captain's smile was faint and wolfish. "Probably had something to do with the peace treaty the New Galvestonians and Kalistans just signed. The *Conquest* captain was evidently afraid they wouldn't get paid if they kept fighting and blew the deal."

"The Dharani are a practical people." She didn't turn her attention from the tube. "When they're not being complete lunatics."

"So I gather." He looked up at the tube with its naked occupant. "Interesting stray you brought home. I'd love to know how you pulled that one off. The Dharani are legendary for their fanatic loyalty."

"I think," Cassidy said softly, "he just fell in love with me."

August looked at her. "Okay, this I've got to hear."

✛ ✛ ✛

THE whole story poured out in a rush. Cassidy didn't hold any of it back, though her face flamed when she recounted her duel with Rune and her subsequent seduction. The captain went dangerously still at that point. She could tell he had grave doubts—until, anyway, she described how Rune had shielded her from Kaveh's beamer blast.

"Then he fired on the *Conquest*," Cassidy finished. "Wasn't actually aiming for the ship; he just wanted to buy us time to get away." She stepped up to the tank, gazing through the faintly glowing gel at her lover's face. "He gave up everything for me, Captain. He can't go back to his people; they'd kill him."

August frowned. "Are you hinting you want me to offer him a berth?"

She turned to face him, her heart in her mouth. "Would you be willing to do that?"

The captain frowned, smoothing a finger across his lower lip as he contemplated the question. "I don't know, Cassidy. Dharani Tribesmen are legendary warriors—God knows I wouldn't mind having one as a member of my crew." He sighed. "Unfortunately, there's more to it than fighting prowess. On the one hand, he turned on his own people, which isn't what I'd consider a rousing recommendation. But on the other, he did it to prevent your being gang-raped, when it would have been easier to let his friends do what they wanted."

She angled her head toward the tube. "Then there's the blast he took for me. If it had hit me, we wouldn't be having this conversation."

"I'm aware of that." August eyed her, bracing his big fists on his narrow hips. "Tell you what—I'll talk to him when he comes out of it. I'm a pretty good judge of character."

She closed her eyes in relief. "Thank you, Captain."

"You might want to hold those thanks, Lieutenant. If I decide we can't take him, what are you going to do?"

Cassidy put out a hand and rested it on the cool, curving side of the tank. "I think . . . I'll have to go with him. I'm in love with him." She stopped, her mouth working in surprise. "Hell, I hadn't realized that until this moment."

August's smile was dry. "Yeah, sometimes it sneaks up on you like that."

"It doesn't make sense—I hardly know him. But . . ."

The captain studied her face. "I suspect you know him a lot

better than you think," he said quietly. "And if you're willing to give up your berth on the *Starrunner* for him, that says a great deal." He smiled and rested a hand on her shoulder. "I've got a feeling he's going to pass my test."

"This is so strange," Cassidy murmured, as much to herself as her commanding officer. "I've only known him a couple of days."

"True, but it's been a hell of a couple of days."

She snorted. "That's putting it mildly."

✦ ✦ ✦

THREE days later Nathan studied Rune Alrigo across the width of his captain's desk. The big Dharani was dressed in a black civilian unisuit somebody—probably Cassidy—had produced from ship's stores. His gaze was as level and respectful as it was wary. Sebastian sprawled in the other chair, green eyes watchful.

"I understand you took a beamer blast for my crewman," Nathan began, his sensors focused on the man. "Was that intentional?"

A hint of defiance heated the pale gaze. "Yes, sir."

Nathan's comp silently confirmed he was telling the truth. Not that he needed the confirmation; it was written all over Alrigo's face.

"Thank you." The captain sat back in his seat, studying him. "Why?"

The Dharani shrugged. "I had vowed to protect her."

"She told me you told her that when she lost that Claiming Duel, she also lost the right to refuse any order you gave her. Wouldn't it have been easier to order her to bang your friends?"

He didn't flinch at the blunt question. "Yes, sir."

Nathan looked at him, silently demanding he elaborate.

"She would not have obeyed, and they would have hurt her," Alrigo told him. His expression tightened with remembered anger.

"So you were willing to betray your friends and your people to keep her safe?"

Temper stirred in those eyes, only to be ruthlessly tamped down. "There is no honor in brutalizing an outnumbered, unarmed woman." He took a deep breath. "Just as there's no honor in turning her into an object of contempt. When I saw the way they were treating her, I realized it would be even worse on the *Conquest*. I couldn't allow that."

"Commendable of you," Nathan said. "And having made that decision, you had to go with her, because they'd have killed you otherwise."

For the first time Rune looked startled. "No. I have always been prepared to die if my people demanded it. I went with her because she couldn't have flown the transport without my codes."

"That's the first half-truth you've told. There's more to it than that."

A muscle flexed in Alrigo's jaw. "All right. I went with her because I had to be with her."

Nathan smiled, recognizing a plain fact even without the comp's confirmation. "So. Interested in joining the crew of the *Starrunner*?"

The Dharani blinked once before the relieved grin spread across his face. "Yes. Cassidy belongs here."

Nathan rose to shake his hand. "And you, evidently, belong with Cassidy."

Chapter Twelve

RUNE'S rich baritone rolled over the docking deck as every man and woman who could get off duty stood listening. When the last notes faded, the crowd broke into whistling applause. Cassidy smiled indulgently at the flush of pleasure on his face as he bowed.

Just about the entire crew of the *Starrunner* had assembled on the launch deck. It was the only place on the ship big enough for a gathering that size, and it was still packed.

Everyone was in a good mood, too, judging by the yells encouraging Rune to sing another song. With a grin, he allowed himself to be convinced.

"All that and gorgeous, too," Trin sighed in Cassidy's ear as he launched into the next song. "It's really not fair."

"And singing is only one of his *many* talents." Cassidy gave her friends a teasing grin.

"I'll bet I can guess what the others are," Zaria said, plucking a canapé from a tray carried by a passing robot. She bit into it and moaned at the flavor. "Food that didn't come from a ration pack. Yum. Your work, Trin?"

Trinity shrugged. "Some of it's mine, some of it is a gift from the New Galvastonians." She'd taken over the hydroponics department after discovering that the crewman in charge had no idea what he was doing. Experienced farmer that she was, she'd soon had it producing fresh fruits and vegetables that were a hit with the crew. "The president sent his personal chef up with a transport full of goodies."

As the robot looped around her on its floaters, Cassidy filched something colorful and exotic from its tray. "Judging from this and the victory bonus they paid, the Galvastonians must be pretty happy with us."

"A lot more so than the Kalistans are with the Dharani, anyway." Trinity's smile was brightly nasty. "I understand all the Tribeships are headed for Kalista. Apparently somebody tried to stiff somebody."

Cassidy smiled grimly. "Which is not the kind of thing the Dharani will take lying down."

"I hope the Tribeships kick their asses," Zaria said. "Serves the greedy bastards right for invading in the first place."

Cassidy raised her glass in a toast. "Here, here."

The three women had become quite close since Trin and Zaria had joined the *Starruner*'s crew. Cassidy was glad to see both of them had settled in well. Sebastian, as executive officer, had quickly put Zaria's genius for organization to good use. Cassidy suspected it wouldn't be long before Captain August made her quartermaster.

God knew Trin's green thumb was certainly welcome.

Her attention wandered back to Rune as the crowd broke into whistles and cheers. She only hoped he settled in as easily as her friends had.

Of course, the *Starruner* was a mercenary vessel, and mercs were used to being enemies with people they later fought beside. She suspected the rest of the crew would come to appreciate and trust Rune quickly enough. Particularly since he'd gained the captain's seal of approval, not to mention a spot in the fighter wing.

The real question was, could Rune put his past behind him with the same ease?

+ + +

CASSIDY keyed open her quarters, and she and Rune reeled inside. He promptly pulled her into his arms. "That was . . . an interesting party."

"There was certainly a lot of newlywed cooing going on," Cassidy said, stepping full against him and hooking her hands behind his neck. "When the women weren't teasing me about my handsome captive."

His eyebrows flew upward. "Captive?"

She grinned up at him. "Maybe it was captor. I keep getting those two confused."

"I noticed," Rune said dryly.

"Kiss me, Captive." She rose on her toes and took his lips. His mouth was silken, soft, a delicious contrast to the ridges and hollows of his hard body. The hands around her waist tightened. They both groaned.

Rune sent his tongue questing delicately between her lips, tasting her, and she swirled her own around it. He cupped her backside, gave it a gentle squeeze, stroked. She angled her head and closed her teeth gently over his lower lip in a teasing bite. The fingers caressing her butt tightened, pulling her against the erection swelling behind the fly of his unisuit. Unable to resist, she rolled her hips as their tongues dueled gently, gliding and retreating in sweet carnality.

When they finally broke the kiss, both were breathing hard. He rested his forehead against hers, panting. His free hand rose to cup her breast. Squeeze. Stroke.

"I love you." The words were out of her mouth before she intended to say them.

Rune went still except for a sudden inhalation. When he lifted his head, there was a surprising vulnerability in those pale eyes. "Are you sure?"

"I don't say something like that unless I am." Which is why she'd never said it before.

Despite everything, a sudden anxiety clutched at Cassidy's chest. Had she misread his feelings for her?

He cupped the side of her face with long, warm fingers. "I know you feel . . . grateful for what I did. Shielding you. Going with you. But—"

"This isn't gratitude, Rune." *He wants reassurance,* she realized, startled. This big, powerful warrior felt as vulnerable as she did. She rested both hands on his chest. The warm muscle flexed nervously under her hands. "I've fought beside men all my life," Cassidy told him softly. "One or two of them has saved my life. But I never felt about any of them the way I do about you."

"I love you." His voice was low, rough. "Finding you was like discovering something that had always been missing from my soul. It's just . . . right."

Relief poured over her. He did feel the same. "Yeah. That's it. That's it exactly."

This time when she kissed him, he pulled her off her feet. With a moan Cassidy coiled her legs around his waist as he turned with her, stepped to the bed. They tumbled to the gel mattress with a soft plop, then promptly began pulling at the seals of each other's uniforms.

Something tore. Cassidy didn't care, too intent on getting at Rune's warm skin. Her boot hit the wall with a thump. He wrestled the other off her foot, then gave it a toss. Pulled her suit the rest of the way down her legs. Stood just long enough to push his own uniform past his hips. His cock sprang out at her, bobbing and flushed with heat.

She sat up and reached for it, closing her fingers around its warm satin width, smiling at his groan of pleasure.

Rune caught his breath as she opened her mouth and took him in, swirling her tongue over the head. "Oh, no," he muttered, pushing her back and catching her behind the knees. Spreading them. "My turn."

She braced on her elbows and grinned. "How about a little sixty-nine?"

Rune lifted a brow, obviously intrigued. "Which is what?"

"You suck me while I suck you."

Instantly grasping the possibilities, he smiled.

✦ ✦ ✦

A moment later they had themselves arranged—Rune on his back with Cassidy straddling his face while she slid his length into her mouth. The sensations he created with the first wickedly skillful stroke of his tongue sent jolts of feral pleasure up her spine.

She tried to distract herself with the hot, smooth length of his cock, swirling her tongue over the velvet head. He groaned against her sex. Purring, she started feeding his length into her mouth, intent on working him completely down her throat.

That should drive him nuts.

But Rune was every bit as skillful as she was, as he demonstrated with swirling tongue flicks that soon had her squirming. A strong finger found her sex, slid inside for a slow, deep thrust. Cassidy moaned. Let go long of his cock enough to pant.

A second finger joined the first. Pumped. "Like that?" he asked roguishly.

Eyes narrowing, she swooped her head down and engulfed him, feeding him completely down her throat. This time it was his turn to groan.

Then he slid a finger up her backside and chuckled at her gasp. Pumped his hand. She almost choked on his cock at the darkly carnal sensation.

Panting, she drew back and released him. Looking over her shoulder at his masculine grin, she gave him a mock glower. "Are you challenging me?"

The grin broadened. "Oh, definitely."

She grinned back. "That's what I thought."

Then they attacked each other. Lips and tongues and teeth, caressing, sucking, and biting. Hands cupping, fingers stroking. Soon every nerve in Cassidy's body was quivering in time with Rune's deep pants.

"God, Rune!" she gasped finally, so hot with need she felt maddened.

He growled.

The next thing she knew, he'd tumbled her onto her back. She spread her thighs wide as he pounced, bracing one hand beside her shoulder as he aimed his cock for her wet sex. His first stroke tore a groan from her lips. She wrapped her legs around his waist and rolled her hips up at him.

Rune bent his head to rake his teeth gently over her nipple. "Ohhh, yeah," she purred, her eyes shuttering in bliss. She threaded her fingers into his short, dark hair and held him close as he licked and played, thrusting slowly, sweetly.

Finally he looked up at her, his eyes blazing. "You taste so good." Driving in a deep, hard lunge that made her gasp, he groaned. "You *feel* so good."

"Mmm. So do you." She ground up at him, enjoying the way his cock shuttled in and out of her slick core, filling her so deeply, so completely. Clinging to his broad shoulders, she stared up into his face, watching pleasure close its grip on him, tighter and tighter with every sweet entry. A flush rose over the brutal cheekbones, and his lips parted.

But there was more than lust in his glittering gaze. Tenderness softened his hard features as he looked down at her. The love there was so pure, so intense, that it took her breath.

Until at last he threw back his head with a shout, driving all the way to the balls in her, grinding deliciously down on her clit. Her orgasm rose in a sudden hot wave and swept her away with a frenzied cry of completion.

Finally Rune collapsed over her, and Cassidy wrapped her trembling arms around his sweat-slicked shoulders. With a groan, he rolled over, tumbling her with him.

Panting, her senses still shimmering from the aftermath, she lay draped across his muscled torso, listening to him breathe. She felt sweetly dazzled, sated.

Long moments passed before she felt capable of speech or thought. Unfortunately, the first thought that occurred to her was a worry.

Stroking her fingertips through his dark chest hair, she said, "You've given up a lot for me. Your people, your home. I hope you won't regret it."

His chuckle vibrated against her cheek. "Oh, believe me, love—I won't. Especially not if you keep rewarding me like this."

She lifted her head and braced her chin on her fist. "That was not a reward fuck."

"No?" His grin was white and roguish. "What would you do as a reward fuck?"

Cassidy sat up. "Be a good boy and find out."

Rune snorted. "I'm not a boy of any kind."

"*That's* the truth." She sobered, frowning. "But seriously . . ."

"I don't think you have to worry about me regretting my choice, Cassidy. That party today . . ." He hesitated, his gaze going distant. "There was such warmth between your crewmates, a sense of camaraderie. It brought home to me how little of that I knew on the *Conquest*. We were too busy guarding our honor and our thoughts. Jockeying for advancement, fighting duels to prove our skill and worthiness. I could never drop my guard, not even with my Wing Brothers. Any sign of weakness would be instantly seized and turned against me."

She frowned in sympathy. "Tough way to live."

He stroked a hand through her long, tangled hair. "I think that's why I was so determined to capture you. I wanted someone in my life I could love without fear of being met with contempt."

Cassidy smiled slightly. "Believe me, Rune—the last thing I feel for you is contempt." She let the smile bloom into a grin as she sat up to straddle him, contemplating his stirring cock. "Now, lust, on the other hand . . ." She stared into his eyes. "Marry me." The question was an impulse, but she meant every word.

Rune smiled, slow and breathtaking. "As I recall, I asked you first."

Cassidy grinned, giddy. "Yes. Oh, yeah."

Then she fell into his arms.